KARSTEN DE BOLT AND ISAAK URIARTE

Midtown: The Forsaken Virus of the Black Realm

Black Brim
Publishing

Contents

Prologue

The wind howled like an ancient spirit mourning its past. It twisted through the crumbling husks of towers and hollow-eyed windows, rattling rusted metal and whispering through the skeletal remains of a city long surrendered to time.

A black SUV crawled over the fractured asphalt as it pulled up to the dead expanse of a once-thriving metropolis, now reduced to a desolate wasteland.

Dr. Elias Kade sat in the passenger seat, his fingers twitching slightly against his knee. The expression on his face was unreadable behind square-framed glasses. His eyes scanned the desolate skyline, carrying reverence and dread.

Ashenfell.

The name had always haunted the edges of his thoughts. He dreaded their arrival, feeling a chill run down his spine.

Behind the wheel, Sergeant Lorne sat with one hand resting lightly on the wheel, his fingers tapping in a slow, deliberate rhythm. A scar split the side of his temple, pale against his dark skin, a reminder of the kind of man who had spent too much of his life standing guard.

Kade didn't know Lorne well, but he trusted him.

In the back seat, Task Force agents Mason and Phil shifted restlessly. The two were younger, sharper, the kind to speak half-jokes to cover nerves.

The team was here to escort Dr. Kade into Ashenfell to retrieve materials for a project that they didn't understand.

The SUV rolled to a stop, the engine humming faintly in the brittle air. Kade stepped out, his boots crunching down on cracked stone, a soft mist of ember swirling up around his ankles. He inhaled and coughed, the taste of old metal and dust scratching his throat. The silence here was wrong. It was thick and heavy, pressing against his ears with a deep pressure.

Ash drifted from the sky, slow and steady. It fell like snow stripped of its beauty, clinging to every surface, painting the world in hues of bone and smoke.

The skyline stretched flat and steel gray above them, no birds, no movement, no sound. Just a hollow echo.

Kade rubbed the back of his neck, his eyes flickering toward the jagged silhouettes of buildings. The city left him feeling uneasy. The only visitors this place got were researchers from Veilhaven, hoping to unlock the secrets of Midtown. As much as Kade hated theorists, he would have loved to see any sign of life.

"I've got the gear," Lorne said, slinging a heavy duffel over his shoulder as he approached. His voice cut through the silence like a blade. "You know what we're here for?"

Kade tapped at his datapad, forcing his voice steady.

"Crystals," Kade answered. "Specifically, the mineral-rich variety found beneath Ashenfell. Old-world remnants. Veins of concentrated power."

Lorne let out a rough grumble, shifting the weight on his shoulder. Kade didn't even bother to attempt a reply. Instead, he turned and led the way.

The group moved forward. The path through the ruins

was slow and winding. Cracked stone streets gave way to collapsed intersections and the occasional rusted signpost jutting up like a tombstone.

Mason drifted a few steps behind Kade, his hand near his sidearm, his eyes sharp and restless.

"This place gives me the creeps," Mason muttered.

"It's just dust and rocks," Sergeant Lorne growled. "Keep your nerves in check."

Phil jogged up beside Kade, his grin thin and stretched.

"So, doc," he said, glancing sideways, "you been to Ashenfell before?"

"A few times," Kade said, his eyes flicking across the datapad screen. "Purely for research. It's been years now, though."

"My folks used to tell me stories about this place," Phil said, his head turning toward the collapsed structures. "They said there was an underground society. Secret tunnels, survivors, even cults."

Kade snorted softly and gave a thin smile. He had heard these rumors before.

"Theories," he said. "Nothing more. We've scanned underground dozens of times. No signs of habitation. The oxygen levels down there wouldn't support a field mouse, let alone a society."

"What about the Protector?" Mason asked suddenly. "Some folks think he's been hiding somewhere here."

That made Kade pause. He lifted his gaze from his datapad, just briefly.

"Believe me," he said, "if the Protector had been holed up in Ashenfell for the last five years, someone would've found him."

"So where do you think he is, then?" Sergeant Lorne asked,

his voice rumbling behind them.

"Somewhere no one would dare to look," Kade replied, pocketing the datapad. "We're here."

The group came to a stop.

Before them stood the gaping mouth of a collapsed transit tunnel, the entrance half-swallowed by dirt and shadow. A cold breath exhaled from within, stale and metallic. The stone around it cracked like fractured bone. The interior was cloaked in a darkness so dense, it felt alive.

"Torches on, men," Lorne commanded.

A chorus of clicks followed as Mason and Phil powered up the tactical lights attached to their weapons. Beams of sterile white carved into the black.

Kade swallowed, his stomach knotting.

"Are those really necessary?" he asked, his voice a little thinner than he liked.

"We don't know what's in there," Lorne replied, drawing a sleek black pistol and extending it toward Kade.

"Oh, I don't use guns," Kade said, raising his hands in protest.

"And I don't go into creepy caves with men who aren't prepared to defend themselves," Lorne replied, his voice more commanding than before. "Take it."

Kade hesitated. For a second, the wind shifted. He thought, just barely, he heard something move in the dark.

He took the pistol.

#

The cave swallowed the group whole.

Boots crunched over loose stones, every step sending faint echoes skittering along the jagged walls, only to be smothered by the suffocating dark. Flashlights cut narrow beams through the black, sweeping across rough rock and cracked walls, slick with condensation.

Each step forward pressed the air flat against their chests, as if the tunnel itself resisted their presence.

Somewhere deep within the cave, water dripped steadily, echoing like a slow and hollow pulse.

The air hung thick and damp against their skin, carrying the sharp scent of wet minerals and something more ancient. Something that made the back of Kade's neck prickle.

Kade adjusted his grip on the datapad, its screen casting a pale glow across his glasses. Coded readings flickered in bursts, though he barely read them. His attention was drawn to the walls.

The farther they descended, the more unnatural the formations became. Twisting spirals of stone that looked like claws, and streaks of color etched in patterns that were too symmetrical. Thin streaks of minerals painted patterns that seemed to shift at the edges when his eyes slid past.

Kade swallowed. His fingers flexed nervously.

"This is real nightmare fuel," Phil muttered behind him, his flashlight wavering slightly. "You're sure nobody lived down here?"

"Nobody who would have survived," Kade replied. His voice sounded thinner than usual as it echoed through the cave.

A sudden tremor rippled softly through the cave. Soft, like a shift. Enough, however, to shift dust from overhead, sending it spiraling through the beam of Kade's light. A faint, hollow thud echoed from deep within the stone far away.

The group froze.

Kade's gaze darted to Lorne, catching the way the sergeant's fingers clamped tighter around his rifle.

"Likely just a pressure shift," Kade offered, hoping to ease the tension. "Underground spaces are known to do that."

The silence returned, much heavier than before, as the group pushed on.

They continued until the tunnel widened into a cavern. A cathedral of stone. Its walls shimmered, dusted with veins of crystalline growth. Stalactites hung overhead like daggers. The ceiling arched above them like a rib cage.

Kade exhaled slowly.

"This is it," he murmured. "Give me a moment. I will scan the mineral deposits and tell you which to collect from."

Kade stepped forward, carefully sweeping his datapad's sensors along a nearby mineral deposit. Soft red pulses blinked in sequence as he muttered under his breath, his eyes narrowed.

He continued scanning deposits, moving farther into the chamber as the agents followed.

Finally, a green flash, a faint confirming beep.

"This one," Kade called out. "Start here."

Mason and Phil approached. Lorne tossed the duffel bag to the ground in front of them. It landed with a thud that shattered the silence.

Kade stepped away slightly, his light drifting across the far edge of the chamber. He approached an area where the walls darkened, where the shadows grew deeper, untouched by the others' beams.

"Where you headed, doc?" Lorne called.

"Just surveying," Kade replied, his voice quiet and distant as he continued to walk. "I won't go far."

His boots echoed differently on this stone. It was smoother, as though shaped and chiseled by a person. The air felt colder. Stiller.

Then, at the far wall, cradled in a split of blackened rock, he saw it.

A crystal, unlike the rest.

Where the others were a pale blue, reflecting light like ice, this one was deeper. Violet, almost black. It nearly vanished into the shadows, threaded with thin veins of faintly pulsing red. It didn't reflect like the others. It seemed to drink the light. It breathed quietly, ominously, like the last ember of a dying star.

The air around it felt even heavier, as though the space itself tensed.

He took one step forward, his heart pounding faintly against his ribs. His hand lifted, trembling slightly, before he even realized it.

He was drawn closer.

A whisper slithered into his mind. Not words—at least, none that he could understand. Just sound. A pressure, a rhythm. Familiar and foreign at once. Like something that had waited for too long.

Kade clenched his jaw, trying to shake it off. *It's the wind,* he thought. *Just the cave settling.*

The moment his fingers brushed it, the sound surged into a silent roar blooming behind his eyes, filling the space inside his skull, rattling against the edges of himself.

He gasped softly, clutching the crystal, pulling it free.

The moment it left the wall, everything went dead silent.

Kade stood frozen, his heart thundering, breath caught in his throat. His hand slipped the crystal into his personal satchel almost without thinking. For a long, trembling second, he just stared at the place where it had been, unable to comprehend what had just happened.

Then, slowly, he turned and walked back.

When he returned to the others, Mason and Phil were sealing the duffel, their faces drawn tight with the kind of tension they didn't want to admit to.

"You find anything?" Lorne asked, watching him closely. His eyes were sharp and steady.

Kade hesitated, the satchel's weight pressing hot against his side.

"Nothing of note," he said quietly. "We should head back."

Lorne's gaze lingered a moment longer. Just long enough to make Kade's stomach twist. Then he gave a sharp nod.

"You don't gotta tell me twice," Mason said, breaking the awkward silence and slinging the bag over his shoulder.

The group turned, retreating into the tunnel's long throat, their flashlights narrowing to thin beams in the dark behind them.

Somewhere, deep within the stone they left behind, the faintest hum pulsed. Faint, patient, and waiting.

#

The SUV rumbled across the broken ground, its tires groaning over fractured stone.

Behind them, ash curled through the air like smoke trailing from a dying fire, swallowing the ruined spires of Ashenfell.

Phil exhaled heavily and leaned his head against the window.

"I swear," he muttered, his breath fogging the glass, "I never want to see that place again."

Mason gave a dry chuckle beside him.

"It wasn't as bad as I expected," he replied. "I was worried we were going to be chased out by cannibals or something."

Up front, Sergeant Lorne kept his eyes fixed on the battered road, both hands steady on the wheel. Still, Kade could feel his occasional glance. A flicker of attention, measured and quiet.

"You good, doc?" Lorne asked at last, voice low.

Kade blinked, dragging his gaze back from the window. He'd been staring at the horizon without seeing it, the desolate landscape smudging into gray streaks of light and dust.

"What?" he said, blinking again.

"You're quiet," Lorne clarified. "More than usual."

Kade adjusted his glasses, offering a faint, mechanical nod. His hand shifted instinctively, resting on the canvas satchel by his side.

"Just a long day," he murmured.

Lorne didn't press. He only shifted slightly in his seat, eyes narrowing faintly before focusing forward again.

Kade leaned back in the passenger seat, exhaling slowly, but his fingers never left the satchel.

He could feel the shape of the crystal through the layered fabric, a faint but undeniable warmth pressing against his leg. He told himself it was residual heat from the cave. From the deep stone.

But even as the thought crossed his mind, another shadowed it.

It wasn't the cave. It wasn't even the stone.

The warmth pulsed faintly, a rhythm too slow, too deliberate, too alive.

Outside, the sun dipped lower, sinking behind a haze of gray clouds. Shadows lengthened across the wasteland, painting the cracked ground in long, dark streaks. The ruined city shrank smaller and smaller in the rearview mirror until only jagged silhouettes remained.

Still, the weight of the crystal pressed hot and certain against Kade's leg.

Not heavy in size, but with something else.

Silent, but not asleep.

Waiting.

1

Who Watches...?

Perched atop the rotting shingles of a forgotten rooftop, Nikki waited. The air smelled of scorched wires and old oil, thick with the tang of rust and the sour stink of trash fires burning far below.

The city stretched before her in broken silhouettes: half-finished buildings, collapsed walkways, skeletal high-rises covered in grime. Beneath her feet, Halvade pulsed in flickers of neon and shadow, alive with hurried shapes darting through narrow streets.

She crouched low, a black sweater clinging tight under her makeshift costume—a violet cloth mask, matching joggers, homemade gear that wasn't much, but was hers.

The underworld of Midtown moves in shadows, Nikki thought to herself. *Secret meetings. Quiet deals. Power shifting hands in the dark. And I am the only one standing in its way.*

CRUNCH!

She bit into a potato chip, the crumbs tumbling down the cracked shingles to the alley below.

Nikki tugged the mask lower over her mouth and exhaled

slowly.

What is taking so long? she thought, very loudly.

Her intel said the deal was supposed to go down half an hour ago. Either they were late, or her intel was garbage. Which, considering almost all her intel came from her best friend, the latter option seemed the most likely.

Her stomach twisted, half from nerves, half from the stubborn knot of doubt that always settled when the wait stretched too long.

She was just about to pull back when the low hum of an engine crawled up her spine. Then, her heart leapt.

Below, a blacked-out sedan rolled into the alley, headlights washing the walls in silver. Its tinted windows gleamed faintly in the haze.

"Finally," she muttered, wiping her fingers on her sleeve and sliding to the roof's edge.

Four men emerged, clad in dark jackets, faces sharp and cold in the headlights.

All right, she thought. *Classic bad-guy look. That's a good start.*

A second car arrived, this one sleeker, cleaner, and polished to a mirror sheen. Nikki's breath hitched as the driver's door opened.

Tall. Broad. Sharp-cut suit straining over a massive, muscular frame.

Frederick.

Nikki's jaw tightened.

He wasn't some street punk. Frederick ran Halvade like a king. If he was there, it meant this wasn't just a minor arms deal. This was big.

Her fingers tightened on the rooftop's edge. She knew she

should wait and investigate a bit more. Moving too quickly could allow them to get away. But this was Frederick—the biggest crime boss in Midtown.

She could feel her pulse hammering. By the time she had finished thinking, they were already halfway to the crate.

She sprang into motion, darting across the rooftop, boots whispering over old concrete and steel. Below, the two groups converged, murmured voices low and quick.

Okay, she thought, forcing herself steady. *Just go down, take a few guys out, and scare the rest away. Main priority? Capturing Frederick. Simple. Right?*

She exhaled hard, rolled her shoulders back, and launched into the descent. She utilized fire escapes, window ledges, and rusted gutters. She moved like a shadow, skin humming with tension.

As she reached the ground, she froze. They were facing her. All of them. As if they had just watched her every move down the building.

"Who's this supposed to be?" Frederick asked, a smirk curling at his lips as he gestured lazily to her.

Nikki stepped forward carefully, trying to project confidence, though her heart rattled painfully in her chest.

"Listen," Frederick went on, chuckling, "this doesn't concern you. How about you turn around and head back to your yoga class or whatever it is you're dressed for?"

The others laughed, sharp and mocking. Heat flushed through Nikki's face.

Wrong move.

She sprinted forward.

Frederick snapped his fingers.

Weapons raised, but too slow.

A violet puff of smoke exploded outward. Shots rang, wild and scattered, punching through empty mist.

When the smoke cleared, she was gone.

"Where'd they go?" Frederick growled, spinning.

CRACK!

Nikki dropped from above, her knees slamming onto a thug's shoulders, sending him crumpling to the ground.

Gunfire. Another puff, another vanish.

Nikki reappeared behind two more, sweeping the legs out from one and driving a punch into the other's jaw.

"Who is this guy!?" one of the thugs shouted as she disappeared again.

Nikki perched on a flickering lamppost, chest heaving, pulse electric in her ears. A grin curled at the edge of her mask. This was going much better than she'd expected.

She dropped, vanished, and reappeared, except this time she caught a sudden, brutal *CRACK* across her temple.

Pain detonated behind her eyes.

She staggered back, hitting the ground hard, vision swimming. Three Fredericks blurred before her, shifting, merging.

That can't be right... She shook her head, fighting for clarity.

"Stay back..." Nikki whispered, making a poor attempt to deepen her voice. She crawled backward, palms scraping cold concrete.

Frederick stepped forward slowly, gun raised, smirk sharpened.

"That smoke trick of yours is cute," he said. "Any other surprises?"

Nikki clenched her fists, anger slicing through the haze.

"I've got a few," she muttered.

A violet mist wrapped around her palm, and with a sharp

burst, a smoke-wreathed scythe crackled into shape.

She hurled it at his gun, knocking it aside in a burst of sparks.

Frederick cursed, jerking back.

Nikki rolled, sprang to her feet, and *POOF*.

She was gone.

Above, her head pounded, breath ragged as she crouched atop the nearest roof. She winced, pressing fingers to her temple.

Suddenly, sirens began to blare, and her eyes snapped open.

No, no, no. Nikki turned and ran to the edge of the rooftop. Red and blue lights painted the alley below. Task Force SUVs skidded to a halt. Agents spilled out, shouting.

Frederick had already disappeared into the dark, his men scattering.

Nikki's eyes darted between him and the crate.

She clenched her jaw, vanished again, and reappeared deep in a side alley, lungs burning, shoulders shaking.

Stupid! she thought. *What were you thinking!?*

She bent over, hands on her knees, trying to force the spinning world still. Then, with one more ragged breath, she teleported one last time.

#

Two Task Force SUVs idled outside the alley, their running lights casting long beams across the mess left behind. Agents moved with brisk, quiet urgency, snapping photos, tagging shell casings, and marking bloodstains on cracked pavement.

A low growl joined the static hum. A sleek gray sedan rolled to a stop behind the SUVs.

From the driver's side stepped out Laura Sinclair. Director of the Task Force. She moved sharply, not a wasted motion, not a moment's hesitation. A tailored slate suit hugged her frame like armor, her ponytail bound as tightly as her expression. Every inch of her radiated command.

From the passenger side, Connor Avery. A contrast in every way. His suit jacket was unbuttoned, his tie loose, his smirk crooked, and his stubble rough. He moved with the easy rhythm of a man who didn't take things too seriously. He had been one of Laura's closest friends since she first joined the Task Force, probably the only reason he still had the job. At least, that was what others might've thought. Laura knew better. Connor was one of the best agents around. His combat skills were unmatched by most. His intelligence, though he masked it with his comedy, was exceptional. There was nobody better fit to be by her side.

They walked side by side toward the scene.

"You think it was him?" Connor asked, stepping over a groaning thug.

Laura crouched beside one of the fallen men, pulling on nitrile gloves. Without a word, she tugged up the sleeve of the unconscious figure, revealing a snarling cougar tattoo wrapped in barbed chains, its body coiled in fog.

Her mouth hardened into a thin line.

"Frederick's working with the Gunsmith," she murmured.

Connor groaned quite loudly.

"Figures," he replied. "That guy's got his claws in everything from back-alley trades to clean contracts."

Laura rose, striding toward the half-cracked crate in the center of the wreckage. She pried it open carefully. Inside were weapons. Task Force–grade, but modified.

She pulled a weapon out and cocked it. Something was off. She popped a round, causing Connor to jump back.

"What the hell?" he exclaimed.

"These guns are faulty," Laura said. "They've been tampered with."

"You think the Gunsmith is purposefully giving Frederick weapons that don't work?"

Laura put the gun back into the crate.

"Who knows?" she replied. "Maybe he's trying to keep the competition at a disadvantage. What I do know is that they weren't expecting *him* to show up."

Connor joined her, peeking into the crate.

"No one ever does," he said.

Laura's brows furrowed.

"Still," Laura said. "He's never gone after Frederick. Not directly."

"Maybe he's stepping up," Connor offered. "Or maybe he's tired of chasing rats and wants to burn down the nest."

Laura didn't reply, sifting through the contents of the crate, fingers brushing against something cold at the bottom. She pulled it free.

A blackened card, smooth and gleaming faintly in the streetlights. Etched on its face was a single name:

The Gunsmith.

She turned it over. Blank. Without a word, she placed it into the hand of an agent.

Connor glanced back at the waiting SUVs, then at the alley beyond, where a trash fire flickered, its sparks bouncing off the walls.

"So," he drawled, "lunch?"

Laura didn't smile, but the sharp tension around her brow

softened, just slightly.

They turned from the scene, footsteps fading.

Behind them, the crate waited. Cracked open and humming with unspoken threats. It was a shadow that would follow Laura into the long night ahead.

#

Bernie's Big Burgers.

A greasy burger joint in the middle of Capital City. Voted "Midtown's Best Burger" four years in a row. Five years in a row before that. The year it didn't win, Bernie was dealing with family problems and had to close shop for a few months.

The place smelled like heaven and heart disease. Charred beef. Fry oil. Toasted buns. That vague tang of melted cheese and something sweet that could never quite be placed. The red vinyl booths were cracked, the flickering overhead lights buzzed softly, and a neon sign above the soda machines blinked: *Eat Big. Live Fast. Tip Bernie.*

Connor stood at the counter, watching his order with the intensity of a bomb technician.

Double cheeseburger. Onions grilled to a crisp. Thin tomatoes. Two sheets of lettuce—not shredded, not chopped. Bernie's secret sauce. A mountain of extra-crispy fries. One oversize strawberry lemonade.

Perfection.

Bernie waddled up with the tray, his stained apron gleaming with fresh grease.

"Thanks, Bernie," Connor said, reaching for the food with a grin. "You're the man."

"Anytime," Bernie responded. "Oh, almost forgot!" He

ducked under the counter and returned with a fistful of ketchup packets, dropping them onto the tray with a satisfying slap.

Connor gave him a salute and made his way to the corner booth.

Laura was already there, hunched over a sad-looking turkey club. Extra tomatoes, no dressing, no indulgence.

How can anyone eat something so plain in a place like this? Connor thought, sliding into the seat across from her.

He immediately stuffed a few fries into his mouth.

"Ohhh," he groaned dramatically, eyes fluttering closed. "Now *this* is food. Want some?"

Laura looked at his plate, then at him.

"I'm good," she said. "Thanks."

"Suit yourself," Connor replied.

He tore into a ketchup packet with his teeth and scooted his fries over, leaving just enough space for his sauce. He continued to pile the condiment, creating his own little dipping pool. Then, he proceeded to scarf down his fries.

"So," he said, voice half-muffled through mouthfuls of food, "what are you thinking?"

Laura exhaled sharply, pinching the bridge of her nose.

"If the vigilante keeps interfering with Frederick's operations, it won't be long before Frederick retaliates. He's not just going to—"

Connor couldn't focus on her words anymore, his eyes inexorably drawn to the glistening tower of his burger. It was begging to be devoured. He lifted it reverently. The scent hit him like a warm hug and a slap in the face. A little spicy, a little sweet. He knew the first bite was always the best, and he would savor it. He brought the burger up to his face and took one more sniff before taking a huge bite. *God, that's good,* he thought as the flavors danced around his mouth. *Life doesn't get better than—*

"Connor!?" Laura yelled.

He froze midbite, burger hovering halfway to his mouth.

"Huh?" he mumbled, blinking at her.

"Did you hear anything I just said?" she asked, pretty angrily.

Connor lowered the burger slowly back onto the plate, chewing and swallowing.

"Yeah, yeah," he replied. "About the vigilante, Frederick, and all the retaliation stuff. Loud and clear."

Laura stared at him.

"Well," Connor said, taking a sip of his lemonade. "We could always...I don't know. Try to talk to the vigilante? Work something out?"

Laura snorted softly, shaking her head.

"Work something out?" she asked. "The only thing I'd work out with them is a prison sentence."

"Oh, come on," Connor said, leaning forward with a playful glint in his eye. "At least they're helping people."

"They're untrained," Laura snapped. "They're reckless. They go out there punching gangsters in alleys while we're trying to build actual cases."

"Yeah, but," he started, "maybe if the Task Force wasn't so short-staffed and politically kneecapped..."

Laura shot him a glare.

Connor grinned nervously and held his hands up in surrender.

"Just saying," he said.

Laura returned to her paperwork, eyes scanning notes, fingers twitching slightly against the edge of the table.

Connor sighed, sinking back into his seat. He tore into his burger, but the taste sat heavier on his tongue now, the earlier joy dimmed.

He would never admit it, but he knew more about the vigilante than he let on. Midtown was changing. Whether Laura liked it or not, the vigilante wasn't the problem. They were a solution.

#

The door shut with a quiet click.

Nikki slipped inside, the silence of the house wrapping around her like a cold, damp towel.

She peeled the mask off her head, her black hair falling loose. A dark red streak curved through her bangs and caught the light.

Her face, still so young, was marked by exhaustion. Her eyes were heavy with more weight than most seventeen-year-olds ever carried.

She moved through the kitchen like a ghost, every step familiar. She didn't bother turning on the lights. She grabbed her usual midnight snack. Two painkillers and a glass of water.

She downed the pills, feeling the knot of frustration still tight in her chest. The throbbing in her head hadn't eased. Neither had the knot of frustration in her chest. She had encountered the most infamous man in Midtown, and he got away.

Glass clinked softly into the sink.

Nikki turned, each step heavier than the last as she crossed the hall.

She passed the bathroom mirror and caught a glimpse of herself. The bruising along her temple had begun to bloom faintly, painting her reflection in streaks of fatigue. She carefully placed her palm on her head and winced. A slight purple mist appeared from under her hand. When she removed her palm, the bruise was gone.

She looked at herself once more and could see how much the stress was affecting her. Pain. Hollow-eyed. Worn. Things her abilities couldn't heal.

Three weeks into fighting crime. Five months of training before that. Trying to learn how to use and control her powers.

Was it enough time? she wondered. *Should I go back to training? What if I'm not ready?*

She let out a slow, shaky sigh and shook her head. She couldn't stop now. She was making progress. Helping people and saving lives. Getting criminals off the street. More than the Task Force was doing anyway.

In the bathroom, she leaned over the sink, turning the tap. Cold water washed over her hands, stung against her bruised knuckles. She splashed her face and felt the cool relief.

Her arms ached. Her ribs pulsed. Her mind swam.

But she was alive.

She turned off the water, and that was when she heard it.

The faint metallic rattle of a key in the front door.

Her breath caught.

In a blur, she darted down the hall, heart pounding.

She tore off her vigilante gear, stuffed it under her bed, and threw on pajamas. Her heart thudded against her ribs as she dove under the covers.

The bedroom creaked open just as she settled in.

Laura stepped in.

"You awake?" she asked gently.

Nikki rubbed her eyes, feigning drowsiness.

"I am now," she replied.

"I didn't mean to wake you," Laura said, stepping farther in. She lifted a small plastic bag with Bernie's logo on it. "I brought you your favorite."

"Thanks, Mom," Nikki said, sitting up slowly and forcing a tired smile. "I'm not really hungry right now. I'll eat it tomorrow."

She was lying through her teeth. Her stomach was growling. She hadn't eaten since that morning. But she didn't want to spend any more time dancing around the truth than she had to. She knew her mom would have too many questions for her to dodge.

"No worries," Laura murmured.

A pause followed. Not awkward, exactly. Just…unfamiliar.

"I was thinking," Laura added. "Maybe we could go out tomorrow. I have Sunday off."

Nikki couldn't help but let out a sarcastic chuckle.

"You?" she said. "A day off? Since when?"

Laura let out a soft exhale.

"It was Connor's idea, actually," she replied. "He thinks I'm pushing myself too hard."

"Is he wrong?" Nikki asked, her words sharper than she intended.

She couldn't help but feel angry at her mom. Ever since the Protector disappeared, Laura had buried herself in work. Whatever bond she and her mother once had… It had fractured, hairline cracks splitting deeper by the month.

"I was hoping to make it a regular thing," Laura said softly.

"Connor's been helping keep things in order at headquarters, and we're really close to finishing a project that could make everyone's lives easier in Midtown. I—"

Laura had a knack for overexplaining and oversharing. It was one of the things Nikki used to love about their talks. These days, it was mostly updates about cases, city troubles, and any other work-related details.

"I want things to go back to the way they used to be," Laura continued quietly. "I want us to go back to normal. To feel like a family again."

Nikki's throat tightened. She wanted that too. But wanting something didn't always make it real.

"We'll see," Nikki finally replied.

Laura nodded and gave a small, tired smile.

"I love you," she said.

"I love you too, Mom," Nikki said, her voice softer now. "Good night."

Laura lingered at the door for just a second longer.

"Good night, my love," Laura said.

Then the door closed.

Nikki exhaled sharply, her whole body sagging with exhaustion.

She turned to face the window. Outside, Capital City pulsed. Sirens threaded through the night air, neon lights blinking from rooftop to rooftop like fading stars.

Her eyes stayed on that skyline for a long time, unfocused and distant.

Then, finally, mercifully, they drifted closed.

For a few precious hours, she rested.

2

Connections

In the daytime, Halvade looked like just another crowded city.

But those who lived there knew better.

The tension never left the air, like a taut wire stretched across the district, always on the verge of snapping.

Everyone felt it.

Everyone but Frederick.

He moved through the bustling sidewalks with the quiet confidence of a man who owned every inch of them. Crowds instinctively parted as he walked by.

Frederick dressed sharply in a dark suit and polished shoes, everything cut to fit his large, commanding frame. He was a warlord dressed as a businessman.

Then again, war *was* his business.

As he approached a cracked intersection near a sagging tenement, his eyes softened.

An older woman—frail, hunched, her arms bent under the weight of heavy grocery bags—struggled up the front steps. The wind tugged at the edges of her shawl.

"Mrs. Carillo," Frederick called gently, reaching out with one large hand. "Why didn't you ask someone for help?"

She flinched at his touch. He was used to this. Most people were startled by his presence, by the sheer weight of him in a space.

"Oh, Frederick!" she said, smiling with worn, creased lips. "You startled me, dear."

Her voice was light but frayed at the edges, like a threadbare blanket.

"Apologies," Frederick said, already relieving her of her bags. "Let's get these up those stairs."

He held the bags with ease on his left arm and offered the other to steady her. They ascended the concrete stairs slowly, his pace perfectly matched to hers.

Inside, the apartment smelled of old lace and lemon cleaner. The wallpaper peeled in long, curling strips. Dust settled on every surface that wasn't sacred. On the counters and shelves sat picture frames, prayer candles, and worn keepsakes.

Frederick stepped into the kitchen and set the bags gently on the table.

"Do you need help putting your groceries away?" he asked.

"Oh, no," Mrs. Carillo replied, waving a delicate hand. "I can manage."

As she moved about, busying herself, Frederick scanned the room. He'd been here just a handful of times. The couch sagged in the middle. The TV was ancient. But the pictures— that was what caught his eye.

Photos of her family. His gaze landed on a frame near the window. Mrs. Carillo's only son, Marco. His thin face stared back, his skin pale, eyes too large for his sickly frame.

"How is Marco doing?" Frederick asked softly.

Mrs. Carillo's hands faltered. She drew a deep breath, seemingly hesitating to answer.

"Not well," she admitted, continuing to put her groceries away. "The doctors say it's spreading again. They recommend a procedure in Capital City, but..." Her voice trailed off. "The cost..."

Frederick exhaled slowly. He reached into his inner suit pocket and pulled out his wallet. Without a second thought, he pulled out several crisp hundred-dollar bills and turned to her.

"Take him tomorrow," he said, approaching her.

He placed the bills into her small, frail palm as she turned to face him. Her hand trembled, tears already brimming.

"Frederick, I can't accept..." she replied.

"You can," he said, gently closing her fingers around the money. "This is what family does. For me, please. Go to Dr. Jennings and tell him I sent you. He'll take good care of Marco."

Mrs. Carillo wiped her cheek and looked up at him, eyes shining.

"Bless you," she said. "You do too much for us little people."

Frederick smiled faintly and leaned down to place a gentle kiss on her cheek.

"Take care of yourself, Mrs. Carillo. Give Marco my love. If you ever need anything else, please don't hesitate to call."

Then he left.

Back outside, the city swallowed him.

The sounds of Halvade rushed toward him. Buzzing neon, restless foot traffic, and street vendors shouting over each other. The moment he hit the sidewalk, he was no longer a man. He was a force.

As he walked down the crowded sidewalk, he couldn't help but think of her words. *You do too much for us little people.* They echoed in his mind. *Who else would, if not me? I, too, was one of the little people of Halvade. I changed that. I made a name for myself.*

The people in my line of business expected me to leave and go to Capital City. I never could. This is my home. The people here are my family.

Midtown may not care, but I always will.

A vibration buzzed in his pocket, breaking the thought. He pulled out his phone.

A blocked number.

He already knew who it was.

"Yes?" he answered.

"We have a problem," said a voice like rusted metal scraping through a modulator.

Frederick's brow twitched faintly.

"I'm heading to my office," he said calmly. "Call me in thirty."

He ended the call.

Sliding the phone back into his pocket, his pace shifted. Quickened.

He didn't look back.

#

The Capital City Mall sparkled with life.

Glass storefronts gleamed under the bright lights. Small vendors packed the walkways, voices calling and shouting for customers. Everyone here looked relaxed. They shopped without concern for how the other cities struggled.

Nikki hated it.

She stood among the crowds, arms crossed, watching strangers live lives that didn't feel real.

All the while, Halvade was barely hanging on. Places like Veilhaven had it even worse. But here? Here, it was all artisan pastries and overpriced hoodies.

She lived in Capital City, technically. But she never felt like she belonged to it.

"Oh, let's go in here," Laura said suddenly, steering toward a trendy boutique with pastel signage and overly happy mannequins.

Nikki sighed.

She'd regretted agreeing to this outing from the moment they left the house. But some part of her still wanted this to work. She loved her mom. She missed her. Rebuilding what they'd lost might be impossible, but trying still felt worth it.

Inside, Nikki glanced around the racks. Sweaters with floral stitching. Jeans, both tight and baggy. Crop tops with glittery slogans. All curated for the bright, bubbly kind of teen Nikki had never been.

Her mom did not know her style at all.

She looked down at her own black tee, dark jeans, and worn sneakers. Then, back at a hoodie that read *Good Vibes Only* in neon pink cursive.

"Yeah, I don't know," Nikki muttered. "Not really seeing anything I'd wear."

Laura was already waist-deep in a pile of knitwear. She turned, holding up a beige sweater decorated with a tiny cartoon graphic of a mushroom slurping noodles.

Nikki snorted. She didn't want to. It just happened.

"See?" Laura said, beaming. "Cute, right?"

"It's cute," Nikki admitted, trying to swallow her smile. "But definitely not something I'd wear."

"All right," Laura replied, folding the sweater up and placing it back on its rack. "Well, where *would* you like to shop?"

Nikki grinned mischievously.

Without answering, she grabbed her mom's hand and tugged her out of the boutique, weaving expertly through the crowds.

Finally, they stopped in front of her favorite store: Buzy Beez.

The second they stepped inside, the vibe shifted.

Loud pop-punk blared through the speakers. This was more her speed.

The walls were plastered with movie posters and blacklight art. Racks were stuffed with graphic tees, enamel pins, and limited-edition sneakers. A corner display featured horror-themed plush animals, all with cute-but-sinister designs.

Nikki made a beeline for a tiny plush fennec fox, fangs blood-stained and its eyes glowing red.

She held it up like it was a holy relic.

"I *have* to have her," Nikki exclaimed dramatically, turning to show her mom.

Laura raised an eyebrow.

"Well...she's fierce," she said.

"Exactly," Nikki replied, hugging the plush close to her chest. "Her name is Foxxy."

"Simple," Laura said, clearly trying. "I like it."

Nikki drifted deeper into the store with renewed energy, combing through clothes. Laura trailed behind, looking politely overwhelmed.

"You should get something," Nikki called over her shoulder.

"Oh, I don't know," Laura responded, hesitantly. "Pretty

sure these clothes weren't made for people my age."

Nikki scoffed and grabbed two matching black T-shirts. A massive teddy bear stared from the front, its eyes glowing. It held a squirt gun in one hand and a bouquet of roses in the other.

"We could match," Nikki said, holding one up. "Twinning is cool again. I read it online."

Laura stared at the shirt, seemingly confused.

"What is that supposed to be?" she asked.

"It's an album cover," Nikki explained. "But that's not the point. It's about fun. Stepping outside your weird mom comfort zone."

Laura gave her a long, flat look.

"Okay," she said. "But if I wear that, you're getting that cute mushroom sweater."

Nikki blinked.

"Wow," she deadpanned. "Blackmail. Real classy."

"Well?" Laura prodded, half-smiling.

Nikki rolled her eyes, but her grin was already blooming.

"Deal."

#

Frederick's office sat high above Halvade, tucked away on the top floor of an unmarked concrete building.

Inside, luxury clashed against restraint. A polished dark oak desk, a few priceless paintings. Everything else was sparse. Controlled. Heavy.

Frederick sat behind the desk, his thick fingers drumming a slow and impatient rhythm across the wood. The laptop screen in front of him glowed softly, waiting.

He leaned back, his broad shoulders pressing into the leather chair, and turned toward the window. From up here, the city looked like a rotting machine. Thin figures moved below like ants, scurrying between jobs, debts, and dead ends.

He couldn't see their faces, but he didn't need to. He could feel the weight they carried. Fear. Exhaustion. Sorrow.

Those were the things Halvade was built on. He had learned how to harvest them.

The laptop chimed. A high, clipped tone.

Frederick turned back, his shoulders squaring. He tapped the screen.

The call opened.

On the other side, a shadow flickered against a black background.

No face. No features. Just a presence.

The Gunsmith.

"Frederick," the figure said, voice low and mechanized, dragging like rusted iron against the speakers. "The delivery was compromised. My weapons are now in Task Force hands. This is unlike you."

Frederick's throat tightened.

He was not a man who bowed to many. But the Gunsmith made something old and primal twist in his gut. The taste of being smaller.

"Apologies," Frederick said, each word carefully measured. "We had an unexpected problem. A masked hero."

The Gunsmith was silent.

"Masked hero?" the Gunsmith asked finally. "Was it—"

"No," Frederick cut in. "It wasn't the Protector. Different abilities. But abilities nonetheless."

"I see," the Gunsmith replied, the faintest hint of disdain

bleeding into the words. "If this vigilante is going to be disrupting your business, perhaps it would be best that we put a pause on our arrangement."

Frederick stiffened. His jaw worked silently for a moment before he answered.

"That won't be necessary," he said, low and tight. "I'll handle it. This won't happen again."

"It better not," the Gunsmith said, so soft it somehow hit harder than a shout. "Efficiency. Discretion. Two things you seem to lack. There will be no more chances."

The call cut off.

Frederick stared at the empty screen, his breath loud in the silent room. Each puff from his nostrils fogged his reflection.

Then, he exploded.

The laptop went flying across the room, smashing into the far wall. Plastic and glass rained down, scattering like shrapnel. His roar filled the office, bouncing off steel and stone.

The door burst open.

One of his men appeared, wide-eyed, frozen at the threshold.

"You all right, boss?" the man asked, half a step from bolting.

Frederick didn't answer at first.

He squeezed his fists, nails biting into his palms until blood welled in tiny crescent moons.

"I want the vigilante," Frederick growled, his voice rough-edged, barely human. He sucked in a deep breath through flared nostrils, steadying himself. "I want them alive. I want to teach them exactly who runs this city."

He rose, moving toward the man, his shadow stretching long under the office lights. The air in the room tightened, as if the weight of his presence had thickened.

"I don't care what it costs," Frederick continued, his voice dropping even lower. "Bring them to me."

#

Nikki bit into a warm pretzel, savoring the salty, buttery taste as it melted across her tongue. She glanced up and couldn't help but laugh.

Across from her, Laura tugged at the hem of her teddy bear T-shirt like it was lined with thorns.

"You look adorable," Nikki teased, licking salt from her fingers.

"I feel like a walking sticker book," Laura said, glaring down at the cartoon bear grinning up from her chest. "But if it makes you happy, I'll live."

The food court was alive around them, buzzing with people. The sounds of people laughing and trays clattering, along with the mingled scents of sugar and grease, filled the air. People indulged in pretzels, pizza, fried chicken, and whatever else they could get their hands on.

For a fleeting second, Nikki let herself pretend that this was normal. That this life was actually *hers*.

"So," Laura said, too casually. "How's school been going?"

The illusion popped like a bubble.

"It's…going," Nikki replied, shrugging and wiping her palms on her jeans.

The truth was, she had been falling behind. Her best friend, Jenna, had tried to cover for her as much as possible. Jenna was Connor's niece. She also knew about Nikki's secrets. She wasn't as supportive as Nikki would have hoped, but Jenna would never let her deal with it alone.

"Well," Laura offered, "if you ever need help with your studies, you know you can always come to me. I was quite the whiz in school."

"Please don't ever call yourself a *whiz* again," Nikki responded, smirking.

Laura chuckled, a real one.

It delicately punched a soft ache into Nikki's chest. Hearing her mom laugh was so rare.

"Jenna's been really helpful," Nikki added.

What she didn't tell her mom was that Jenna would often use her hacking skills to bump Nikki's grades up.

"That's good," Laura responded. "I'm glad you've had her in your life."

Then, there was a pause.

Laura's hands drifted toward each other, fingers twiddling. It was a rare crack in her mom's always-composed exterior. Something was coming. A conversation they'd both danced around for far too long.

Nikki decided to break the silence before it swallowed them both.

"You know," Nikki said, "it's okay to talk about Dad."

Laura froze, just for a second. Her shoulders stiffened. Her face tightened, as it always did when she was uncomfortable.

"I know how hard it was," she said finally, her voice softer now. "Him leaving. And I know I haven't been there for you. Not the way I should've. But I'm trying. I want to fix this, Nikki. Maybe it'll never be exactly like it was…but I want us to be close again. You're still my number-one priority. You always have been."

And for the first time in a long time, Nikki believed her.

Not because of what she said, but because of *how* she said it.

BUZZ!

Laura's phone vibrated across the table, loud enough to snap the moment in half. She picked it up, grimacing when she saw the screen.

"It's Connor," she said. "I'm sorry, do you mind if I—"

"It's fine," Nikki said automatically.

But it wasn't. It never was.

She watched as her mom stepped away, phone pressed to her ear, voice low and serious. Another secret. Another emergency. Another thing Nikki would never be allowed to understand.

She took another bite of her pretzel, but the flavor was gone now. Just heatless dough and salt in her mouth. Heavy and hollow.

Laura returned a minute later, guilt etched into every line of her face.

"There's an emergency at work," she said, carefully. "They need me to come in."

Nikki exhaled slowly through her nose, masking her disappointment behind a small smile.

"I get it," she said. "Work's important."

"I'll make it up to you," Laura promised. "We'll have a full day. Just you and me. No phones. No interruptions. I swear."

She extended her pinky, a playful old habit from when Nikki was little.

Nikki rolled her eyes, but she couldn't hide her smile.

"You better not break it," she said, linking her pinky with her mom's.

Laura leaned in and kissed Nikki's forehead.

"I love you," she said, then vanished into the crowd.

Nikki watched her disappear into the river of shoppers, feeling that ache return. For one tiny moment, it had felt like they were getting back to who they used to be.

She wrapped her arms around herself, holding on to the feeling and the promise. Because deep down, she wasn't sure when, or if, she'd ever get that day.

3

The Project

The Task Force Headquarters loomed in the heart of Capital City like a watching god. Its spires of glass and steel rose sharply against the smog-thick skyline. It served as the city's authority and its governing office. Nothing happened in the world of Midtown without the Task Force knowing.

Inside, the air was chilled and sterile. White floors, chrome walls, and cameras were embedded like blinking eyes.

Laura's heels struck the marble floor in a rhythm sharp as a metronome, each step echoing like a countdown. Her mind wandered despite herself, lingering on Nikki's smile, the soft moment in the mall food court. She'd meant everything she'd said. She wanted to be the kind of mother Nikki needed. But the city had its claws in her. And it never let go.

She reached the secured elevator and entered a code. A biometric scanner slid from the wall and bathed her face in a narrow band of blue light.

"Laura Sinclair," the automated voice confirmed. "Access granted."

The elevator sank, descending past the visible floors into the buried heart of Headquarters.

When the doors parted, the lab opened before her like a second world. A sprawling network of white corridors and glass-walled chambers. Machines hummed in constant motion. Screens flickered. Containment units blurred with pulsing lights inside. Scientists in fitted coats drifted from station to station like ghosts of progress.

Connor stood near the back, arms crossed, midconversation with Professor Vincent.

Vincent, the Task Force's chief scientist, didn't look like he belonged in a facility like this. He looked like he should've been cataloguing dusty books in a forgotten cathedral. Gaunt. Twitchy. Wisps of silver hair stood wild over a lined, clever face. But no one questioned his brilliance. Not if they wanted to keep their jobs.

Connor caught sight of her first.

"What the heck are you wearing?" he asked, one brow arched like a dare.

Laura glanced down at the teddy bear T-shirt she'd forgotten to change out of. A sigh escaped her.

"I was out with Nikki," she said.

"Honestly, it suits you," Connor said, deadpan.

She didn't dignify him with a reply. Just gave him the kind of stare that made lesser men evacuate entire rooms.

Professor Vincent stepped forward, wringing his hands.

"Director Sinclair," he said. "The recovery team returned this morning. We now have sufficient crystalline material for activation."

Laura's posture straightened. Her pulse quickened beneath the calm.

"Show me," she said.

They crossed the lab and entered a sealed chamber on the far end. The ceiling rose high, filled with scaffolding and reinforced beams. In the center stood the portal. It was massive, metallic, and unfinished. It looked like a cathedral door wrenched from some forgotten god's church—arched, ringed with conduits, its center dormant.

Wires sprawled across the floor like roots searching for water. Engineers worked in focused silence, calibrating instruments, fingers flying over holographic keys.

Waiting beside the frame were three men from the recovery team. Sergeant Lorne, Agent Mason, and Agent Phil. And behind them, *silent as shadow*, stood Dr. Elias Kade.

Lorne stepped forward and saluted.

"Director Sinclair," Sergeant Lorne said. "Permission to speak freely?"

Laura gave a curt nod.

"What exactly is this project?" Lorne continued.

Laura's eyes held his. She hesitated before answering.

"What I am about to share with you does not leave this room," she replied. "Is that clear?"

"Yes, ma'am," the agents chorused.

She stepped closer to the portal, its cold frame humming beneath her fingertips.

"This device is a gateway," she said. "A portal to other realms. Professor Vincent and his team have potentially found a method to stabilize cross-dimensional travel. We believe this device could connect our world to others. Realms where protectors still exist. If we're right, this portal could give us allies..."

"And if it doesn't work as intended?" Lorne asked bluntly.

Laura hesitated for a fraction of a second. She knew how bad things could get if this project failed. Then she straightened her shoulders.

"It will work," Laura replied.

Vincent gestured toward a nearby chamber, an oblong core with crystalline ports.

"It's time to load the power chamber," he explained. "The crystals will break down into a pure energy form. Once converted, it should be enough for a single ignition. A test run."

Mason and Phil opened their duffels, revealing crystals that pulsed with soft, alien light—glowing shards the size of fists. Milky, green-blue, and edged in mineral veins. They fitted them into the chamber, one by one, the room darkening slightly as each locked in.

Laura stepped aside to observe. But her gaze caught a flicker of motion.

Dr. Kade.

He moved slower than the others. His coat was stiff, his hands pale and trembling. From his satchel, he withdrew a smaller crystal. This one was darker. A deep bruised purple, with veins of red that pulsed.

"What's that?" Laura asked, her eyes narrowing. "It's different than the rest."

"Stronger," Kade said, his voice rasped. "It will work, just as the others…"

Laura turned to Vincent.

"If Kade says it will work, then I trust him," Vincent replied. "There's a reason he was chosen to lead the extraction team."

Laura let out a soft exhale. Without another word, Kade tucked it into the chamber. Still, something about it unnerved her. A ripple of unease passed down her spine.

Before she could give it a second thought, Vincent was already confirming the sequence.

The machine began to whir. A low, grinding thrum. Sparks raced along the cables toward the portal's frame. The entire chamber seemed to breathe.

"How long does the process take?" Laura asked.

"A few hours," Vincent replied. "The energy conversion should be complete before nightfall."

"The moment it is ready, you let me know," Laura said.

She returned to the main room of the lab, where Connor was waiting.

As she glanced back, she noticed Kade slipping away. His gait was off, his shoulders hunched. He seemed to be folding in on himself. Under the lab lights, his skin had taken on a sickly pallor, like wax left too close to the heat.

Something was off.

"Doctor Kade," she called out.

He froze.

When he turned, his eyes were…wrong. Sunken. Too still. Like they were staring out from inside a cave.

Laura approached him carefully.

"Are you all right?" she asked him.

"I-I'm fine," he said too quickly.

His gaze darted across the room, never settling on her.

"You look exhausted," Laura said. "Why don't you take the rest of the day off?"

"No!" he snapped violently. The air in the room shifted.

A dozen eyes turned toward them. Silence fell.

Laura's expression didn't change. But for just a second, the hairs on her arms rose, as if static had whispered across her skin.

"Excuse me?" she said, her voice hardening.

Kade seemed to realize how badly he had messed up. He flinched.

"I'm sorry," he muttered. "I didn't mean to snap. It's just…I want to be here for the activation. I'll go home and rest. I'll be ready when you need me."

Laura held his gaze for a long moment. Then gave a single nod.

"When the test begins," she said, "we will contact you."

Kade nodded and hurried off, almost stumbling as he vanished through the doors.

Laura watched him go.

Connor stepped up beside her.

"What was all that about?" he asked.

"I have no clue," Laura replied, lowering her voice and folding her arms. "Something's off. I want someone to keep a close eye on him. Have Lorne and his men stay outside of his house. He's not to leave until the test is done."

"You got it," Connor said, walking away.

Laura turned back toward the glowing frame, its power rising like a tide.

Whatever was happening to Kade…she wouldn't allow it to threaten this project. Not when they've come this close. Not while Midtown's future was at stake.

#

The shed smelled faintly of oil and old wood. A string of mismatched fairy lights drooped along the low ceiling, casting flickering halos over faded posters and rust-speckled shelves.

Tools hung from nails like museum relics. In the corner, an old electric heater buzzed faintly, barely cutting the cold.

Nikki sat stiffly on a sagging couch, her arms locked tightly across her chest like armor, her jaw clenched, her stare fixed. She looked like she was trying to hold herself together with nothing but friction and breath.

Jenna paced the floor with nervous energy, her sneakers scuffing lightly against the cement. Upbeat indie music played from her open laptop, bouncy, bright, and mocking in the tension-thick room.

She stopped pacing long enough to glance at Nikki.

"Why aren't you saying anything?" Jenna asked carefully. "Please say something. I can't take the silence. It's making me nervous."

"You knew," Nikki said, her voice low. "You knew that Frederick was going to be there. Why didn't you say anything? Not even a warning."

Jenna winced, as if the words had slapped her.

"Okay, to be fair, I didn't actually know," she said. "Not for sure. I only...suspected. Plus, I thought you wouldn't want to go if you knew he might show up. I really thought you could handle it."

"You *thought* I could handle it?" Nikki shot back, jumping to her feet. "You're kidding, right?"

"I didn't think it would go sideways like that!" Jenna's voice rose, but her eyes stayed apologetic. "You've faced some pretty tough guys. You always stay on your feet."

"I nearly died, Jenna. Do you get that?" Nikk's fists trembled at her sides. "If I hadn't teleported in time, I'd be dead. Gone. Just another body they dragged off."

Jenna looked away, guilt burning behind her eyes.

"I thought if you caught him…" she started, struggling to get the words out. "I thought the Task Force would finally take you seriously. That, maybe, your mom would stop treating you like a kid. Maybe you could finally come clean."

"So you gambled my life on a *maybe*?" Nikki replied, her voice staying sharp.

Silence.

"I'm sorry," Jenna whispered. "I wanted to help. Ever since you told me about your abilities, I've done everything I could. But you're the vigilante. You've got powers. You get to save people and be the hero. And I'm just…stuck here. Hacking cameras. Watching. Waiting. I wanted to do more. To *help* more. I really thought this would be your moment."

"Jenna—"

"Don't," she said, sharper now. "You don't get it. You don't know what it's like to lose everything and then just be expected to move in with your uncle and pretend everything's normal while the world ends outside your window."

Nikki's breath caught.

"I'm sorry," Jenna said, blinking fast. "I didn't mean—"

"No," Nikki said, quieter now. "I know how hard it's been since your mom…I haven't been much help. Not like you've been for me."

"No one talks about it," Jenna said, shrugging and biting her lip. "Connor doesn't. I think he thinks if we don't talk about it, we won't fall apart."

A long pause.

"I know that feeling," Nikki said. "Pretending helps…until it doesn't."

Jenna sat on the couch, letting a soft exhale out.

"I didn't mean what I said," she said, looking up at Nikki. "If anyone knows what I'm going through…it's you."

Nikki nodded and sat next to Jenna.

"Jenna, you help a lot," she said. "You help more than anyone else, actually. Without you, I wouldn't be able to do what I do. I'm not angry, I just… Last night was reckless. It can't happen again."

"You're right," Jenna said. "I messed up. And I promise, it won't happen again."

Nikki hugged her, and the tension cooled.

Then a sharp alarm blared from the laptop.

Jenna jolted and rushed over, fingers flying across the keyboard. The alarm died. Surveillance feeds filled the screen in flickering squares.

"What is it?" Nikki asked, the steel sliding back into her voice.

"One of the cameras in Halvade just flagged activity," she replied. "Frederick's men, they're moving something. Might be a weapons drop."

Nikki's body coiled, fists already clenched.

"Is *he* there?" she asked.

"Nik…" Jenna said, hesitating.

"Is he there?" she repeated, voice like the snap of a whip.

Jenna sighed and scanned the feed. Her expression tightened.

"Yeah," she said. "He's there."

Nikki's shoulders rose and fell with one steady breath. Her eyes narrowed with quiet fire.

"Send me the coordinates."

Jenna turned, worry etched deep into her brow.

"Nikki, you're still recovering," she said. "This isn't strategy. It's revenge."

"I know what it is," Nikki said. "Just give me the location."

Jenna bit her lip.

"Okay," she said. "But if you're going, you're taking comms. You have to keep me in your ear the whole time. Promise me that."

"I promise," Nikki said, already grabbing her gear.

Jenna entered the coordinates and synced Nikki's device. The silence stretched between them again.

Nikki paused at the door.

"This time," she said quietly, "I'm not going in blind."

The door creaked open, and she vanished into the night, fire in her chest, purpose in her stride.

No more surprises.

No more mistakes.

Only payback.

#

The abandoned building groaned beneath Nikki's weight as she crouched at the ledge, peering through a jagged window frame. Below, trucks idled like metal beasts outside the warehouse. Their headlights sliced through the fog, halos stuttering in the mist—yet no drivers stood nearby.

"There's no one outside," Nikki whispered, pressing two fingers to her earpiece. "Are the trucks already empty?"

"Affirmative," Jenna's voice crackled back. "No movement. No one's exited the warehouse either. Frederick should still be inside."

Nikki's gaze swept the empty street. Not a single figure. No footsteps. No engines. No voices. Just a brittle hush that pressed in from all sides.

"Too quiet," she murmured.

"You need to activate your bodycam," Jenna said. "We've got no visual down here."

Nikki tapped the pin-size device under her collar. A faint *beep* answered.

"Got it," Jenna confirmed. "I'm online."

"What's the play?" Nikki asked, brushing a damp strand of hair from her cheek. "Any quiet ways in? I'd prefer not to walk in to a dozen rifles on casual mode."

"Give me a sec," Jenna muttered, fingers clicking furiously on her end. "There's a maintenance hatch. Center-left on the roof. Small, rusted. That's your best shot. And Nikki…no noise. Please."

"Define *noise*," Nikki said, as she sprinted.

Midleap, she vanished in a burst of violet smoke, reappearing above the warehouse in a whoosh of displaced air. Her boots struck the metal rooftop with a dull *thud*, skidding slightly on the rain-slick surface.

"I said *no noise*," Jenna sighed.

"Come on," Nikki muttered, brushing off her knees. "That was pretty stealthy. For me."

The roof creaked under her weight as she crept forward. Wind hissed through rusted seams, shadows peeling and folding across the steel. Her pulse beat like a signal drum in her ears.

"Where's this hatch?" she whispered.

"Middle of the roof," Jenna replied. "Didn't you listen the first time?"

"Did *you* forget who's dangling off rooftops right now?" Nikki hissed.

"Fair," Jenna said. "Still. Less sass, more stealth."

Nikki smirked and kept moving.

Finally, she found it: a square panel of rust-flecked metal, barely the size of a crate lid. Her fingers curled under its cold edge. Inch by inch, she eased it open. The hinges groaned, loud in the stillness.

Then, darkness.

She dropped in.

She hit the iron scaffolding with a metallic *clang*, echoing faintly. Nikki crouched, one hand steadying herself.

"I'm in," she breathed.

The warehouse yawned below her like a metal skeleton. Steel beams stretched out like ribs, dividing space into crosshatched shadows. Crates rose in uneven towers. The far corners dissolved into black.

Something was wrong.

"Uh…" she whispered. "It's empty."

"That can't be," Jenna replied. "No one's left. I've had eyes on every exit. You should see someone. Anyone."

Nikki crept along the catwalk, her steps slow and deliberate. Below, something shifted. Barely a flicker behind the crates.

"Wait," she said. "I think I see someone."

"Don't engage," Jenna warned. "It's too dark. I can't see anything."

But Nikki was already climbing down.

Her boots kissed the concrete with barely a whisper. Her breath fogged faintly in the warehouse chill.

The figure lay slumped at the base of a crate. No blood. No wounds. No breath.

Nikki knelt beside him, shook his shoulder.

"Hey," she whispered. "You okay?"

Nothing.

Dread coiled inside her, cold and low.

"Nikki," Jenna said sharply. "Get out. Right now. I'm calling the Task Force—"

The lights snapped on.

Buzzing fluorescents exploded to life, blinding and brutal. Nikki threw up an arm, squinting hard. Shadows fled in every direction.

Crates burst open.

Men poured out like floodwater, armed, fast, and precise. Tactical gear gleamed. Rifles locked. Boots slammed.

A trap.

"Nikki, run!" Jenna shouted.

Too late.

The exit slammed shut behind her with a final echoing *bang*.

And from the shadows, Frederick stepped forward. Two brutes flanked him, rifles slung on their arms.

"What's the matter?" he said, voice low and amused. "Wasn't expecting to *actually* find me here?"

Nikki took a step back, hands raised. Her eyes flicked to the exits. Blocked. Too many bodies. Too little time.

"You cost me a lot the other night," Frederick said, circling. "Almost lost a client I spent *years* building trust with. And that kind of mistake"—he grinned—"doesn't sit well with me."

Her heart thundered like a war drum. But her grin came quick and cruel, sharp as broken glass.

"Can't we talk this out?" she asked lightly. "Maybe settle this like friends?"

Frederick chuckled. Dry and hollow.

His men raised their weapons.

"I guess not," Nikki muttered.

Her fists clenched. Violet light surged under her skin,

crackling at her knuckles.
She wouldn't go quietly.
Not this time.

4

The Doorway

Dr. Elias Kade twisted violently in his bed, his body slick with cold sweat. The sheets tangled around his limbs like restraints, as if the bed itself refused to let him go. Every nerve screamed.

Darkness smothered the room, thick and unbroken. Not even the bleeding glow of the city lights slipped through the blinds. The shadows here felt deeper. Hungrier.

He clutched his abdomen, fingers digging into flesh as something inside writhed—a sharp, sickening pressure that felt less like pain and more like invasion. His skin had taken on a corpselike pallor, clammy and wet. No matter how often he wiped his face, the sweat returned, heavier than before.

He hadn't slept since leaving Ashenfell.

Every time he drifted near the edge of unconsciousness, the whispers would start.

Soft at first. A slithering under his skin.

Then louder. Sharper. Inescapable.

"We will come," they said. *"We will take your world. You will help us. You belong to us."*

Kade gripped his skull with shaking hands, pressing his fingertips so hard into his temples they left dents.

"No…" he rasped. The word crumbled on his tongue. "No, please…"

A spike of pain lanced through his forehead. He rolled out of bed, staggering blindly into the dresser. A lamp toppled and crashed to the floor, shattering with a brutal crack. Glass burst in a shriek.

His knees gave out.

He collapsed onto the hardwood, heaving, but nothing came out. Only dry sobs. He felt fire in his throat.

The world around him flickered. It *shifted*.

He was no longer in his bedroom.

He stood on barren soil, cracked and black. Above him stretched a sky that bled. Crimson lightning splintered the heavens. Cinders swirled, carried on winds that stank of rot and ozone.

Figures emerged from the haze. Tall, twisted things. Eyes like pits of burning coal. Their shapes blurred the line between flesh and machine, between nightmare and creation.

They moved toward him.

"You belong to us!" they shrieked in a voice that was not one but hundreds, layered and discordant.

Kade screamed. He clawed at his scalp, tearing at his own skin. Blood mixed with sweat. His mouth opened wide enough to crack.

"GET OUT OF MY HEAD!"

His world fractured again. The nightmare bled into reality.

The room warped, the ceiling bending, the floor tilting, the darkness folding in on itself. He collapsed again, sobbing, barely human.

For a long, breathless moment, there was only the sound of his shallow, desperate breathing.

Then… a hand.

A black, shadowy, distorted hand.

It palmed Kade's head.

And in an instant, it disappeared.

Silence.

Kade's eyes snapped open.

They were no longer his own.

They glowed a deep, blistering red.

Slowly, unnaturally, he rose. Bones creaking. Muscles tightening.

His lips peeled back into a grin. Wide and sharp.

The man who had been Elias Kade was gone. Something else wore his skin now. Something that had been waiting.

#

Gunfire tore through the warehouse like a thunderstorm of bullets.

Nikki dove behind a stack of crates as bullets shredded the wood inches from her skull. Splinters rained like shrapnel. The deafening cracks of rifles swallowed every other sound, even her heartbeat. Breath came in ragged bursts. Her chest felt crushed from the inside out.

"Nikki!" Jenna's voice screamed through her earpiece. "You need to get out of there, *now!*"

"No," Nikki hissed. Her voice shook, but her grip didn't. "I'm not leaving without Frederick. Not this time."

Power burned beneath her skin, itching to be freed.

Violet smoke curled at her fingertips. Her scythes materialized, solid and hungry. She planted her boots, spine braced against the crates, grounding herself as another storm of bullets chewed the space around her.

Then she ran.

Mid-sprint, she vanished in a burst of violet smoke, reappearing in the middle of a knot of armed men.

Her scythe swept in a wide, brutal arc, ripping through one man's ribs. He dropped, gasping. She spun, heel crashing into another's jaw with a sickening crack. A third lunged. She caught his swing, twisted, and drove the scythe's handle into his temple.

Another enemy raised his weapon—

She blinked out of sight before he could fire, rematerializing behind him. One clean sweep of her blade and he collapsed with a grunt.

But the fight was catching up to her.

Every teleport drained her like blood from a wound. Every swing took more than it gave. Her limbs trembled. Her balance faltered. She staggered sideways, gasping, scythes wavering in her grip.

Just a second. Just a breath.

Then back in.

She struck again. Elbows to jaws. Knees to stomachs. Scythes carving through the chaos. Violet smoke trailed behind her like a storm.

But no matter how many she dropped, more kept coming.

Then, a blunt impact slammed into her ribs.

Pain exploded. Her breath vanished.

She hit the ground hard, spine smacking concrete. The world spun. Light blurred. Her limbs refused to move. Every breath she took burned. Her lungs had tightened.

Fear wrapped around her like ice.

Hands grabbed her. One at her arm, another at her leg. She was dragged across broken concrete, skin scraping against splinters. Her vision returned just long enough to catch the boots marching toward her.

Then she was yanked up and slammed back down.

A moan escaped her lips. Her ears buzzed. Jenna's voice crackled in her earpiece, frantic, but it was all static now.

Across the warehouse, Frederick approached.

Calm. Smiling.

"Well, well," he said. "This all feels familiar."

Nikki snarled and twisted, but the men held fast. Their grips were iron, dug deep into her limbs.

"Take the mask off," Frederick ordered, stepping closer. "I want to see who's caused me this much trouble before I put them down."

A heavy hand reached toward her face.

Panic ignited.

Her chest locked. Her throat seized. Her mask was the last line. It was her identity, her shield, her lifeline.

She couldn't scream.

Couldn't move.

Couldn't breathe.

But something inside her could.

It had waited long enough.

Power surged.

It *burst*.

A pressure boiled out from her center, violent and pure, like a star igniting inside her ribs.

BOOM!

A shockwave of violet light erupted from her body.

The men holding her were hurled backward like rag dolls, crashing into crates, pipes, and support beams. Screams echoed. Bones snapped. Some didn't get back up.

Frederick staggered, shielding his face. Smoke coiled around him like something alive. His men reeled, disoriented. The air reeked of scorched ozone.

Nikki gasped, one hand pressed to the floor. She pushed herself upright.

Her legs trembled. But they held.

The ache was gone. The exhaustion burned away. Electricity sizzled beneath her skin.

The warehouse swirled with violet haze. Threads of light danced along her arms. Her fingers sparked. Her body buzzed.

She stood at the center of the chaos, trembling.

Smoke radiated from her skin.

Frederick lowered his hand. His smile had vanished.

He was still angry, but beneath it, something else had crept in.

Uncertainty.

For the first time, he looked at her not like a nuisance.

But like a threat.

Nikki stepped forward.

Then again.

She didn't wait for permission.

#

The Task Force SUV idled beneath a flickering streetlight, the only movement in an otherwise silent street. The night air was thick, as if the shadows were waiting for something.

Inside the vehicle, Sergeant Lorne sat behind the wheel, arms folded and eyes locked on the house.

Something felt *wrong*.

"Are we seriously pulling an overnight on babysitting duty?" Phil grumbled from the back seat. "This is beneath us."

"We have orders," Lorne replied dryly. "We follow them. Even the boring ones."

Mason propped his boots on the dash and let out a long, lazy breath.

"I just want to say," he started, "I'm not the only one who noticed how *off* the doctor's been, right?"

Lorne glanced at him. Then at Phil, who now leaned between the seats, the tension in his face sharper than his sarcasm.

"Oh, *absolutely*," Phil said. "He looked hollow. Like something crawled into his skin. The dude is off."

Lorne's jaw tensed.

"We aren't the only ones who noticed," he said finally. "That's why Director Sinclair wanted eyes on him. Whatever is going on, it's not exhaustion. Something happened to him in Ashenfell. I just don't know what."

Silence fell again. Even the crickets had gone quiet.

Then...

CREAK.

The front door opened.

Lorne sat up straighter. A figure stepped out beneath the porch light, casting long, unnatural shadows across the steps.

It was Kade.

But it also...*wasn't*.

He moved like a marionette, limbs jerking with no rhythm, no sway, no soul. His walk was steady, but there was no humanity in it. Just motion. Just intent.

Lorne opened the door slowly, stepping into the cool night. His hand hovered near his holster.

"Doctor Kade?" he called out, keeping his voice level. "Everything all right?"

No answer.

Kade kept walking.

Lorne motioned subtly to the others.

Mason and Phil slipped out, spreading wide without a sound. Years of conditioning kicked in. Their weapons were ready, but their eyes showed hesitation.

"Doc?" Phil tried now, approaching with one hand extended. "Hey, you can talk to me. Tell me what's—"

CRACK!

Phil's scream tore through the night.

Kade had seized his wrist and *snapped* it like a twig. Bone burst through skin, the sound nauseatingly loud.

Before anyone could react, Kade *flung* Phil across the street like a pile of wet laundry. He crashed into a parked sedan with a metallic crunch. A moan slipped from his lips, but nothing more.

"*Get back!*" Lorne barked. He drew his weapon in a single practiced motion. "Stand down, *now!*"

Kade turned to him, slowly. His eyes met Lorne's.

They were…empty. No fear or rage. Just red.

Lorne fired. Once. Twice. Center mass.

The bullets hit, but Kade didn't even flinch.

Mason charged in, swinging the stock of his rifle at Kade's jaw with all his weight behind it.

Kade didn't blink.

He caught Mason by the throat and *lifted* him off the ground.

Mason kicked. Struggled. His face flushed purple. His fingers clawed at Kade's wrist, desperately trying to escape.

Lorne fired again, this time aiming for his head.

But Kade spun, using Mason's body as a shield.

The bullets struck flesh.

Lorne stopped, too late.

Kade dropped Mason like a broken doll and turned.

One blow. A fist to Lorne's chest. It felt like being struck by a sledgehammer.

Ribs *snapped*. Pain detonated behind his eyes as he was launched backward into the SUV, crumpling the door on impact.

He gasped, his lungs refusing to fill.

Before he could rise, Kade's boot drove into his gut. Lorne's body *skidded* across the pavement, coming to a stop near the curb in a twisted heap.

Everything burned.

His vision smeared like paint on a wet canvas. Blood pulsed in his ears. He couldn't feel his legs. Couldn't move his arms. He could feel his life fading.

But he saw, blurry and distorted, Kade climbing into the Task Force vehicle.

The engine rumbled to life.

Headlights lit the street in a harsh white glow.

Then the SUV pulled away, slow and quiet.

The only sound left behind was Lorne's shallow, gurgled breath. The wind whispered over the lifeless bodies of his team.

As the strength left his body, so did his last breath. His eyes slipped closed. Darkness followed.

#

Connor sat at a sleek steel table in the Task Force lab, absently twirling a stylus between his fingers. His eyes bounced between the dormant portal frame and Laura pacing like a caged wolf.

"Why don't you sit down?" he asked, his voice taut with unease. "You're making me nervous."

Laura didn't stop.

"Laura," he said again, sharper now, cutting through the hum of generators.

She halted, finally, and spun on her heel.

"What?" she snapped.

"Sit," he replied. "Before you wear a trench into the floor."

She exhaled hard through her nose and dropped into the chair opposite him. Arms crossed. Shoulders coiled tight as steel cables.

"How was bonding time?" Connor asked, lacing his voice with mock-casual levity.

Laura's posture softened, only by a fraction.

"Honestly," she said, "it went better than expected. We actually talked. She even smiled."

Connor could see Laura's eyes glossing, just a bit.

"It's weird, but… that scared me the most," Laura said.

"What do you mean?" he asked.

"Seeing her happy," Laura replied. "It reminded me of that little girl she used to be. And how devastated I would be if I lost her."

Connor waited a moment before replying.

"She misses you," he said, quieter now. "The job has swallowed everything else. You barely look at her anymore."

"That's not my fault," she replied, looking away.

"I know," he said, lifting both hands, placating. "Not blaming. Just…observing. You said she was happy. That counts for something."

Laura's gaze drifted toward the flickering panel lights.

"That's what this is all about," she said. "The portal. This project. If it works, if we make contact… Maybe I won't have to be everything, all the time."

"You really think this will fix it all?" Connor asked.

"No," she admitted. "But it might give us a chance. Midtown can't survive another crisis alone. Not without another protector."

The word hung in the air.

Protector.

Laura usually made it a point not to talk about him, as if he didn't exist anymore. Though sometimes Connor couldn't help but feel that way too.

He looked away.

"I…I've never asked how you've been doing," Laura said.

Connor looked back at her. He knew what she meant, but he was never one to talk about his emotions.

"How is Jenna?" she asked.

"She's been…holding up," he said. "But she's different. She doesn't talk about her mom. Not even once. I keep wondering if I should bring it up or just let it sit."

"You've taken on a lot," Laura said, her voice softened.

"I didn't really have a choice," he said with a small, hollow laugh. "After the accident, she had no one else. It's just been the two of us in that drafty apartment. Me pretending to be a father figure while still figuring out how to help keep the city from falling apart."

"I'm sorry," Laura said quietly. "I should've checked in. With both of you."

Connor looked at her and smiled faintly.

"You've had your own grief to carry," he said. "Plus, Nikki's helped a lot. Keeping her company. Hell, Jenna practically worships her. I think being close to her is the only thing keeping Jenna from spiraling."

Laura nodded, eyes distant now.

"She's lucky to have you," she said.

"I hope she still feels that way in ten years," he replied.

The hum of the machines shifted, deeper now, like a growl echoing through the walls.

BWAAAANG.

The building's alarms screamed to life.

Connor was on his feet instantly, hand snapping to his weapon.

A *crash* came from behind the elevator door.

Then the door flew inward, ricocheting off the wall with a thunderclap of steel.

Dr. Kade walked through the threshold. Blood soaked his front, bullet wounds gaping and dry. His skin had turned the color of old wax, his veins pulsing black beneath the surface. His eyes now glowed like dying stars. Red and endless.

"Doctor Kade?" Connor called out, trying to steady his breath. "What the hell is going on!?"

No answer. Kade's gaze locked onto the portal, and he moved toward it without hesitation.

"He's going for it!" Laura shouted. "Stop him!"

Connor raised his weapon and fired. Two clean shots to the side. Kade kept walking.

The portal began to whine, its frame vibrating like a tuning fork.

"Shut it down!" Laura barked.

Professor Vincent scrambled to the main console. His fingers flew across the keyboard.

"It's not responding!" he yelled. "The system's rejecting input!"

Connor and Laura rushed Kade together.

They hit him like battering rams, but it was like slamming into steel wrapped in skin.

Kade *roared*, a sound twisted and inhuman, and hurled them both across the lab.

Connor hit the tile hard, ribs grinding. Laura slammed into a support beam and crashed into the ground, coughing.

Connor forced himself up on trembling limbs, vision swaying.

Across the room, monitors exploded into static foreign symbols flashing like a virus spreading across the lab.

"Elias, please!" Vincent begged. "This isn't you! You must fight this!"

Kade seized him by the collar and tossed him aside.

Vincent hit the ground with a grunt, unmoving.

Kade raised his hand and pressed it to the control panel.

The portal roared to life.

A swirling mass of violet-blue energy coiled into existence, electricity snapping along its edge. The air warped. The floor trembled beneath their feet. It was alive and *angry*.

Connor charged.

He tackled Kade from behind, dragging him to the ground. The doctor thrashed beneath him like a feral beast.

Connor drew his sidearm, desperation raw in his voice.

"Don't make me do this!" he shouted. "Elias—!"

Kade turned. Eyes burning. A twisted smile.

BANG!

Connor fired. The bullet struck clean between Kade's eyes.

His body jerked. Then fell still.

And then, the portal *exploded*.

Light swallowed the room. A burst of energy cracked the walls. Consoles shattered. Connor was hurled backward, slamming into a steel beam hard enough to drop him.

Sparks rained from the ceiling like falling stars. Glass shrieked. Then...

Darkness.

#

Nikki surged forward, nerves stinging like a rising fire. The warehouse blurred around her, shadows twisting, crates toppling, and muzzle flashes slicing through smoke. Her scythes flared, larger than before. Their edges were alive with dark violet arcs of energy. The air cracked with each pulse, as though the storm inside her had found a shape.

She struck like fury unchained.

Each attacker who charged her was met with brutal pre-cision. Bone crunched beneath her blows. Blood sprayed across the dusty air. Scythe. Elbow. Kick. Her body moved on instinct, pure reaction honed by rage and fear. She felt untouchable.

Then she saw him.

Frederick—slipping through the chaos, using his men as a human wall. His eyes darted toward the exit like a rat sensing a fire.

Not this time.

With a breathless snarl, Nikki vanished in a burst of violet smoke and reappeared between him and the door, boots slamming into the ground. Her scythe snapped upward, inches from his throat.

Frederick skidded to a halt. His expression cracked. Fear was behind those cold, calculated eyes.

"No," Nikki growled, low and shaking. "You're not running again."

He turned to bolt, but she was faster. She grabbed him by the collar, yanking him backward. He hit the ground hard, gasping, as she loomed over him. She held her scythe to his neck, the once thick and dull blade now sharpened as smoke wrapped around it.

His breath hitched.

"Nikki," Jenna's voice buzzed in her ear, soft but urgent. "What are you doing?"

The sound of Jenna's voice cut through the noise in her head. Nikki's grip faltered. Her hand trembled. She hesitated.

And in her hesitation, Frederick twisted, driving his elbow into her ribs. She grunted, staggering back. His men surged in like a tide.

They overwhelmed her. Fists, boots, hands dragging her down.

She fought back, but there were too many. By the time she broke free, bodies collapsing around her, Frederick was gone. Vanished like mist into the night.

She screamed, but it was swallowed by a roar.

The ground lurched beneath her.

A low yet thunderous groan, like the city itself was in agony, rippled through the warehouse. Crates toppled, metal screamed, and the roof buckled above. A quake, violent and sudden.

She fell to one knee, losing her balance.

"It's a quake!" Jenna's voice rang in her ear. "Nikki, get out of there—*now!*"

She tried to teleport—but nothing happened.

Her powers flickered, then died. She gasped, the emptiness in her chest worse than pain. It was an absence, like her core had been drained.

She stumbled forward, dodging a crashing beam. Rubble split the floor open like a wound. The air reeked of dust.

She ran.

Her muscles ached. Her vision blurred. But she didn't stop.

A final chunk of ceiling tore loose behind her, just as she burst through the warehouse doors and slammed into the pavement outside. She landed hard, hands scraping raw across the asphalt. Her body trembled. Sirens echoed in the distance.

Black SUVs tore away down the road. It had to be Frederick's convoy, vanishing into the chaos.

She didn't have the strength to follow.

"What the hell was that?" she asked breathlessly.

Nikki rose slowly, her breath ragged. Every muscle ached. Her scythes faded to mist. She turned in place.

The city was unraveling.

Emergency lights flashed across the skyline. Fires lit the horizon. Civilians screamed in the streets. Buildings cracked like bones under strain.

"That… That quake…" Jenna said, her voice tight with disbelief. "It wasn't just Halvade. That quake hit everywhere. Capital City, Veilhaven… The entire world just shook."

Nikki stood still, watching red and blue lights flicker in the smoke.

"You need to get back here," Jenna urged.

Nikki's hands trembled at her sides. The guilt swelled, raw and acidic. She'd lost control. She'd let Frederick slip away again. But now…the world was bleeding.

She turned her gaze to the fractured skyline.

"I can't," she said quietly. "They need me."

5

Aftermath

The air in the lab was thick—choked with smoke and the acrid stench of scorched circuitry. Emergency lights flickered against the walls in warning pulses, casting red shadows over overturned desks and fractured screens. Somewhere beneath the chaos, the hum of the backup generator kicked in, groaning to life like the heartbeat of a wounded beast.

Laura groaned, pressing a trembling palm to her forehead. A sharp throb pulsed behind her eyes, each pulse a hammer strike in her skull. She pushed herself upright, blinking through the haze. Her vision was blurred. Her ears rang with high-pitched static.

"Connor?" she called, her voice barely above a whisper. "Connor, are you okay?"

A muffled grunt responded.

"Still breathing," Connor muttered, coughing as he pushed a beam of shattered conduit off his chest. He staggered to his feet, one hand gripping the edge of a broken desk for balance. "Mostly, anyway…"

Laura stood, shaky and sore. Around her, scientists and Task Force engineers moved like ghosts through the rubble, stunned, burned, and limping. Sparks sizzled from frayed wires. The portal frame lay in a smoldering heap, its center blackened, its limbs twisted into something unrecognizable.

As she scanned the room, she saw Professor Vincent motionless on the ground behind the portal's control panel.

"Vincent!" she yelled as she hurried over to him.

She knelt and carefully turned him on his back.

Vincent's body shifted under her touch. A gasp tore from his lungs as his eyes fluttered open, dazed and bloodshot.

"W-what happened?" he asked, wincing in pain as he sat up.

"Easy," Laura said, easing him back with one hand. "There was an explosion. We lost the portal."

Vincent's face twisted in confusion, then horror.

"What!?" he replied. "What? No...no, that's impossible. It was stable. I ran the diagnostics myself! Where's Kade?"

"He's dead..." she said softly.

Vincent's shoulders slumped. He let out a long, rattling breath as Laura helped him to his feet.

Connor arrived at her side, offering his support as they guided Vincent to a chair.

"Don't worry," Connor said. "We're going to get you medical attention. We'll figure out what happened."

Laura looked over the wreckage one last time, her jaw tight.

"We need to get up to the command floor," she said. "We have to assess the damage and coordinate a response."

She turned and led the way out of the lab.

When she and Connor entered the main building, they found chaos.

Lights sputtered. Ceiling panels had collapsed. Agents

shouted into radios, rushed across flooded hallways, and ducked sparks from broken wiring. The air reeked of burnt steel and ozone.

"This is bad, Laura," Connor said, looking at the destruction.

"Yes…" Laura replied, distracted as her eyes scanned the shattered ops room.

"Lorne and his team were supposed to have eyes on Elias," Connor said. "Do you think…"

"He had to have gotten to them," Laura replied. "Lorne would never have let him out of his sight. Not without a fight."

Before they could linger on the matter, an officer ran over to them.

"Director," he said, "the entire Task Force is awaiting orders. How should we go about this situation?"

"We need to evacuate the building and check for casualties," Laura replied. "Assist our injured and see if the blast affected any civilians outside."

"And what about the rest of the city, ma'am?" the officer asked.

"Excuse me?" she replied.

"The rest of the city," he said. "And the others? What should we do?"

"What do you mean?" she asked, confused. "What happened to the other cities?"

"Ma'am…do you not know?" the officer asked, his expression shifting. "The blast…it wasn't just an explosion. It was a quake."

"How bad is it?" Connor asked, while Laura stewed on the information.

"Bad," he said. "It wasn't just Capital City. Reports are

coming in from all over Midtown. Veilhaven, Halvade, everywhere. Global impact."

Laura gathered herself.

"Do we have recovery units on the streets?" Laura asked.

"We have units patrolling as many areas as possible," the officer replied. "But it's bad out there. Too much ground to cover.

"It doesn't matter," Laura declared. "Get everyone out there if you have to. Every available agent needs to be out in the field. Every. Single. One. Make sure the public sees we're doing something. They need to know someone's in control."

"Yes, ma'am," he replied, rushing off.

Connor placed a hand on her shoulder. She turned to him, her expression unrelenting.

"Laura," he began, voice gentle, "we need to get checked out. That blast nearly killed us."

"We don't have time," she said. "Whatever corrupted Kade… it came from that portal. A portal *I* authorized. And for all we know, he wasn't the only one exposed. We don't know the scope yet. We don't even know if—"

Her words caught.

"Nikki…"

She turned and bolted.

Laura burst into her office and snatched the phone from her desk. Her fingers punched the numbers with frantic speed.

"Come on, come on. Pick up."

It rang.

And rang.

"Damn it!" she hissed, slamming the receiver down.

Connor stepped into the office, eyes on her.

"What's the matter?" he asked.

"It's Nikki," Laura replied. "I can't get ahold of her."

"Call Jenna," he said. "Nikki was supposed to hang out with her today."

Laura dialed the number and waited.

After two rings—

"Hello?" Jenna's voice answered, startled.

"Jenna!" Laura yelled. "It's Laura. Is Nikki with you!?"

"Yes, Ms. Sinclair," Jenna replied. "She's here. We're all okay. We're just…shaken up from whatever just happened."

"Thank goodness!" Laura replied, exhaling a shaky breath as relief washed through her like a tide. "You tell her to stay there with you. Tell her I will go get her after I deal with this chaos."

"Okay, I will."

The call ended.

Laura remained still, fingers gripping the desk as she steadied her breathing.

"Laura," Connor said, "seriously. We need to breathe. Even just for a moment."

She straightened, jaw clenched. Then moved to the window.

From her vantage, the city was burning.

Smoke coiled into the sky. Sirens howled in every direction. Buildings crumbled. Fires raged. Somewhere out there, people were dying. Families were screaming. The world was unraveling.

"We don't have a moment," she said.

She turned back to Connor, her voice clear, commanding.

"The world needs the Task Force right now," she continued. "I need you with me. I need you to be focused. Can you do that?"

Connor looked past her, out at the shattered skyline.

She grabbed his face and looked him in the eyes.

"Connor," she repeated, firmer now. "Can you do that?"

"Yes," he said quietly.

Her eyes softened.

"Then let's get this under control."

#

Nikki ran through the streets of Halvade, her breath heavy and muscles burning with every step. Smoke curled up from burning buildings, casting shadows over shattered glass and splintered stone. Sirens wailed from every direction, blending with the panicked screams of civilians in a symphony of chaos.

"Nikki!" Jenna's voice cracked through her earpiece, strained and urgent. "Your mom just called. I told her you were with me, but she's going to expect you here when this is over. Please, you need to come back."

"Not yet," Nikki panted. "I need to help as many people as I can."

Up ahead, a building had crumbled, burying the sidewalk in jagged debris. Dust swirled in the air. A small crowd had gathered nearby, pale and paralyzed.

"What's going on?" Nikki asked, skidding to a halt.

A man turned to her, eyes wide.

"Someone's trapped," he exclaimed. "A kid. We tried…he's stuck."

Without another word, Nikki dropped to her knees and started digging. Concrete, beams, glass, she tore through it all with shaking hands. Her fingers bled. Her back cried out in protest. But she didn't stop.

She found him beneath a slab of drywall and twisted pipes,

a boy, maybe six or seven, his tiny body trembling beneath the weight. Coughing, crying, and scared.

"I've got you," she whispered, lifting the rubble away and cradling him in her arms.

A woman screamed and rushed forward.

"No, no. I've got him, I've got him!" she cried, clutching the boy and collapsing around him, sobbing. "Thank you. Thank you..."

Nikki staggered back, breathless, sweat pouring down her face. Her chest heaved. Around her, the crowd that had once stood frozen now stared at her in awe.

For a flicker of a moment, she wasn't just a girl with powers. She was a protector.

But the moment was shattered with a blast of heat and light. Another explosion rocked the street. Just ahead, flames engulfed a small house. From inside came the unmistakable sound of screaming.

Nikki was already moving.

The front door buckled under her kick, smoke flooding out to claw at her throat. The fire inside snarled like a living thing, walls crackling as embers danced through the hall.

"Nikki!" Jenna's voice buzzed. "That house isn't stable. The smoke will kill you. You've done enough, just...just stop!"

"There are people in here," Nikki snapped, coughing. "I'm not leaving them."

She pressed forward, dodging falling plaster and burning beams.

"Where are you!?" she shouted.

"In here!" a voice cried.

She kicked through a splintered door and found a woman and a little girl huddled in the corner of a bedroom, coughing and crying.

"Can you walk?" Nikki asked.

"Yes," the woman coughed, pulling the girl closer.

"Good. Take my arm. Stay behind me and move fast."

They reached the hallway just as the ceiling gave out. A support beam crashed behind them, sealing the way they came. The girl shrieked. Fire roared on either side.

Nikki turned to the window. The glass was already spider-webbed from heat.

"Nikki, stop!" Jenna shouted. "Don't break the glass. The heat could cause it to explode. You could seriously hurt them."

Smoke filled Nikki's lungs. Her powers pulsed inside her, flickering like a dying flame.

A burst of violet smoke engulfed them. When it cleared, they were outside.

Nikki collapsed to the pavement, coughing hard, her arms wrapped protectively around the woman and child. The mother sobbed as she held her daughter.

"Thank you," the woman whispered, cradling Nikki's head. "Thank you..."

The little girl touched Nikki's arm gently.

"Are you an angel?" she asked.

Nikki gave a tired smile.

"No," she replied. "Just...someone trying."

She pushed herself to her feet. The street was chaos—sirens, fires, screams. Another explosion rumbled in the distance.

"Jenna," she rasped into the earpiece. "I need your help. Tell me where to go."

There was silence.

Then, Jenna's voice returned, quiet. Different.

"This is too much," she said. "It's not just Halvade. Every

city's on fire. Veilhaven, Capital City…Nikki, you can't fix this. You'll die trying."

"I can't stop," Nikki said. Her voice trembled. "*He* wouldn't stop. They need help. They—"

"They need you alive," Jenna interrupted, firm now. "You saved people. You're saving people. You are not him. If you keep going, you're going to burn with the rest of this city."

Nikki didn't respond. Her hands shook.

"Nik," Jenna said again, voice raw now, no longer composed. "Please come back. Please. You're not alone in this."

For a long moment, Nikki stood in silence, the weight of the world pressing down on her shoulders.

Then finally, with tears in her eyes, she whispered, "Okay…"

She turned toward the cracked skyline, took one more look at the smoke and fire behind her.

And then she vanished into the storm.

#

Two Task Force agents guided Professor Vincent through the rubble-strewn entrance of Headquarters, the air sharp with smoke and the cries of sirens. His legs barely obeyed him. Pain throbbed through his skull in heavy pulses, each step dragging him further from clarity.

"Easy, Professor," one agent said, tightening his grip. "You're almost there. Just hold on."

Vincent glanced up, squinting against the glare of flashing lights. A medical transport waited at the curb, its back doors open and its engine growling low. A medic stepped out to greet them.

"We'll take good care of you," the driver said gently. "What are you feeling?"

"My head…" Vincent groaned, wincing. "It hurts…so bad…"

The medic helped him into the back of the vehicle, guiding him onto a stretcher. Vinyl cracked beneath his weight. His body was damp with sweat.

"Here," the driver said, handing him a bottle. "Drink."

Vincent downed it like a man who hadn't tasted water in days. The pain in his skull dulled to a throb. He lay back and closed his eyes, letting the world blur around him.

The vehicle jerked into motion.

Outside, chaos reigned. The sirens wailed like dying animals. Screams rose from all sides. Glass shattered. Fires crackled. The road trembled beneath the tires as the vehicle sped over potholes and broken asphalt.

But inside…silence.

A gnawing unease crept into Vincent's gut.

He cracked his eyes open and turned his head toward the rear window. What he saw beyond the glass made his pulse spike.

This wasn't the route to the hospital.

"Hey," he called out, throat dry. "What's going on out there? Where are we going?"

No response. Vincent's gut twisted with anxiety.

The vehicle swerved, jolting him hard in the stretcher. He grabbed the rail, heart pounding now. He looked outside again. Alleyways now, dark and deserted, buildings looming like tombstones.

"Hey!" he shouted louder. "What's going on? Where the hell are we?"

Still no answer.

Then, with a sharp hiss of the brakes, the vehicle came to a stop. For a moment, the only sound was the cooling engine.

And then…silence.

Vincent stared at the rear doors.

They creaked open slowly, spilling in the cold breath of the alley.

No one stood outside.

Vincent blinked. His hands, without realizing, had already unfastened the straps. His feet found the floor. He moved as if pulled by invisible strings.

A voice echoed from the dark.

"Step closer."

Vincent's blood ran cold. His body continued to move before his mind could manage a thought.

"Who's there?" he asked, trying to keep his voice steady.

The voice responded—low, ancient, inhuman.

"It matters not who I am, Vincent. Only what I need."

Vincent's blood turned to ice.

"How do you know my name?"

A chuckle, twisted and metallic, rattled through the night. It didn't echo in the air. It echoed in his mind.

"I know all."

The shadows shifted.

"Come closer."

Vincent tried to resist. His body ignored him. One foot moved, then the next. The darkness swallowed him whole. Shapes danced just beyond his vision. Whispers in shadow.

Then he saw it.

A silhouette, titanic in size, standing at least seven feet tall. Its limbs were thick, unnaturally proportioned. Mechanical. Alive.

Vincent's mouth went dry.

"What do you want?" he asked.

"To reshape the future," the voice said. "You will build me a new portal."

Vincent's fear sharpened to defiance.

"No," he said, backing away. "I won't."

A pause. Then, calmly:

"This isn't a request."

The darkness moved.

A colossal figure stepped forward, its body made of burnished black metal streaked with glowing red veins. Wires wrapped around its limbs like sinew. Its face was bizarrely humanoid. It wore a cold smirk. A mouth, sculpted into a mocking expression, curved beneath burning crimson eyes that seemed to look straight into Vincent's soul.

The Virus.

Vincent stumbled back in horror.

"I-I won't..." Vincent said, struggling to get his words out.

The Virus stepped closer. His hand extended, not in violence, but with something far more terrifying. Control.

"Yes," the Virus replied. "You will."

His palm touched Vincent's temple. Fingers clamped tight. And then fire.

Vincent screamed as pain exploded behind his eyes. His back arched, his body spasming violently. The scream was long and raw, echoing down the alley like the last cry of something human.

Then silence.

Vincent's eyes dulled. His muscles relaxed. His mind erased.

The Virus tilted his head, his smirk still carved in steel.

"Much better."

6

Revelations

Laura had been trained to lead through crisis. But nothing in her life had prepared her for this—a city crumbling, agents scattered, and no one left to command.

She stood motionless amid the chaos, her boots rooted to fractured pavement as if gravity had grown heavier. Her eyes swept the burning skyline; ashen clouds blotted out the sun. Sirens howled through the streets like wolves circling a dying herd. Task Force vehicles weaved around collapsed lamp posts and shattered barricades, their red and blue lights casting frantic pulses across broken glass.

"Director Sinclair!" an agent shouted, sprinting toward her. "Several buildings have collapsed. We're getting calls for reinforcements!"

"Send units three and seven," Laura demanded.

"Ma'am, those units are already en route to Halvade's Children's Hospital."

"Then *find* someone who isn't!" she snapped, her voice sharper than steel.

The agent nodded and rushed off into the crowd. Through the blur of movement, Laura spotted Connor weaving between civilians and agents alike, his expression grim.

"Laura," he said, slightly breathless, "we're running out of people to send. We've got nothing left."

"You think I don't know that?" she replied, her voice raw. "Midtown's in ruins. No protocol. No precedent. We were never prepared for this. We're barely holding it together."

She turned away, her eyes landing on a high-ranking officer coordinating triage beside a smoldering bus.

"You!" she called. "Report. Now."

The agent hurried over, eyes wide.

"We've deployed units to every corner of Midtown," they said. "Veilhaven, Halvade, outer districts. All boots are on the ground."

"How many agents?" Laura asked, her voice cold.

"Ma'am?"

"How many Task Force agents do we have in the field?" she asked, patience wearing thin.

The agent hesitated.

"All of them, Director," he said, finally. "Every single one."

The words hit Laura like a brick to the chest.

Her control was slipping. No reinforcements. No backups. Only fire, screams, and fading hope.

She pushed past the agent, her steps heavy as cries from the crowd filled the air like static. The pressure grew tighter with every breath. Nikki's face flashed in her mind, again and again. It was like a blinking warning light.

Then gunfire. Close.

Laura's instincts ignited.

She sprinted down a side street, rounding a corner toward

the sound. Two Task Force agents stood with rifles raised, facing a frantic group of civilians.

"Stay back!" one shouted. "This area is under lockdown!"

"What the hell is going on!?" Laura shouted, charging up to them.

The agents turned, their faces strained.

"Looters," one said. "They're from Halvade. A bunch of them made it here looking for shelter. And now they've started breaking into stores."

"Get it under control!" Laura yelled. "The last thing we need is Midtown turning on itself!"

"The Task Force doesn't care about us!" a civilian cried. "Where the hell were you when the quake hit?!"

"You let us burn!" another voice roared.

The crowd surged with anger, their screams a tidal wave of fear and betrayal. Laura stepped back, struggling to catch her breath. Then, she centered herself.

"Listen up!" she shouted, projecting her voice like a banshee. "Effective immediately, I want Task Force Headquarters and any stable buildings converted into shelters. I want trauma teams, water, food, beds, anything we can spare. Pull anyone unfit for the field and put them on relief detail. Now."

"Yes, ma'am," the agents said in unison. "You heard her! Let's move!"

As the crowd began to disperse with their guidance, Connor reappeared at Laura's side.

"What now?" she asked, not looking at him.

"It's the vigilante," Connor said. "They're in Halvade. Helping civilians."

Laura's shoulders tensed.

"Perfect," she muttered. "Just what we need."

"You mean…isn't that a good thing?" Connor asked. "They're helping. Taking some of the weight off us. We need help."

"No," Laura snapped. "This sends the wrong message. If the public sees some masked crusader doing our job, they'll think the Task Force is unfit. They already doubt us. This just cements it."

Connor's voice softened.

"Laura…we're already spread too thin," he said. "Maybe they *are* helping. Maybe we need to stop trying to carry the world on our backs and just take this one step at a time."

"One step at a time?" she said, her voice breaking slightly. "There *are* no steps anymore, Connor. The stairs have collapsed. People are dying. They need heroes, and we're not enough."

"You don't have to be enough alone," he said. "We do what we can. That's all anyone can do."

She looked at him then. Her jaw trembled. Her knees felt unsteady.

"I'm not built for this," she whispered. "He was. *He* was the one who could handle this."

She didn't have to say the name. Connor knew.

"And now he's not here…"

A moment of silence passed between them.

Connor stepped closer, placing his hands gently on her shoulders.

"You're wrong," Connor said. "You've kept this city, this world, standing longer than anyone expected. You're still standing now. Without you, Midtown would have crumbled a long time ago."

Laura's expression buckled.

"Nikki's with Jenna, right?" he asked softly.

Laura flinched. The realization crashed over her like a wave.

"Nikki…I haven't even called. I haven't heard her voice. I need to—"

Connor tightened his grip.

"Stop," he said. "Breathe. Let's go check on her. Together."

Laura nodded, eyes glassy but focused. The commander had cracked.

But the mother still stood.

#

Nikki lay stretched across the battered couch in Connor's shed, one arm draped over her stomach, the other holding a damp cloth to her soot-stained face. Ash clung to her skin, streaked in patches where sweat had cut through. Her muscles ached, a dull, stubborn pain throbbing just beneath the surface, but it was less than before. A light purple smoke radiated off her body. She was healing. Fast.

"Hey," Jenna called from across the room, where she sat surrounded by blinking monitors and tangled wires. "How're you holding up?"

"Better than I should be," Nikki admitted, her voice rough but steady. "It's weird. I've never bounced back this quickly before."

Jenna swiveled in her chair, brows pinched in curiosity.

"Well, you've never blasted half a warehouse with purple lightning before," she said. "Or teleported two people out of a burning building. So maybe your body just…leveled up."

"Leveled up?" Nikki asked.

Jenna smirked faintly.

"I mean, abilities are weird," she said. "We don't really know *how* they work. But you were under extreme pressure tonight. Something new must have clicked. It could also explain why you were so exhausted. You pushed your body pretty hard."

"Do you think there's more I could do?" Nikki asked, sitting up. "What if there are abilities that I haven't even discovered yet?"

"I think we could find out," Jenna said. "But to do that, we need to return to training. It's the only way we can safely push your limits. You can't go back out there half-aware of what you're capable of."

Nikki forced a small laugh.

"I think I should be out there anyway," Nikki replied. "Just for a little while longer. There are still people who need help."

Jenna's expression tightened.

"Nikki, no," she said. "You barely made it back here. If you push yourself too hard again—"

"I won't," Nikki interrupted, firm but not unkind. "I'm already feeling way better as it is. And I'll come back if I feel myself slipping. I promise. But I can't just lie here while people are dying."

Three loud knocks suddenly shattered the moment.

BANG. BANG. BANG.

Nikki's gaze snapped to the back door.

BANG. BANG. BANG.

"Let me in!" a familiar voice called. "It's me. Connor!"

Nikki exhaled in relief.

"Geez," she said, relaxing. "Just let him in before he breaks the door down."

Jenna hurried over and unlatched the door. Connor stepped in, breath short from rushing. His eyes scanned the room, and then Laura stepped in behind him.

Nikki's stomach dropped.

Laura's sharp gaze swept over the mismatched tech and glowing screens. Her expression shifted, confused, then darkened.

"What the hell is all this?" she asked, stepping farther inside.

Nikki panicked, jamming her mask between the couch cushions, but it was pointless. She was still in her full vigilante suit, the black armor scuffed and smudged with ash. The smoke around her body had faded, but the truth was plain.

Laura's eyes locked onto her.

"Nikki?" she said, voice cracking slightly as she rushed to her daughter's side. "What happened to your face? Are you hurt?"

She pulled Nikki into a tight embrace. Nikki winced as her bruised ribs pressed against her mother's arms.

"What are you wearing?" Laura said, examining Nikki once more.

"I—I..." Nikki started. She couldn't answer. Her mind scrambled for something, anything, that might soften the blow.

"Laura," Connor said, stepping forward. "Before you continue to freak out, you need to know something."

Laura looked especially confused now.

"What is going on here?" she asked. "What aren't you telling me?"

"She's the vigilante, Laura," Connor said.

Laura froze, staring at Nikki now.

Nikki could feel her heart stop. No matter how hard she tried, no words could come out.

"What is he talking about?" Laura asked, her voice broken.

"He's…He's telling the truth," Nikki replied, finally.

Laura's expression slowly shifted to anger. She turned to face Connor.

"You knew about this?" she asked. "How could you—how could *any* of you—hide this from me?"

"It's not his fault, Mom," Nikki said. "I asked both of them to keep my secret. I just…I didn't know how to tell you. When I found out I had powers, I was scared. I wanted to tell you right away, but I thought you'd be just as scared as I was. And after everything with Dad…I didn't want you to make me hide them."

Laura stayed silent. Nikki could see that the information was stewing in her brain.

"I only told Jenna so I wouldn't deal with it alone," Nikki continued. "And Connor found out while I was training. He offered to help."

Laura exhaled.

"Nikki, you hid this from me," Laura said. The hurt in her voice hit harder than yelling would have. "What if something had happened to you? I wouldn't even know. I couldn't survive that again."

Nikki's throat burned.

"I didn't want to scare you," she said. "I just wanted to help."

"She's been helping," Connor said. "I've seen it. She's good, Laura. Smart. Careful. She's not running around like a reckless kid. She's saving lives."

Laura rubbed her temples, the weight of it all collapsing on her shoulders.

"I can't believe this…"

"Mom," Nikki said, stepping closer. "I'm sorry. I never wanted to lie. I did it to protect you."

Laura met her eyes.

"You think I need protecting?" she asked, her voice softer.

"No," Nikki said. "I think you've carried too much for too long. I just wanted to share the weight."

The silence thickened. Only the hum of the monitors remained.

"I couldn't stand watching you work yourself to death trying to keep this city safe," Nikki said, voice trembling. "I thought if I helped…you'd sleep more. You'd breathe easier. You'd be more comfortable. And then…then we could spend more time together."

Laura's lip quivered.

"I'm sorry," she said. "I'm sorry that you didn't think you could tell me. I…You should never have to feel that way. Not with me."

Nikki hugged her mom as tightly as she could.

"I love you, Mom," she said. "I know I should have told you…I'm sorry. I just wanted to make you proud."

Laura tightened the hug.

"Oh, Nikki," she said. "You already have…"

They stayed there, mother and daughter wrapped in each other's arms, just for a moment. Their grief and pride tangled like roots beneath the surface.

Nikki pulled back and looked her mom in the eyes.

"Does that mean I can help?" she asked.

Laura was silent, biting her lip.

"Laura," Connor said. "I've seen her in action…She's a tough kid. We could use her help."

Laura exhaled and nodded.

"Okay," she said. "You can help. But we do this together. No more secrets."

"Deal," Nikki replied, smiling through tears.

Jenna let out a breath and slumped back into her chair, her face pale with the aftershock.

"That was intense," she said, wiping tears from her cheeks.

Nikki laughed softly. Then she looked back at her mom.

"How can I help?"

7

Control

The warehouse stood like a corpse on the edge of Halvade: hollow, cold, and forgotten. Its bones were steel and concrete, its lungs long collapsed. What light remained filtered through jagged skylights like fractured halos, casting spectral beams over rust-flecked girders and broken machines.

The wind slid through its cracked ribs, whispering across chains and ruined tools. The air was thick with the scent of oil, rust, and something older—blood dried into the floor, stubborn and permanent.

Then came the hum.

Low. Constant. Not mechanical, not human. Something deeper. A resonance beneath reality.

At the center of the vast, decaying space, Professor Vincent stood hunched over a scorched metal workbench, his shoulders curled like wilted wings. Around him: scavenged cables, melted equipment, scrap tech bent into unnatural shapes. His hand, shaking unnaturally, scrawled lines across yellowed parchment. Symbols spiraled outward from the center like a

91

curse. Some equations held structure. Others defied logic.

He didn't know what half of them meant. But his hand kept moving.

He couldn't stop it.

Behind him stood the architect of his agony.

The Virus.

Towering. Still. A sculpture of cruelty wrought in chrome and shadow. Armor fused to wire, limbs encased in jagged plating, his face a blank mask save for the eyes, two burning red coals that pulsed with rhythmic malice. Every inch of his form radiated pressure, as if the air itself recoiled from him.

"How soon can this be done?" he asked. His voice was rot through a speaker. Muffled. Multiplied. Drenched in static.

Vincent didn't answer at first.

Because Vincent, truly, was no longer in command.

On the outside, he appeared calm. Precise. A man deeply at work.

But behind his eyes, his soul beat fists against a glass wall. *I'm still here,* he wanted to scream. *This isn't me.*

He couldn't move. Couldn't cry. Couldn't blink unless permitted.

He was conscious. Awake. A prisoner in his own nerves.

Finally, his mouth opened. Not by choice.

"Weeks," he said, voice flat. "Maybe months. Without the proper tools or assistance, the construction will take time. The last portal barely held. It fractured the fabric of our reality. If I'm to build another…I'll need simulations. Stabilizers. I can't guarantee structural integrity without—"

"We don't have months," the Virus interrupted, stepping forward. The floor trembled beneath its weight. "Even weeks is impossible. Accelerate your work. Tell me what you need.

I will obtain it."

Vincent hesitated. Not of will. Of instinct.

"The crystals," he said. "They are the main component. Not the forged cells; they can be replicated. But the source material can't. They're only found in one place. A ruin. Far east. Ashenfell."

The Virus paused. A long silence settled.

"Ah, yes," he replied, voice colder. "The city that buried your gods. I can sense the taste of it."

Vincent's throat tightened. Some part of him recoiled.

"Then…you know it's not an easy journey," he said. "And I'll need more than materials. I'll need…people. A team. I can't build this alone."

"You'll have them." The Virus's neck twitched as he turned. "Leave the bodies to me."

He began to circle the workbench. Slow. Purposeful. Like a beast surveying its kill.

"Your Task Force gathered the wrong crystals," he murmured. "They worked as a power source, yes, but they were not strong enough to open the portal. Had Elias Kade not interfered, the gate would've remained sealed. But he heard the crystal. It sang to him. He took one. Only one. It was not enough to hold the portal. But it was enough to let *me* through."

Vincent's head twitched. Something inside him sparked.

"What… *is* this crystal you talk about?" he asked.

The Virus stopped walking. He didn't speak at first. When he did, his voice had shifted. Quieter, but laced with ancient memory.

"A shard of history," he said. "Forged in the rupture. When the lattice of worlds cracked and bled. They are older than time. They not only channel power, they *are* power. They *command* it."

He stepped closer, and the red glow of his eyes intensified.

"They are the price of passage," he continued. "You cannot walk between realms without them. And when your machines cracked open the sky…they did more than open a door. They screamed. They called across the vastness. They sent a signal."

The Virus tilted his head.

"That signal brought me here."

Vincent's body didn't flinch. But inside his skull, he screamed.

"Then…" He choked, voice struggling against its leash. "Then I made a mistake."

"No," the Virus said, almost kindly. "You fulfilled prophecy. Because of you, this realm will be remembered. Etched in the memory of something far greater than your dying world."

He turned away. The emergency lights flickered, casting his silhouette against the broken walls like a demon-shaped wound.

"Begin," he said. "When I return, I expect progress."

Vincent's body obeyed.

It bent once more to the parchment, hands sketching feverishly. His fingers ached. His wrist screamed. But they would not stop. Runes bled onto the page. Equations layered over blueprints he didn't recognize. His own handwriting, now a stranger's.

Inside his mind, Vincent wept.

But no one could hear him.

#

Fires still clawed at the skeletons of buildings in Halvade, painting the sky in sickly hues of orange and gray. Smoke spiraled upward like mournful banners, and screams, thin and broken, echoed from every direction. Rubble crunched beneath bootsteps. Blood mixed with dust.

And it still wasn't enough.

Task Force agents darted through the chaos like ants in a drowning hive, trying to hold back a flood with bare hands. But the city continued to bleed.

Frederick moved through the wreckage with six of his men. They carried crates of salvaged supplies—water, rations, medical kits scavenged from pharmacies and abandoned Task Force outposts. Their sleeves were rolled, their eyes ringed with ash. They wore no uniforms. No one in Halvade would follow a uniform anymore.

"Next street, boss?" one of them asked, his face streaked with sweat and soot.

Frederick gave a silent nod.

They turned the corner, and his heart stopped.

Where Mrs. Carillo's home had once stood, there was only a heap of shattered stone and splintered beams.

He didn't think. He moved.

"Go!" he barked, dropping the crate with a crash.

He sprinted across the street and dropped to his knees, clawing at the debris with frantic, brutal strength. Wood snapped beneath his hands. Plaster dust filled his lungs. Every pull of his muscles came with the promise of *please, please let me be wrong*.

He knew her address. He knew this was the spot. But maybe she'd left. Maybe she and Marco had gotten out.

His fingers brushed fabric.

Frederick froze.

Then he dug harder, ripping aside the collapsed frame of a doorway, his hands blistering on twisted metal.

He found her.

Mrs. Carillo lay twisted in the rubble, one arm curled protectively over a smaller form beneath her.

Marco.

Her son.

Frederick stared, paralyzed.

Her eyes were open but empty. Her lips were caked with dust. Her hair was matted with ash. And her arm, bruised and bloodied, still cradled Marco like a mother shielding her child from the end of the world.

Frederick reached out with trembling fingers and touched the back of her hand.

Cold.

No. Not her. Not them.

A sound clawed its way out of his throat. Low at first. Then rising.

It built into a roar. A scream of grief so deep it rattled the broken buildings around him. It echoed off scorched walls and rippled through smoke-choked air. It made the flames falter. Somewhere in the distance, dogs howled back.

"Boss," a voice called gently behind him. "We need to move. There are still people who need us."

Frederick turned, eyes burning with rage.

"You don't—!"

But the street was empty.

His men were gone. So were the wounded. The world itself had gone silent.

The smoke thickened. Ash danced in the air like falling

snow.

And then, a voice.

Low. Metallic. Measured.

"They didn't have to die."

Frederick spun, his hand snapping to his pistol.

A figure stood atop the wreckage, cloaked in shadow and flame.

The Virus.

His red eyes burned behind his mask like dying suns. Smoke curled around his limbs as if drawn to it. Metal joints gleamed faintly in the firelight.

"Don't move," Frederick barked, raising the gun.

The Virus didn't flinch.

He stepped down from the rubble with slow, deliberate grace and knelt beside Mrs. Carillo's body. One gloved hand, blackened metal and humming circuitry, brushed her cheek.

"You loved them," he said softly. "You tried to protect them. But love isn't enough when you have no power."

"I said don't move!" Frederick shouted. "Back away from her!"

The Virus looked up, red eyes steady.

"They were innocent," he said. "And your Task Force failed them. The people in charge failed them. Again."

Frederick's grip tightened on the pistol.

"Who the hell are you?"

The Virus rose to his full height, standing tall above the wreckage. He looked like something born from the apocalypse, a prophet of ruin.

"I am the answer to your city's suffering," he said. "I can give you the strength to make sure this never happens again."

Frederick's lip curled.

"You think I haven't heard that before?" he replied. "Task Force speeches. City council promises. All of it's garbage."

"And yet," the Virus said, spreading his arms, "I'm here. And they are not."

"You're a monster," Frederick replied.

The Virus tilted his head.

"Then we are not so different," he said.

The words cut sharper than they should have.

Frederick flinched. Just a flicker. But enough.

"I watched this place burn," the Virus continued. "And so did the world above it. They let it happen. But you. You ran *toward* the fire. You tried to hold it back. You clawed at death itself, bare-handed."

Frederick looked down at Marco's face. Ash clung to the boy's lashes like frost.

"I was too late," he whispered.

The Virus stepped closer, voice quiet and low.

"Then help me build something that cannot be ignored," he offered. "Let them fear you, if they won't listen. Let them remember what happens when they forget your people."

Frederick didn't speak. He stared at the boy's still face. At the fire, painting the world in shades of loss.

He wanted justice.

He wanted the world to *feel* this.

He lowered the gun.

"What do you need?"

8

Assistance

Inside the hollowed remains of the steel mill, the Virus stood motionless near the far wall. His colossal frame hunched like a war relic abandoned in peacetime. Still. Silent. Looming.

The red glow in his eyes dimmed. Then it vanished.

And the world peeled away.

The air turned brittle. Cold. Lights flickered and twisted into unnatural patterns before melting into darkness. The groan of fractured beams. The hum of broken generators distorted. Then, everything disappeared.

Shadows bled from the corners like spilled oil, thick and hungry. They slithered across the steel walls, climbed the rafters, and seeped through the concrete floor. They curled around the Virus's frame, devouring light, color, and space itself.

Then, *nothing*.

The Virus now stood in a realm without geometry or air. No ground. No sky. No edges. Just a vast, impossible dark, so cold it scraped at thoughts.

A voice ruptured the stillness.

It wasn't one voice, but many. Layered. Ancient. Inhuman. Like cracking stone. Like stars dying.

It came from all around and nowhere at once.

"You have yet to take the realm," it called. *"Tell me, why do you fail?"*

The Virus did not flinch.

"I breached their world," he replied, his voice sluggish, dragged by the gravity of this place. "The portal was unstable. I nearly perished…but I now control their architect. He will build another."

A long pause. The silence was colder than the voice.

"You were meant to guide my army," the voice replied, *"not creep through a crack alone. If you are unfit to lead—"*

The Virus stiffened. Its metal fingers curled into fists.

"I will restore the gateway," he said. "I only require—"

Pain.

The Virus's body jerked.

Something unseen wrenched his limbs backward like chains made of gravity and wrath. His torso buckled inward with a metallic scream. Sparks burst from its spine. One knee hit the void.

"Do not interrupt me with your demands!"

"N-not…a demand," the Virus rasped. "A…request…"

The force lifted.

The Virus gasped, though he had no lungs, and dragged himself upright. Metal groaned as he straightened, his body trembling with the memory of pressure. He said nothing.

The voice spoke instead.

"I am to trust you?" it asked. *"After you have proven yourself unworthy? Unable. You weak and insignificant pawn!"*

The Virus bowed his head slightly.

"I have gathered allies," he replied. "Ones who know the cracks in this world. I only need—request—time…and resources. Then the portal will be built. Stable. Permanent."

A beat.

Then the void rumbled.

From below, a massive metallic casing rose, wide as a sarcophagus, black and steaming. Its edges hissed and clicked as it turned, then cracked open with a hiss.

Inside was a *body*.

The Virus's *true* form.

Half-organic, half-machine. Pale flesh fused with tubing, limbs suspended in glassy fluid. A face partially hidden behind a breathing mask, its eyes closed.

A prison. A memory.

A soul now trapped.

The voice returned, slower now. More deliberate.

"Do not forget, foolish slave. I own you. Your body is mine. As is your soul. Should you fail again..."

The rumble returned. This time, the body inside of the container convulsed and shook.

The Virus could feel pain radiating from within his mind.

"Is this clear enough?"

The rumble stopped. The body rested once more.

The Virus stared. His fists clenched again, tighter this time. Sparks jumped from his wrists. Rage seethed just beneath his steel.

But he did not speak in anger.

"I understand," he said, calm, cold, and contained. "I will not fail."

The voice said no more.

Instead, the dark receded.

Red light surged back into the Virus's eyes.

The steel mill bled back into reality, hissing welders, groaning rafters, buzzing wires. The shadows vanished like smoke. Light returned in fractured waves.

And the Virus was back.

In the world he would conquer.

In the body he was given.

In the life he was forced to live.

#

The sky above Capital City was a suffocating slate, choked with black smoke that devoured the morning sun. It hung like a burial cloth over the city, turning day into dusk. The air was thick and unbreathable. Every inhale tasted of scorched plastic, melted steel, and something older…something like grief left out too long in the heat.

Nikki walked beside Laura in silence, the two of them moving down a fractured boulevard littered with shattered glass, burnt-out vehicles, and debris that told stories no one had the strength to explain.

She wore her mask again.

The black-and-purple suit clung to her like skin. Smoke-stained, ragged at the joints. Her limbs ached. Her back throbbed. Her hands trembled from time to time. But she was healing. Quicker than before. She could feel her strength returning.

The street wasn't quiet. Not truly. There were no screams now, no sirens or thunderous destruction. But the silence was worse. It was the sound of what came after. Survivors gathered in clusters, slumped on sidewalks or hunched in doorways, hollowed by what they'd lived through.

Some cried softly. Others just…stared.

A voice crackled through Nikki's comm.

"Guys," Connor said, "I've signed us into the Task Force communicators and cameras. We're going to do our best to guide you through the chaos."

"I see something," Jenna said. "A cluster of people surrounding the old transit station. Structural integrity's likely shot. No Task Force units in range."

Laura glanced sideways.

"It's like having two Connors in my head," she said.

"We can still hear you, you know," Connor said through the comms. "And you would be lucky to have me in your head."

Laura groaned.

They passed a burned-out town house, its frame skeletal, one side caved in. On the curb sat a little girl no older than five. Her hair was singed, matted with ash. She clutched a stuffed bear, half-burned, clinging to it like it could anchor her to something.

Nikki slowed. Her stomach turned.

"Hey," she said, crouching carefully beside the girl, lowering her voice. "You okay?"

The girl looked up.

Her eyes, for the briefest second, flashed crimson.

"You let this happen," the child whispered.

Nikki's breath caught. She blinked hard.

Gone. The girl disappeared within a moment, as if she hadn't been there to begin with.

Laura's hand touched her shoulder. Nikki flinched.

"Easy," Laura said softly. "It's just me."

Nikki turned away, blinking the sting out of her eyes.

"It's fine," she said. "I just…It's been a long night."

"Look, if this is too much…" Laura started.

She was cut off by the scream of a nearby civilian.

The two turned and saw a man rushing toward them.

"Help!" he shouted. "The train station, it's collapsed! There are people trapped under it. We need help! They can't get out!"

"I can get them out," Nikki said.

"Ni— um…," Laura said, "Vigilante… the rubble there could weigh tons. Not to mention, if a gas line has been punctured, it could light in an instant. I can call in for a heavy-lifting unit—"

"There's no time," Nikki said. "If we wait, they die."

She held Laura's gaze. Neither blinked.

"Okay," Laura replied quietly. "I trust you…"

As they made their way to the station, they could see a crowd of people surrounding the wreckage. The transit station was unrecognizable, the entire block swallowed by a sinkhole. Jagged steel beams jutted skyward. Chunks of asphalt tilted like tectonic plates midshift. A sparking traffic pole teetered at the crater's edge.

Nikki surveyed it with a grimace.

"Does anyone know how many people are stuck in there?" she asked.

"At least eight," someone replied. "The kid I babysit is down there. Please, you have to help them! He has asthma."

Nikki looked around and spotted a rusted sedan jammed partway into a narrow gap. A possible tunnel.

"That's the exit," she muttered.

She crouched low, planted her feet, and grabbed the twisted

frame. Purple smoke coiled up her arms as she gritted her teeth and lifted.

The metal groaned, resisting. Her muscles screamed.

Then it gave.

She hurled the car aside with a guttural roar.

It slammed onto the street, echoing like thunder.

Nikki leapt into the crater.

"Hey!" she called into the dimness. "I'm here to help! Tell me where you are!"

Hurried footsteps answered. Dust-shrouded faces appeared. Men, women, a crying teenager holding her brother's hand.

"Anyone hurt?" Nikki asked.

A man pointed to the back.

"There's a kid back there," he said. "He's coughing like crazy. He's having trouble breathing."

As Nikki went to check on the boy, the ground above began to give.

"Get behind me," Nikki said.

Concrete and rebar began to crumble and formed a wall of ruin. She clenched her jaw and raised her arms, shielding the people.

"All right," she said. "You all need to follow me."

She moved forward and began ripping pieces loose. Her vision blurred with sweat. Her arms shook.

The world above groaned.

The crater's edge fractured and fell.

Nikki threw herself under the collapsing slab, bracing with both arms. Her feet skidded, knees nearly buckled. But she held. She pushed it up, just enough to leave an opening.

"Go!" she screamed.

The civilians crawled past her, pulled up by Laura and the

surrounding civilians. Nikki's breath rattled. Her muscles gave out, but she wouldn't drop it. Not until the last person was gone.

"That's all of them!" Laura shouted from above.

Nikki screamed and threw the slab aside. It crashed beside her as she collapsed to one knee.

She clawed her way up the crater wall, fingers bloody.

And Laura was there, reaching. Pulling her up.

"You okay?" she asked.

"Are they safe?" Nikki replied. "Where's the boy? Is he okay?"

Laura nodded, moving so Nikki could see the boy being cradled and helped by his babysitter. An inhaler was held to his mouth.

Nikki slowly rose, and Laura pulled her into a tight hug. Nikki clung back, holding on as if her life counted on it.

#

The steel doors groaned open, dragging across the warehouse floor like the gates of a tomb. Dust stirred in the stale air.

Frederick stepped inside, flanked by six of his most trusted men. Soldiers forged in smoke and fire.

Their boots echoed through the chamber, rhythmic and commanding.

The room was a collage of chaos and precision. Flickering lights cast warped shadows across glyphs etched deep into the walls. Schematics cluttered long tables, some singed at the edges, others freshly inked in strange languages. Machinery thrummed in the dark like sleeping beasts.

Then came the sound.

Thoom. Thoom. Thoom.

A pulsing weight in the air.

From the far edge of the hall, two red eyes flared to life.

The Virus emerged from the shadows, towering, metallic, and monstrous.

Frederick's men raised their weapons instinctively. Tension crackled.

"Stand down," Frederick said, calm and commanding.

The men obeyed. But their eyes didn't leave the figure before them.

Frederick eyed the Virus without flinching.

"Where have you been?" the Virus asked.

"You know how many abandoned warehouses I had to look through?" Frederick asked. "You ain't exactly got a sign outside the door."

The Virus ignored this and turned.

They walked side by side deeper into the warehouse, past Vincent, who was still hunched at his workbench, scratching otherworldly runes into a slab of steel. His eyes were glazed, haunted, and mechanical.

Frederick watched him carefully.

"What's his problem?" he asked.

"He is bound," the Virus said. "He will finish the portal. And when he does, everything changes."

Frederick crossed his arms.

"You've said that before," he replied. "But talk is cheap. I don't buy into gods and monsters without proof."

The Virus halted.

"Then let me show you the cracks in your world," he said, turning to Frederick. "The Task Force has failed. Your world's protector is gone. Halvade rots in the dark. Capital City burns.

You see what I see. Collapse."

Frederick's expression didn't change, but the flicker behind his eyes was sharp.

"I see opportunity," he replied. "Not surrender."

"Exactly," the Virus replied. "Together, we can build something stronger. With order. With fear. With power."

"Then let's get to the part where you tell me what you want," Frederick said, his voice dropping to a near growl.

"Manpower," the Virus said. "Obedience. I have my own army, but they cannot join us until the portal is complete. I cannot wait that long."

Frederick studied him.

"And in return?" he asked.

"You expect payment of some sort?" the Virus asked.

A long silence stretched between them.

"You want my loyalty," Frederick finally said. "My people. My weapons. Yes, I do expect payment. In the form of Halvade."

The Virus tilted his head.

"Halvade?" he asked.

"That city's been abandoned by the Task Force," Frederick said. "It survives because of me. My protection. My rules. If I'm going to back you, I need something real in return. I want Halvade. Fully. Sovereign. No interference. No red eyes wandering in. I rule it. Alone. If you need me so bad, if you expect to rule together, I won't just be a lapdog."

The Virus said nothing.

Sparks trailed down his arms as he considered the words. The weight of Frederick's demand.

Frederick didn't waver.

"Or you can kill me now and start from scratch," he said.

"Good luck finding another who can keep an army loyal when the world ends. An army half as large as mine. I am the only person who knows the ins and outs of Midtown in a way that guarantees victory. It's how I got into my position of power."

The Virus stepped close, towering above him like a storm ready to break.

"You're bold," he said, voice colder now. "Perhaps too bold."

Frederick didn't blink.

"I built my empire from dust and ruin," he replied. "I earned everything that I have. I don't answer to you. Never will. This only works as a partnership, not a leash."

The Virus was quiet for a long moment.

Then he extended a hand.

"Halvade is yours," he said. "When the realm has been taken, you will have your kingdom."

Frederick stared at the hand.

A pause. Then a smirk.

"Deal."

He took the hand.

The Virus stepped past Frederick.

"What are you doing?" Frederick asked.

"Turning your soldiers into savages," the Virus replied.

The Virus lifted its hand.

A pulse of energy swept the room. The soldiers froze. Their eyes turned crimson, glowing faintly in the dim warehouse light. Their skin paled. Their veins pulsed, running with red lightning beneath the surface.

"There," he said. "Now…Midtown will be ours."

The Virus and Frederick stood, watching as the men turned into beasts.

Two kings. One war on the horizon.

9

Awakening

T he gymnasium stank of ash and loss.

What had once been a place of laughter and cheers now stood hollowed and broken, hastily converted into a survivors' shelter. Rows of thin cots crowded the scuffed hardwood floor, separated by makeshift aisles and tangled hope. Families huddled beneath silver emergency blankets, their faces waxen under the harsh strip lights. The sharp buzz of overworked generators bled into the air, mingling with the cries of children and the ever-present sting of smoke curling through cracked vents.

Laura moved down the central row with a clipboard in hand, though she wasn't reading it. Her eyes drifted instead to the faces of survivors: ashen, their eyes red-rimmed and emptied. Men held silent children. Women whispered lullabies to no one. An old woman stared at the ceiling as if daring it to fall again.

There were no screams anymore. Only the stillness that followed the quake. The stillness of loss.

From across the room, a voice rang out.

"Water and blankets, over here!" Nikki called, balancing two crates against her chest.

Laura paused.

There she was. Her mask covered her face, but Laura could tell how determined Nikki was to help. Her arms were streaked with soot. She was bruised, limping slightly, but still moving. Still giving. There was something in her daughter's posture that Laura hadn't seen in a long time, something beyond strength. *Conviction. Purpose. Grit.* A swell of pride pushed into her chest, thick and sudden. But beneath it, something colder stirred. Fear. Fear for what Nikki might become. Fear for what she'd already given.

Then a voice cut through the haze.

"Where were you?"

Laura turned. A man approached, wrapped in a foil blanket that fluttered with each step. His eyes were bloodshot, his jaw clenched. Grief rode his shoulders like armor.

"Where were you?" he repeated, louder now. "When the buildings came down? When my wife was screaming under the concrete for three damn hours!?"

Laura faced him. Calm. Controlled.

"I'm sorry," she said quietly. "We're doing everything we can—"

"It's not enough!" someone shouted.

A woman across the aisle had risen, fists clenched, tears carving streaks through ash-caked cheeks.

"We saved our neighbors with our bare hands," she yelled. "The Task Force didn't show up until hours later. My brother died while waiting!"

Others stirred. The room cracked open. Murmurs sharpened into words. Pain, fury, and panic. The air turned brittle with heat.

"I understand," Laura replied, lifting her voice. "I do. We were unprepared—"

"Unprepared?" the man growled. "This city had a protector. We had someone who could have stopped this. If he hadn't abandoned us—"

"But he did," Nikki said.

Her voice cut through the chaos like a blade. Clear. Hard.

The room fell quiet. All eyes turned.

Nikki stepped forward, the crates forgotten behind her. Her eyes blazed, not with anger, but something rawer. *Truth.*

"The protector abandoned you," she said. "He abandoned all of us. And when the sky tore open and the ground swallowed families whole, did he return? Did he stop it?"

She looked around the gym. Every face was watching. Every breath was held.

"Who pulled your neighbors from rubble?" she asked. "Who carried strangers across the fire line? Who wrapped children in blankets, who fought to keep people alive?"

Her voice cracked slightly, but she didn't stop.

"You did. I did. The Task Force did. The medics. The survivors. All of us."

She let the silence breathe for a moment.

"We didn't wait for a hero. Midtown stood on its own. Even without its protector, we endured."

A few people nodded. Some looked down, ashamed of their rage. One woman closed her eyes, tears slipping silently down her cheeks.

"Who are you?" someone asked.

"She's that vigilante," another voice whispered. "The one from Halvade. Are you...Are you the new protector?"

Murmurs spread, rippling through the gym like smoke.

Laura stepped forward, standing beside her daughter.

"She's here," she said, voice firm. "That's all that matters. Not why. Not how. She's here. And she cares about this city. About all of you."

She turned to face the crowd.

"We all do," she said. "And I know this isn't enough right now—not words, not promises. But we're going to rebuild. One street at a time. One family at a time. You have my word."

A silence settled again. A different kind of silence. Not despair, but hesitation. The man who had confronted her stood motionless for a long moment...then gave a slow, reluctant nod. Others followed. A fragile kind of peace.

Laura exhaled. Her shoulders sagged. Nikki approached.

"You okay?" Nikki asked, voice gentler now.

Laura looked at her, eyes tired but proud.

"I am now," she said. "Thank you."

"What are partners for?" Nikki asked.

Laura gave a dry laugh.

"Let's not get carried away," she said.

Then the gym doors burst open.

Connor strode in, breathless, eyes sharp. The sound of his boots across the warped floor turned every head.

"Laura," he said, voice low. Urgent.

Laura turned to him, already bracing.

"Please," she muttered. "No more bad news. I'm hanging by a thread."

Connor didn't smile.

"There's...There's something in Capital City," he said. "They've taken out a squad of our agents. I don't even know how to explain it."

"Connor, calm down," Laura replied. "What do you mean *something*? What is it?"

"I don't know, Laura," he said. "I haven't seen anything like it. But they need us out there."

"Then let's go take care of it," Nikki said.

Laura looked toward the crowd one last time. Survivors. Mothers. Children.

She nodded.

"Okay," she said. "Let's go. Quietly. Just us. No chaos. No spectacle."

#

The streets of Capital City had gone quiet—eerily so.

Most civilians had been evacuated. What remained were scorched storefronts, shattered windows, and the smoke-stained bones of a city choking on its own ruin. Streetlights flickered dimly overhead, casting a sickly yellow glow on cracked pavement and trails of ash. Somewhere, distant metal groaned, warping in the heat. A banner fluttered from a blown-out balcony, half-torn and broken down.

Laura walked in stride with Nikki and Connor. The silence wasn't peace. It was the breath before something broke.

Then they saw them.

Four men, their bodies distorted and twisted. Clothes torn and tattered. Skin pale and clammy.

Laura recognized the look. They looked similar to Elias Kade, but a bit stranger.

The men were aimlessly tearing apart a Task Force vehicle. Near it were two dead agents.

"What are they?" Nikki asked. "They look like people, but...

possessed…"

"The same possession that must have taken over Elias Kade," Laura replied. "We need to stop them, now."

Laura pulled her weapon out, but Connor grabbed her shoulder.

"Laura, wait," he said. "Remember how hard it was to take Kade down? How are we supposed to take four of them out?"

"What do you suggest?" she asked. "We can't just let them run around killing people."

"I'm so lost here," Nikki said. "Who is Elias? What made him so tough?"

"It's a long story," Connor said. "All you need to know is he had superhuman strength. Our bullets barely affected him. He almost killed us all. This whole quake happened because of him."

"Okay, but you guys didn't have me," Nikki replied. "I'm strong, I can take them."

Before Laura could respond, a voice called out.

"Well, well, well," it said. "Look who came to join the fun."

Laura's heart hardened. The group turned and saw Frederick as he stepped toward them. The grotesque men fell in line, staying behind him.

"Frederick," she replied, voice clear and cold. "I should have expected you to have a part in this. Even for you, this is low. Attacking the city in the middle of a crisis?"

Frederick smiled slowly, that familiar smirk already curling across his face.

"What exactly is the crisis, Director?" he said, his tone smooth and unbothered. "The only crisis I can see is with the Task Force and their inability to protect our world."

"You've assaulted our people," Connor said, voice clipped.

"You've killed agents. What do you gain from this? What's the endgame here? Chaos for the sake of chaos?"

Frederick gave a small, humorless laugh.

"'Our people'?" he echoed. "You mean *your* people. Capital City's polished elite. Midtown's golden center. Meanwhile, Halvade rots. It has rotted for years."

"That's because of men like you," Laura snapped.

The smirk disappeared. Frederick's eyes sharpened.

"No," he said quietly. "That's where you're wrong. Men like me exist because of the Task Force. Because of you. You needed someone willing to crawl through the filth while you stood in your glass tower writing reports."

He stepped forward slightly, his voice gaining weight.

"I made sure the sick got food. That the orphans had shelter, even if it was under a ceiling made of rusted tin. I used what you left behind. I used the scraps."

"You turned those scraps into weapons," Laura said.

"I turned them into survivors!" he growled. "Don't you dare confuse the two."

Then his gaze shifted. He locked eyes with Nikki.

"And now look at this," he said, venom curling in his words. "You're standing beside them. The masked brat who's been disrupting my operations for months. One of your *most wanted*, Director. Now she's your partner?"

"Given the state of things," Laura said coolly, "we're accepting help from anyone willing to fight for the right reasons."

"We're not the same," Nikki said, stepping forward.

Frederick tilted his head.

"Aren't we?" he asked, curious. "You fight for Halvade. So do I. You go outside the law. So do I."

"I don't profit off pain," Nikki replied. "I don't trade in

suffering and call it leadership."

Frederick snorted.

"Grow up," he said. "There is no clean solution. Midtown is rot stacked on rot. All that matters is who's willing to keep the roof from collapsing."

He raised his hand slightly, and his men moved.

Four pairs of boots hit the pavement. Perfect unison. Too perfect. Mechanical.

Laura's gut twisted. She raised her pistol in warning. Connor mirrored her, weapon snapping into position.

"Call them off, Frederick," Connor said. "We don't want this to escalate."

"It already has," Frederick said.

One of the men cocked his head, birdlike. The men moved, lunging forward like wolves unleashed.

#

Dark clouds churned above the scorched skeleton of Ashenfell.

What remained of the ancient city was a graveyard of broken towers and shattered temples, left to rot in time's mouth. But the quake had deepened the wounds. Fresh cracks spread like spiderwebs through the earth, columns lay broken and half-buried, and ash swirled like ghosts disturbed from sleep. The wind keened through hollow stone, carrying the scent of sulfur.

The Virus moved through the ruins like a shadow given shape. Vincent trailed close behind, his satchel bouncing against his leg, followed by two of Frederick's silent men. None spoke. The air was thick, not with smoke, but pressure.

As if the mountain itself was holding its breath.

Vincent's voice broke the silence.

"We should be close," he muttered, barely louder than the wind. "There's a cavern west of here. Our researchers found crystals there. The ones we used for the portal."

"No," said the Virus.

Just one word. Calm. Final.

"I…I don't understand," Vincent replied. "That's where—"

"You found scraps," the Virus said. His head turned slightly, red eyes glowing faint beneath the hood. "Echoes. The leftovers of a harvest long past."

"Then…where's the real source?" Vincent asked. "The one the others missed?"

"Deeper." His voice was almost reverent. "Buried beneath the bones of gods. Left untouched since the Sundering."

Vincent hesitated.

"That ground's unstable," he finally said. "We'd risk collapse. We could—"

But the Virus was already walking.

Vincent and the men followed him down into the city's crumbled heart, where ruins twisted into unnatural shapes. Walls fused with ancient roots and half-sunken stairways that led nowhere. Eventually, they reached a plaza, deep, circular, and rimmed with spires that looked more like teeth than architecture.

The Virus raised a hand.

The ground trembled. A low, ancient hum vibrated up through their boots as stone shifted. Rubble rolled aside like it had been waiting to move. Obsidian slabs rearranged themselves into a spiral stair that plunged into the dark.

Vincent watched in stunned silence.

The Virus descended first, his red eyes casting faint halos. The others followed, footfalls swallowed by the silence of the deep.

The walls began to glow.

Veins of violet light pulsed from within the stone, flickering like blood under skin. The deeper they walked, the brighter the light became, until even the Virus's glow dimmed beneath it.

Then they reached the bottom.

A massive subterranean chamber unfurled before them. The ceiling was lost in shadow. Crystals jutted from every surface; twisted, spined, hungry things. Each glowed with a purple core that pulsed like a second heartbeat.

Vincent stepped forward, breath caught in his throat.

"What is this…?" he asked.

The Virus did not answer at first. He stared at the crystal forest with something almost like awe.

"This is the breath between realms," he said softly. "Born from the moment the door closed…and the world was torn in two."

Vincent's fingers hovered near one crystal. He stopped. He could feel the crystal, as if it watched him back.

The Virus moved to the center, where a single monolith rose from the ground like a jagged tower. Its core throbbed with a violent light, brighter than the rest. It felt…awake.

He placed his hand upon it.

Instantly, his body jerked. A low, mechanical snarl ripped from his throat as arcs of energy surged through him. His spine arched. Red sparks burst from his skin. For a moment, his body flickered, shifting between metal and something more ancient.

He tore his hand away.

Smoke hissed from his palm where the crystal had left its mark, a violet sigil, burned and glowing.

Vincent rushed to his side.

"What—what happened?" he asked. "Are you—?"

The Virus straightened. His breathing slowed. He looked at the mark, then closed his fingers into a trembling fist.

"Collect the crystals," he said. "Move as swiftly as possible."

Vincent hesitated.

"Why?" he asked. "What's wrong?"

The Virus turned. His eyes blazed brighter than before, heat radiating from his skin. His voice was lower now. Hungrier.

"I can feel it," he said.

His next words were barely a whisper, yet they echoed through the chamber like prophecy:

"He has awoken."

#

Nikki's chest heaved as she crouched behind the rusted husk of an overturned truck. Her back scraped against scorched metal and her palms trembled. Her scythes, once sharp and solid, now flickered in and out of form, each reappearance more unstable than the last.

Ash churned in the air like smoke from an old fire.

Beyond the wreckage, the fight raged.

She heard her mother grunt with effort; Connor shouting, breathless. The heavy thuds of fists hitting flesh. They were surviving, but only just.

Nikki gritted her teeth, wiped blood and soot from her face, and moved.

She vaulted over the hood, charging toward the chaos. One of the enhanced men, tall and broad, a red glow bleeding from his temples, raised his fist to strike Laura.

Nikki slammed into him shoulder-first.

The impact jolted her spine, but the man flew backward through a building wall, giving Laura space to breathe.

A second enemy—leaner, faster, red veins tracing his neck like circuitry—lunged at her. His punch slammed into her ribs, lifting her off her feet. She hit the ground hard, the air leaving her in a gasp. Her scythes vanished in a sputter of violet sparks.

"Get up," she hissed at herself.

The leaner enemy stalked forward, steps crunching over ash. Nikki rose, summoning the blades again. They flickered into existence, unstable but sharp.

She struck.

One slash across his chest.

A second across his jaw.

He staggered, but didn't stop.

He lunged again, wild and silent, until Connor and Laura grabbed his arms from behind.

"Hold him!" Nikki shouted, stepping back.

"We're trying!" Connor snapped, digging in his heels.

The enemy roared, a monstrous sound that didn't belong in a human throat. He whipped his arms downward. Connor and Laura crashed to the pavement, dazed and groaning.

"Mom!" Nikki screamed. Fury exploded through her.

She lunged and drove a scythe into the man's chest with every ounce of strength she had.

The blow sent the enemy crumpling to the ground.

Breathing hard, Nikki dropped to her knees beside Laura.

"Are you okay?" she asked, voice breaking.

"Just…winded," Laura gasped, trying to sit up.

Connor pushed himself to his knees, blood streaking from a cut above his brow.

"We can't hold them," he said hoarsely. "They're too strong. There are still two more."

Nikki looked up.

Across the street, another enemy, a bulky one with no shirt, skin spiderwebbed with red, was rushing in.

Beside him, a female. Her eyes glowed like lit coals.

"We need backup," Connor said.

"There is no backup," Laura replied, voice flat. "We can't call for help. Anyone else will die."

Nikki staggered to her feet. Her scythes reformed with a crackle, barely more than shadows now.

"Then we don't stop," she said. "We fight until they stay down."

The enemies roared as one and charged.

Nikki took a step forward.

Then—

CRACK.

THUD. THUD. THUD.

A shockwave tore through the air like a cannon blast. All four enhanced soldiers were ripped from their feet and thrown backward, skidding, tumbling, and crashing into rubble. Their bodies hit the ground like sacks of bone and iron, and this time, they didn't rise.

Silence followed. The wind moaned through the ruins.

Nikki's chest heaved.

"What the hell…" Connor whispered, blinking in disbelief.

Laura pulled herself up, one hand clutched to her ribs. She

placed her other hand on Nikki's shoulder, steadying both of them.

Smoke curled in the street.

And then they saw him.

A tall figure stood among the wreckage, cloaked in a worn brown robe. Broad shoulders. Back turned to them. Boots wreathed in swirling dust.

In one hand, lifted effortlessly by the collar, Frederick dangled, snarling, thrashing, and utterly powerless.

The man turned slightly.

A bald head. A hard-set jaw. Eyes that shimmered.

Nikki froze.

Her vision blurred. Her breath caught.

No...

It couldn't be.

"Dad...?"

10

The Protector

ive years ago...

The Sinclair home glowed with warmth, not just from the golden fire crackling in the hearth, but from the laughter that echoed through its walls. Soft jazz hummed from the radio like a sleepy heartbeat, and the scent of Laura's evening stew drifted from the kitchen. Onions, thyme, and something just on the edge of burning.

Alex Sinclair lay stretched across the living room couch, one arm tucked behind his head, the other lazily tossing a rubber ball into the air and catching it with a soldier's precision. Though his age far outpaced any mortal calendar, his appearance spoke of a man barely thirty. He had a head full of dark red hair slicked back, beard trimmed to a disciplined edge. Even at rest, he radiated calm authority.

The ball sailed higher on the next toss, nearly brushing the ceiling.

WHAM.

A shriek of laughter pierced the air as a twelve-year-old blur crashed into him from behind.

Nikki.

She tackled him like a bolt of joy, clinging to his back, her arms wrapped around his shoulders.

Alex grinned, catching her with one arm while his other hand snagged the falling ball midair.

"Well, look who finally got the drop on me," he said, hoisting her higher with a playful grunt. He swept the dark red bangs from her eyes, the one thing she'd inherited from him. Luckily, she shared most of her looks with Laura. "Where's Mom, lovebug?"

"She's on the phone," Nikki said, chin pressed into his shoulder. "I think it's work again."

"Of course it is," Alex replied with exaggerated annoyance. "Come on. Recon mission."

He carried her piggyback down the hall, her giggles echoing behind them. As they reached the office door, Alex gave it a gentle kick.

Inside, Laura stood behind her desk, the soft glow of her desk lamp casting long shadows across the papers sprawled in front of her. She wore a black suit jacket, unbuttoned, sleeves rolled up to the elbows. A phone was tucked to her ear, but she glanced up and smiled at the sight of them. Just for a moment, the tension in her shoulders released.

She mouthed *troublemaker* at Nikki, then stood and approached.

"Connor?" Alex guessed, setting Nikki down gently.

Laura nodded, holding up a finger.

"Yes…" she said, speaking into the phone, "keep Lorne and the others circling. I'll send Alex in now."

She hung up and pressed her fingers to her temples, exhaling slowly.

"Everything all right?" Alex asked.

Laura offered a tired shrug.

"Stolen gear out of Veilhaven," she said. "High-grade Task Force tech. Grenades, rifles, probably more. A group of lowlifes tried to hit a cash transport in Halvade. Now they're holed up in an office building. Our agents are pinned down."

Alex's brow furrowed. Then, like muscle memory, a grin cut through the concern.

"I'll be back before dinner."

He kissed her forehead gently and gave Nikki's hair a quick tousle on his way toward the door.

"Don't let your mom burn the stew," he said.

But just as his hand reached for the knob, Laura's fingers closed around his wrist.

"Hey," she said softly.

He turned, sensing the weight behind that single word.

Her gaze searched his, her voice quieter now.

"These weapons..." she said. "They're Task Force issue. Prototype-level. We were supposed to dismantle them months ago. But some got out."

Alex blinked.

"Why would thugs have access to—?"

"I don't know," she said, cutting him off. Her voice was tight, controlled. "But they're not standard-issue. They're... advanced. And they weren't designed for the average criminal."

The silence swelled, thick between them.

Alex studied her face. Measured, composed, but not unreadable. Beneath her control was something else.

Worry. Fear. Guilt?

"You think a few black-market toys are going to stop me?"

he asked with a half-smile.

Laura managed one in return, but it didn't quite reach her eyes.

"It's my job to worry," she murmured. Her thumb brushed against the fabric of his sleeve, drawing a small circle without thinking. "Just…be careful. Please?"

"I will," he said, brushing a strand of hair behind her ear. "It's my job to come home."

He turned without waiting for a response. A second later, a soft gust of wind filled the hallway. Outside, a boom like distant thunder rolled through the quiet neighborhood.

Laura stood in the doorway long after he'd vanished into the sky. One hand rested lightly on the frame, her fingers still tingling with the memory of his warmth.

She didn't move.

#

Alex dropped from the sky like a shadow, landing in the middle of a broken, smoke-veiled street.

Ahead, a cash transit vehicle lay gutted, its rear doors blown wide open, flames licking at twisted metal. The air stank of ozone and burning plastic. Medics crouched beside wounded Task Force agents, wrapping bandages and checking pulses. Sirens wailed faintly in the distance, too far to matter now.

Alex strode to one of the medics kneeling beside a bloodied officer.

"What happened?" he asked, voice low and firm.

"They've got some kind of advanced weaponry," the medic muttered without looking up. "Stuff I've never seen. Armor-piercing, concussive—tore through us like paper. They're holed up in that office building."

Alex's eyes followed the medic's gesture to a squat, concrete structure streaked with soot.

"How many?"

"Three," the medic said, hands trembling as he tightened a tourniquet. "We tried to breach, but…it wasn't even a fight."

Alex gave a grim nod and walked toward the building. He pressed his palm to the scorched metal door, warped and warm, then shoved.

The door blasted off its hinges, crashing inside.

Dust swirled in the flickering half-light of the ruined lobby. Three men stood at the far end, jittery and armed, backs to duffel bags overflowing with cash, the bills fluttering like dying leaves.

"You know…" Alex said, stepping inside, voice calm but thunderous. "You hurt good people today. For what? A payout you won't live to enjoy?"

His gaze dropped to their twitching trigger fingers.

"Drop the guns," he continued. "Leave the bags. I walk away, and we forget the part where you used Task Force weapons on Task Force officers."

Silence.

Then one of them lifted his weapon.

Alex sighed.

"No? Suit yourself."

He took a step forward.

Without warning, the first blast hit him square in the chest.

A shriek of energy punched through the air, slamming him backward. He staggered, boots grinding against the concrete, the burn mark smoking through his shirt.

Pain. Real pain. Not the muted sting of bullets or bruises.

A second blast hit harder, sending him crashing into a filing cabinet, which folded beneath him.

Alex groaned, rising. His ribs ached. His pride, more so.

"All right," he growled. "Last warning."

The second man fired.

Alex raised his fist and struck the blast midair. It cracked against his knuckles, bursting in a hiss of steam. Smoke curled from his hand.

His jaw clenched.

No more games.

He launched forward. A sonic shock cracked the tiles as he blurred across the room. In one motion, he tore the weapon from the first man's hands and flung it across the room.

The second raised his gun again. *Too slow.*

Alex drove an elbow into his chest, lifting him off the ground before slamming him into the wall.

But the third had a clear shot.

The blast caught Alex on the side of the head. His scream echoed off the concrete. Static exploded through his skull. He dropped to one knee, eyes swimming, vision doubling.

He hadn't felt this kind of pain in years.

The three scrambled, grabbing duffels and making for the exit.

Adrenaline surged.

Alex roared, springing from the floor. He grabbed two of them by their collars midrun and hurled them across the room. The third spun to fire again, but Alex was faster now. He drove his palm into the man's chest with bone-cracking force, dropping him instantly.

Silence.

Alex stood in the aftermath, chest heaving, eyes wide. His

hands trembled.

Not from injury.

From doubt.

He stared down at the fallen weapons, their cores still humming with residual energy.

He grabbed the duffels and the weapons. When he stepped outside, the sun had dipped behind the skyline, bathing the street in cold twilight.

The medic looked up in disbelief as Alex dropped the bags at his feet.

"Tell Connor to meet me at my house," Alex said, voice like iron wrapped in frost.

Before the man could reply, Alex shot into the sky, leaving only the whisper of wind and the screech of distant sirens.

#

The wind howled as Alex landed, the force of his descent cracking the concrete beneath his boots. Dust swirled at his feet as he marched across the lawn, his eyes burning with fury and disbelief. In his arms were the weapons, now stained with the weight of their implications.

A car door slammed behind him.

"Alex," Connor called, jogging across the street, hands raised in a pacifying gesture. "Let's just talk for a second, all right?"

Alex didn't slow. He stopped only when he'd reached the edge of the driveway and threw the weapons at Connor's feet. They crashed to the ground in a violent chorus of metal and synthcore plating, the sound sharp and damning in the silence that followed.

"What are these?" Alex asked, his voice a low growl, like an animal restrained by will alone.

Connor hesitated.

"It's complicated," he finally said.

"*Simplify.*"

The front door burst open. Laura rushed down the steps barefoot, still in a T-shirt and joggers, the look on her face one of dread and inevitability.

"What's going on?" she asked, her voice taut, fragile.

Alex didn't look at her at first. His eyes stayed fixed on the twisted remains of the weapons.

"That's what I want to know," he said, finally raising his gaze. "Because those things hurt me, Laura. *Actually hurt me.*"

Laura stopped short. For a moment, words failed her.

"I-I didn't think they'd ever be used," she said at last. "They were prototypes."

"Prototypes?" Alex repeated, voice rising. "Prototypes of what, exactly?"

"They're designed to counter high-threat–level entities," Laura said carefully. "Beings who pose risks we can't neutralize with conventional weapons."

"You mean beings like me?" he asked. The words hit the air like thunder. His jaw flexed. "Say it."

Laura looked away.

"Alex, come on," Connor said, approaching cautiously. "We needed contingencies. You know better than anyone how dangerous things have gotten."

Alex turned on him, eyes flaring.

"And your 'contingency' nearly killed me!" he shouted. "These weapons were in the hands of street thugs, Connor. *Civilians.* You want to tell me how that happened?"

"It wasn't supposed to go that way," Laura said, stepping

closer. "They were stored securely. Someone must've—"

"They got out," Alex snapped. "That's all that matters. You built weapons that could hurt me, and now they're out in the world. You didn't think to tell me? You didn't even warn me before sending me into that fight blind."

He was breathing hard now. Not from exhaustion, but from something worse. Hurt. Betrayal.

Laura reached out and placed a hand on his shoulder.

Alex flinched away, eyes narrowed.

"Don't."

"Alex, please," she said softly. "This won't happen again. I promise."

But the words rang hollow.

He turned to the weapons, jaw tight, and raised a boot. With a single stomp, he shattered the core of the first gun. Then another. And another. Sparks flew as delicate systems crumpled under his heel.

When the last weapon broke, he stood over the wreckage, shoulders heaving.

"I gave everything to this world," he said, his voice low but resonant. "Every scar. Every moment. I protected it without asking for anything. And now you think you need weapons to defend yourselves...from *me*."

Laura stepped forward, eyes glossy.

"That's not what this is—" she tried.

"It is," Alex said, cutting her off. "You just won't admit it."

He looked at her. Really looked. And for the first time in a long time, he saw her as someone he didn't fully recognize.

"I'm the protector of this realm," he said. "But maybe it's time I leave it to the people who think they can do it better."

He walked past them, into the house.

The door closed behind him with a click that echoed like finality.

#

The Sinclair home had fallen into silence.

Not the kind born of peace, but the heavy, suffocating kind—dense with everything unsaid. The fireplace flickered low, casting faint amber halos on the living room walls, where shadows danced like memories that wouldn't leave.

Upstairs, Laura lay curled on her side, her body still but her mind anything but. Sleep didn't come. It hadn't even tried. She stared past the dresser into the dark, watching nothing, just the soft blur of regrets stacking quietly in her chest like folded letters never sent.

Regret, she'd learned, was a patient thing. It didn't scream. It whispered.

A soft creak broke the stillness.

She sat up, her breath catching.

Another creak—this one closer. She rose and stepped into the hallway barefoot, careful not to disturb the silence further. Around the corner, she saw Alex.

He was slipping into Nikki's room, a duffel bag slung over one shoulder. His silhouette leaned down over their daughter, tucking the blanket gently around her, then pressing a kiss to her forehead. Tender. Final.

"Alex?" Laura whispered, the word barely more than a breath.

He turned, raised a finger to his lips.

She nodded, heart thudding.

They moved down the stairs together in silence, the wood

beneath their feet groaning like old bones mourning the moment. In the dim light of the living room, with the fire reduced to embers, she finally asked the question already burning behind her ribs.

"What are you doing?"

Alex adjusted the strap on his shoulder.

"I have to go," he said.

"Where?" she asked.

"You know I can't tell you that," he replied.

Laura looked around at the life they'd built. The family photos on the wall. The half-folded blanket over the couch. The house that had once felt like shelter now felt hollow, each familiar thing a reminder of what she was about to lose.

"So that's it?" she asked, her voice cracking. "You're just... leaving? After everything? What about Nikki?"

"I'm not abandoning her," he said softly. "Or you. But after what happened today...I need to be better. Stronger. I need to find answers. About myself, about Midtown, about everything."

Her arms crossed, not in defiance, but in self-preservation. As if trying to hold herself together from the inside out.

"And you think leaving us is the answer to that?"

He paused, then looked down at his hands.

"If I stay..." His voice tightened. "I'll break. I felt it today. That edge. Something inside me cracking. And if that part of me gets out...I don't know if I'll be able to stop it. I won't risk becoming a danger to the people I love."

The words hit her like a wave. Cold, slow, and irreversible.

Alex stepped forward and pulled her into an embrace. She didn't resist. She leaned in, buried her face into his chest, and let herself pretend, for just a second, that this was any other night. That the fire hadn't dimmed. That they still had time.

"Nikki will be safe," he whispered into her hair. "You're the strongest person I know. You'll protect her. You'll protect this city."

As he started to pull away, Laura caught his hand and held it tight.

"I didn't want this," she said, voice shaking. "I should've told you about the weapons. I should've trusted you. You were right to be angry."

Alex nodded slowly, eyes gentle, as if memorizing every detail of her face.

"You did what you thought was right," he said. "So did I."

A pause.

"I'm sorry," he added softly.

"So am I," she said.

He lingered in the doorway, silhouetted against the pale light spilling in from the porch. For a heartbeat, he looked like a stranger carved from memory. A man already halfway gone.

"You'll understand one day," he said. "Why I had to go."

And then he stepped outside.

The door closed with a quiet click, but it echoed like a slammed vault inside her chest.

Laura stood there in the stillness, arms loose at her sides, lips slightly parted. The room felt suddenly larger, emptier. Colder.

And when the tears finally came, they did so silently.

They slid down her cheeks and fell with soft, aching taps onto the floor, like rain against a window that no longer opened.

For the first time in years, Laura Sinclair felt powerless.

#

Far above the clouds, Alex flew, an arrow loosed into the waking sky. Wind tore past him, cold and biting, but he didn't feel it. His mind churned with memory and silence, the echoes of what he'd left behind still rattling inside him.

The sun had risen fully now, casting long golden beams over the curve of the world. But Alex soared higher, beyond cities, beyond valleys, into the untouched cold of the far north.

At last, he slowed.

Before him stood a range of ancient mountains, their snow-crusted peaks rising like the spines of sleeping titans. At their heart, one mountain loomed above the rest. Taller, darker, and older. Carved into its cliffside like a secret too sacred for the world below was the temple.

Snow fell in fragile flurries, vanishing as they kissed his warm skin. Alex descended in silence, his boots crunching into the powdery earth as he landed. Each step forward echoed against the stone.

The stillness was thick. Deep. Not with emptiness, but presence.

He crossed the outer threshold, entering the temple's heart. Smooth stone, cold underfoot. The air hummed with memory, though no words were spoken.

He found the courtyard fountain, cracked by time but still flowing. Kneeling beside it, Alex dipped his hands into the water. The chill cut to his bones, but he held it anyway. He exhaled, a slow, trembling breath, and brought the water to his face.

A soft wash.

A letting go.

A beginning.

Footsteps emerged behind him.

He rose to meet them.

Monks in weather-worn robes stepped from the shadows. No weapons. No expressions. Only presence. Among them came the elder, his beard long and silver, his face etched by decades of peace hard-won.

Without a word, the elder took Alex's hand and placed a small white flower in his palm.

A welcome.

A reminder.

A vow.

Alex bowed, closing his fingers around it.

The weeks that followed tested every part of him. His body. His resolve. His regret. Nights brought no sleep, only the relentless drum of memory. Days were filled with labor, breaking stone, lifting trees, and hurling slabs of granite into the river.

He shaved his head. Not as a symbol of humility, but of surrender. The man who had arrived would not be the man who remained.

He trained in the forests until his fists cracked bark and split boulders. But strength was never the goal. It was discipline. Precision. Presence.

"It is not the power of your strike that protects the realm," the elder told him. "It is the clarity of your heart."

Alex rose each morning before the sun. He meditated in gardens choked with frost. He read ancient scrolls by candlelight, some written in languages long dead. Each page revealed truths about the multiverse: How it was forged, where it fractured, and the fragile threads that still held it together.

"You cannot protect a world you do not understand," the elder said. "And you cannot understand anything while your mind is at war with itself."

The days blurred. The seasons passed in silence. Alex had no mirror, but he didn't need one.

He *felt* the change.

Where once there had been fire, now there was balance. Where once there was fear, now stood stillness.

And yet, always, he missed them.

Laura's laughter echoing from the kitchen.

Nikki's small arms around his neck.

The scent of woodsmoke curling from the fireplace.

He folded these memories like pages into a sacred book, unread, but never forgotten.

In his fifth year, Alex stood shirtless on the edge of a frozen cliff, breath misting in the air. His skin was raw from the cold, but his eyes were steady. Around him, four monks bowed in defeat. He had bested them, not with force, but with calm. Every movement had purpose. Every strike, restraint.

He closed his eyes.

The wind howled.

And then, it stopped.

A jolt. Not pain. *Presence*. Something had awakened.

His eyes snapped open.

The sky pulsed faintly. The mountain trembled beneath his feet. Birds scattered in spirals. Deep in his chest, a new rhythm beat faster. More urgent.

Visions pierced his thoughts:

Glowing red eyes.

A monstrous form of metal and smoke.

Cables twisted like veins.

Midtown engulfed in ash and flame.

And Nikki was older now. Stronger. But alone. Her eyes wide with terror.

Alex staggered back, one hand clutching his chest.

He turned and sprinted into the temple.

The elder was already waiting in the prayer hall, bathed in the flickering glow of candlelight. He said nothing.

"You felt it," Alex panted.

The elder nodded once.

"The world trembles," he said. "A great shadow moves again."

"I can't let it happen," Alex replied.

He turned to leave.

"The world you return to is not the same," the elder warned. "It will test you in ways you cannot yet see. You must remember what you've become."

Alex paused.

Then he knelt.

Eyes sharp. Voice clear.

"I remember everything," he said. "I will carry your teachings to the end. I won't fail her."

The elder placed a weathered hand on his shoulder.

"Then you are ready."

Alex stood.

Fastened his robes.

And stepped outside.

The wind greeted him like an old friend, roaring across the cliffs.

With one last breath, he soared skyward, through snow, through cloud, through light itself.

A streak of silver cut across the sky.
The Protector was going home.

11

Home

resent day...

P *resent day...*
The street was still.

Alex stood in the center of the broken road, bathed in the dying glow of a ruined skyline. His robes whispered in the wind, the tattered fabric fluttering like a banner of a war long thought lost. In one hand, he held Frederick by the collar, lifted as easily as a rag doll. Around them, Frederick's enhanced soldiers lay scattered and broken, their limbs twisted at unnatural angles, armor cracked and smoking, chests heaving in shallow, unconscious breaths.

Even the wind seemed to hush around Alex. As if the city itself had paused. As if it remembered him.

Then, from behind the rusted husk of a truck, a voice cracked through the silence.

"...Dad?"

Nikki's voice was hoarse, paper-thin. Her fists trembled at her sides, her entire body locked tight, like it was taking every ounce of willpower not to run or collapse.

Alex turned his head. Just slightly. His eyes found her.

And then he let go.

Frederick crumpled to the ground with a groan, coughing, the breath knocked from him. His eyes were wild, fixed on Alex like he was staring at something inhuman. A ghost wrapped in skin. A legend returned.

Before Alex could take a step, Laura moved.

She didn't walk; she charged. Straight to him. Her arms wrapped tightly around his chest, her breath hitched, fingers clinging like she wasn't sure he was real.

Alex didn't move at first. Then, slowly, his arms raised to hold her back.

SLAP.

Her palm cracked across his face with a sound like breaking glass. His head turned from the force, but he didn't blink. Didn't flinch.

"You *bastard*," Laura whispered, her voice choked and shaking. "You don't get to just show up. Not like this."

Behind her, Nikki took a step forward.

Her face was hidden behind her mask, not revealing her emotions. Something she hadn't allowed herself to feel in years. Her scythes had faded. Her arms were smeared with blood and dirt. Every breath she took looked like it hurt.

"Is it really you?" she asked quietly. She slowly took the mask off her face. "Or am I just losing it now?"

Alex looked at her fully, his eyes soft, searching. He took her in. The angles of her face, the fire in her jawline, the ache in her eyes. So much older than she should have been.

"It's me," he said. His voice was raw. "I'm sorry. I'm so, so sorry I wasn't here."

Nikki stared. Her lips parted, like she wanted to say something else, but her voice caught on the edge of memory.

Then, like glass giving under pressure, she broke.

"Sorry?" she snapped. "You vanished. No message. No warning. We buried you. We mourned you. Then we had to keep going without you."

Her voice rose, louder now.

"Mom had to carry the entire Task Force on her back. And me? I had to figure out who I was without a father. I had to become something I didn't even understand."

She stepped closer.

"And now you just *appear*? Like nothing happened?"

Alex looked down. His jaw tightened. His fists clenched at his sides.

"I don't expect things to go back to the way they were," he said. "I don't expect forgiveness. But I had to go. What I trained for, what I learned, was bigger than me. It was important."

"And we weren't?" Nikki shot back. Her voice cracked like ice. "We weren't worth staying for?"

The silence that followed was deafening.

Connor stepped forward.

His coat was torn at the shoulder, and a smear of dried blood crusted along his lip. He glanced at the wreckage around them, then looked at Alex, then Laura, then Nikki.

"I know this isn't the best time," he said, voice carefully casual, "but maybe we table the Sinclair family reunion until we're not standing in the middle of a battlefield?"

No one laughed. But the moment let them breathe.

Laura turned, still trembling. She knelt beside Frederick, who groaned and tried to shift.

"What did you do to them?" she asked. Her voice was cold now, clinical. "How the hell did they become this strong?"

Alex stepped forward. His shadow fell across Frederick's battered form.

"It wasn't him," Alex said. His voice cut through the air like a blade. "Something else has entered our realm. He's helping it."

Without warning, he yanked Frederick off the ground by the front of his shirt. Frederick winced, letting out a strained breath through his teeth.

"Talk."

Frederick coughed. Blood flecked his lips. But then, through swollen eyes, he smiled.

"Why don't you ask your wife?" he replied.

Alex froze.

Slowly, his head turned toward Laura. Not angry. Just… quiet. The wind moved again, whistling through the wreckage.

"What did you do?" he asked, his voice lower than before. Almost a whisper. But somehow more dangerous than shouting.

#

The Task Force station was one of the last buildings still standing in Midtown: cracked, scorched, but upright. Its windows were dust-streaked, the overhead lights humming dimly with emergency power, casting sickly shadows over the walls.

In one of the quieter rooms, the group waited.

Alex stood against the far wall, arms folded, robes scorched and stained with ash and blood. His silence pressed on the room like gravity. He hadn't said a word since they'd left the street.

Laura sat on the edge of a dented steel desk, elbows on her knees, eyes unreadable. Her hands fidgeted without her realizing it.

Connor leaned against the opposite wall, chewing the inside of his cheek, one leg bouncing.

Nikki stood near the window, arms folded, her face ghosted by the light filtering through grime-streaked glass. She stared at the skyline like she wanted to disappear into it.

The air crackled with unspoken things.

Then Alex spoke.

"I didn't expect to be gone that long," he said, trying to make a defense.

It was quiet. But his voice filled the room like thunder.

Everyone turned to him.

Connor exhaled sharply and pushed off the wall.

"I'm gonna go check on Frederick," he muttered, brushing past them. The door shut behind him with a dull *clunk*. The tension thinned, but didn't leave.

Laura didn't look at Alex. Her jaw flexed once.

"To be fair," she said softly, "none of us expected you to come back at all."

Alex nodded slowly, his gaze distant.

"I had to be ready," he said. "I told you when I left…I told you it was necessary."

There was a pause.

Nikki turned from the window. Her face twisted.

"Wait, *what?*" she said, her voice sharpened. "You *told* her?"

The room went silent once more.

Laura finally met her daughter's gaze. Her expression was pained, hesitant.

"Nikki…" she began carefully. "It's not that I didn't want to tell you. It's just…it was complicated."

"You *knew*?" Nikki stepped forward, her words now jagged and full of disbelief. A violet mist slowly curled around her arms. "You knew he was leaving? And you didn't say anything?"

Laura stood slowly.

"I was trying to protect you," she explained.

"From *what*!?" Nikki's voice cracked, the hurt breaking through the anger. "Why did you leave, Dad? What are you guys *still* not telling me?"

Alex hesitated.

Then Laura answered.

"He left because of me," she said quietly.

Nikki froze.

Laura swallowed, eyes glassy.

"Because of the Task Force," she continued. "Because of something I authorized."

She stepped forward, her voice low but steady.

"We were developing weapons. Prototypes. Things meant to protect the city from…high-level threats. People like your father. As a last resort."

Nikki said nothing. Just stared.

"But one of the shipments was hijacked. And those weapons were used. On him."

"And they worked," Alex said, his voice bitter. "They tore through me like I was paper."

"So you ran?" Nikki asked, her words trembling now. "You ran because you were scared?"

"No," Alex said. His voice was iron. "Because if something in this world could *kill* me, then I couldn't protect anyone. I had to disappear. I had to understand my limits. Train. Adapt. I had to become more than I was."

"But we were *left* without a protector," Nikki said. "We didn't have a choice."

She took a breath.

"I stepped up."

"...You?" he asked, his brow furrowed slightly.

Nikki's jaw tensed. She hadn't meant to say it like that. But the truth was out.

"I have powers, Dad," she said.

That landed. Alex's face didn't shift much, but something flickered in his eyes.

"I've been using them," Nikki went on, voice firm now. "At night. In secret. Helping people. Trying to protect what I could. I thought it was what *you* would've done."

Alex studied her carefully. No shock. No denial. Just... understanding.

Laura noticed it.

"You don't seem surprised," she said.

"I'm not," Alex said. He stepped closer. "I didn't get my abilities until I was around her age. My father was the protector before me. When he died, something inside me awakened. I always suspected it would happen to her too."

He looked at Nikki.

"You don't have to carry this alone anymore," he said. "Let me help you. Train you. Prepare you for what's coming."

Nikki flinched.

"I don't need your help," she replied. Her voice came out sharper than she meant, but she didn't take it back. "I've been doing this without you. I had to lie to Mom. I had to rely on friends. *Connor* was there. He helped."

She crossed her arms tighter.

"You don't get to come back and play father just because the world's on fire again."

Alex looked down.

There was nothing to say. Not really.

"I never wanted this for either of you," he said softly. "Not this burden. Not this war."

A silence fell between them, deep and aching.

Then Nikki broke it.

"You want to help me?"

Alex looked up.

"Yes."

"Then fix this," she said. "Save the world. Start there. And *maybe* we figure ourselves out after."

Alex stared at her for a moment longer.

Then the door creaked open.

Connor stepped inside.

"We should start the questioning," he said.

Alex gave a quiet nod, then turned to follow.

He didn't look back.

#

The lights above flickered, casting jagged shadows that danced across the cracked concrete walls. The interrogation room smelled of dust and old metal, like the remnants of old wars and older secrets.

Frederick sat alone at the table.

His suit jacket was torn, one sleeve nearly ripped clean off. Blood dried in the corner of his mouth. His hands, cuffed to a rusted ring, drummed lazily against the steel, tugging the chain with bored indifference.

To him, this wasn't punishment. It was an intermission.

The door creaked open.

Alex entered first, robes streaked with ash, expression carved from stone. Laura followed, her movements sharp and restrained. Connor stepped in next, jaw tight, arms folded. Nikki was last, silent and unreadable, her stare locked onto Frederick like a blade waiting for a reason to swing.

The door clanged shut behind them.

Frederick looked up, his eyes gleaming with exhaustion and arrogance.

"Uh-oh," he said, "looks like I'm in trouble."

No one replied.

He gave a chuckle.

"So," he drawled, his attention shifting to Alex, "the *Protector* returns. Was vacation getting boring? Or did you finally remember Midtown existed?"

Still, nothing.

He glanced at the others.

"Ah, and the rest of the welcoming committee. Good cop, bad cop…emotionally unstable teenager?"

He smirked.

"Precious."

Still, silence.

Laura stepped forward.

"Tell us what you've done," she said, her voice demanding.

Frederick cocked his head.

"So, you do speak," he replied. "Director Sinclair. Still leading with the moral high ground, I see. I love the shirt, by the way. New uniforms?"

Laura didn't blink, but her fists clenched at her sides.

"Your men," she said coldly. "They were enhanced. How? Who are you working with?"

Frederick shrugged.

"You're cute when you try to be scary," he said, smirking again.

Then he looked at Nikki.

"And you," he said. "You've been quite the trouble. Who would've thought my biggest problem would be a child?"

Nikki stepped forward, fast.

Alex raised a hand. She stopped, seething.

"Talk," Alex said. One word. But it hit the air like thunder.

Frederick sat back, the chain rattling softly.

"I'm not your enemy," he said. "Not *really*. I'm just smart enough to know when the tide's turning. You opened the door. You invited him here."

"Who is *he*?" Laura asked.

Frederick smiled, slower now.

"He calls himself *the Virus*," he replied. "A mind. A machine. A god in exile. He came through the portal you built so desperately. He speaks in circuits and symbols and prophecy. I listened."

"Where is he now?" Alex asked.

Frederick hesitated. A flicker of something crossed his face. Discomfort, maybe.

Then he straightened.

"Ashenfell," he said. "Digging. Feeding. Growing. He's looking for something down there. Gathering enough power to rewrite the world."

The group pulled into a quiet huddle in the corner. Their whispers were urgent, too low for Frederick to hear.

He rolled his eyes.

"Look at them," he muttered to himself. "Plotting their brave little suicide mission."

Laura turned and stepped back toward the table.

"Why are you telling us this?" she asked. "If you're on his side, why help us at all? Is this just misdirection? A trap?"

"I'm not on *his* side," Frederick replied, his posture shifting. "I'm not on *your* side either. I'm on *mine*. That's the difference."

He shrugged, the cuffs clinking as he moved.

"If you win? I end up in a cell—which, let's be honest, we both know won't hold me forever. If you lose? I inherit the new world. Either way, I *survive*."

"You think he'll honor that?" Connor scoffed. "He's a machine. He'll crush you the second you're no longer useful."

Frederick's eyes snapped to him, cold and fearless.

"Then I'll die standing," he said. "Not groveling."

A pause.

Then he smiled again. A little sadder now.

"You think I'm doing this for power?" he asked. "For kicks? Halvade was dying. Forgotten. I gave it order. Gave it strength. People followed me because I delivered."

He looked at Nikki.

"I didn't become a monster. I became a king. Because someone had to. I didn't see it at first, but maybe me and this *Virus* have a lot in common."

Alex stepped forward.

"You helped him kill innocent people," he said.

"And so did you," Frederick shot back. "You vanished. You're just as much to blame as I am." Frederick shrugged. "He's nearly ready. You want to stop him? Go to Ashenfell. Try your luck. But don't say I didn't warn you."

Alex turned to leave.

The others followed.

Frederick called after them:

"When the world burns…remember who warned you."

The door slammed shut behind them.

Frederick exhaled, alone once more.

The light buzzed above.

The shadows on the wall shifted.

He looked toward the far corner of the room, where no one stood.

A whisper, low and wet, crept into his mind like smoke.

"You gave them too much."

Frederick's jaw clenched.

"Trust me, I gave them just enough," he muttered, barely audible. "Now you just have to finish it."

No reply. Only silence.

12

Ashenfell

The aircraft cut through the sky like a blade through flesh, its engines thrumming beneath the howl of wind and storm. Outside, the clouds twisted like dark spirits, riddled with forked lightning that briefly illuminated the ruin below. Ashenfell was painted with fractured highways, collapsed buildings, and scorched valleys stretching like veins across a dying world.

Inside the cabin, silence reigned.

Nikki sat near a reinforced window, her mask resting like a hollow skull in her lap. Her fingers tapped a nervous rhythm against her knee, steady, controlled, but betraying the storm inside. Her muscles still ached from the rescue, bones worn down by the weight of survival. But pain wasn't what stirred in her now.

It was anticipation. It was reckoning.

Across from her, Laura sat rigid on a bench, her eyes fixed on the datapad in her hands, though she hadn't read a word in the last twenty minutes. Her shoulders were drawn tight, tension climbing her spine like frost. She looked like a commander holding herself together by the edges. And Nikki saw it. Not just the strain of leadership, but the slow erosion of someone trying to carry grief and duty in the same hands.

"Welp," Connor said from near the cockpit, gripping a ceiling rail as turbulence rocked the cabin. "Nothing like a good old-fashioned suicide mission to bring the family together."

His voice echoed with that trademark levity, too light, too sharp. It was armor. They all wore some kind of armor.

Jenna walked out of the bathroom in the rear. She wiped her mouth with a small tissue. Her face was pale, almost green.

"You sure you've flown in this thing before?" she asked, eyeing the blinking lights and sleek controls.

"Plenty," Connor replied, pretending confidence. "Back when we weren't flying straight into the jaws of doom."

"Only when we had to," Laura murmured, her voice brittle. "Alex…usually flew solo."

Alex stood near the ramp, unmoving, the ash on his cloak dusted from a world still burning. His silhouette loomed like a shadow from another time: quiet, statuesque, carved from regret. He didn't speak. Didn't need to.

Jenna sat near him, taking a deep breath.

"You might not remember me much," she said, looking up at him, "but I remember you."

"You're Lucy's kid, right?" he asked, looking down at her. "You and Nikki had a few playdates whenever she'd come around with Connor. How is she?"

"Well—" she started, but stopped.

"Dad," Nikki said, shooting Alex a look.

Alex shrugged, looking confused.

"No, it's okay," Jenna said. "She died. Last year. I've been staying with Connor ever since."

Alex's expression eased.

"Oh, I'm—I didn't know. I'm sorry."

"How would you?" Connor said, his eyes still focused on Ashenfell's horizon. "You haven't been here."

The thunderclouds began to thin. Below them stretched a jagged range of volcanic rock, seething with pulses of red. The aircraft slowed, descending toward what looked like an obsidian scar carved deep into the earth.

Connor leaned forward to peer through the glass.

"All right, ladies," he said. "There it is. I hate to say it, but there's no turning back now."

Laura moved closer, her datapad casting a pale blue glow across her focused face.

"The readings are unstable," she said. "Magnetic interference, heat spikes, and seismic anomalies all across the crater. There's no clean way in."

"Good," Alex said quietly. "He'll know we're coming."

A brief silence settled over the group as the aircraft lowered to the ground.

"So," Nikki finally said, breaking the quiet, "is that the new superhero look?"

Alex glanced down at the ash-streaked robe.

"It's not a costume," he said. "It's what we wore at the temple. Simplicity. Focus. It's…all I've known for years."

Nikki raised a brow.

"Fashion-forward monks," she said. "Got it."

Before Alex could reply, the aircraft jolted, hydraulics groaning as the landing gear met fractured stone. Smoke crawled up through the ramp's seams like fingers reaching for them.

Connor moved into the cockpit, flicking a series of switches. The back ramp began to lower, and the sound of the storm filled the space like a rising tide.

"Well," he said, glancing over his shoulder, "game plan?"

Alex stepped into the center of the cabin, his voice even.

"The Virus will be expecting us," he said. "He'll most definitely have more of those enhanced men. We'll let them strike first. I'll draw their attention. You focus on each other."

"And if it's a trap?" Jenna asked, her eyes scanning the terrain.

"It is," Laura answered flatly.

"We go anyway," Alex said.

A deep boom rolled across the land. The aircraft shuddered, the wind howling louder now.

Connor exhaled slowly.

"This might be the dumbest thing we've ever done," he said, readying his weapon.

"We'll make it work," Alex replied, his voice low and certain, like steel drawn from a scabbard. "It's now or never."

Nikki stood.

She lifted her mask, fitting it into place. Her eyes burned beneath it. Not with fear, but with certainty.

She was ready.

#

A breeze filled the cavern like a breath from the underworld.

It pulsed with violet light, uneven and alive. Warped shadows danced across jagged walls. Crystals jutted from the stone like the ribs of a buried titan, each one humming with raw, unstable power. The air shimmered with distortion, as if reality itself was unraveling at the seams.

At the center of it all stood the Virus.

The crimson glow that once coursed through his veins had faded to a dim ember, a flicker where there had once been a second sun. His armor, streaked with ash and blood, no longer radiated. It pulsed weakly, struggling to contain the dying god within.

Before him, Frederick's soldiers stood in a tense formation. Their breaths came in ragged pulls. Their eyes were rimmed in red, their veins crawling like roots beneath their skin. Their bodies trembled, strained, like cages cracking from the inside.

The Virus raised his arms.

"I give you my strength," he said.

His voice echoed like a death knell, hollow, melodic, and soaked in finality.

From his palms, darkness poured.

Not smoke. Not mist. Something thicker. Viscous. Alive. It unfurled like sentient ink, writhing through the air, slithering into nostrils, mouths, open wounds, anything that led inward.

The soldiers convulsed.

One dropped to his knees, screaming as glowing fissures split across his body like molten fault lines. Muscles swelled, tendons tore, and then stitched themselves anew. Another twisted sideways, arms cracking and reforming into clawed extensions, half-bone, half-steel.

Their humanity melted away.

They were no longer men.

At the edge of the cavern, Vincent stood still. Watching. In his hands, a sack of jagged, obsidian crystals pulsed with faint light. The same crystals that had poisoned the earth above. His face was unreadable, but his eyes, narrow and frantic, betrayed the panic clawing at his mind.

The Virus lowered his arms.

He staggered. Servos in his chest whined with strain. The glow at his core died down to embers. His breath, once mechanical and metronomic, now rasped like air dragged through rusted gears.

Vincent stepped forward, hesitant.

"You're draining yourself," he said, barely audible above the cavern's hum. "If you keep pushing—"

"I know," the Virus snapped, voice glitching with static. "This is all I can give them. It must be…enough."

He stumbled. His boots scraped stone. His frame sagged under the weight of something unseen.

"You have the crystals?"

"Yes." Vincent nodded. "They're ready. But…how are we supposed to return to the city? We won't make it through them."

The Virus turned.

One blackened hand gripped Vincent's shoulder, heavy as iron.

"*We* will not," he said. "Only you."

Vincent blinked.

"*Me?*"

"You will finish what we began," the Virus continued, voice hollow but unwavering. "You have the knowledge. You've studied the breaches. You know how to open the next gate."

"I can't do this without you," Vincent said. "I'm not…I'm not strong enough."

"In this form," the Virus rasped, "I am of no use. If I flee, they will find me. Tear me apart. But they do not fear you. That is your weapon."

Vincent stared at the ground. His jaw clenched. Dust floated in the air like ash in still water.

The Virus leaned closer. His voice dropped low, guttural, almost human.

"Finish the portal. When the breach opens again, I will return. Not flickering. Not hollow. Whole. And ready to erase them."

Vincent hesitated, lips parted with questions he didn't dare speak.

"No more," the Virus said. "Time is gone."

He raised a trembling hand and pressed it to Vincent's chest.

A flare of crimson erupted, blinding and crackling with energy. The crystals lining the chamber vibrated violently as the light coiled around Vincent and the sack, encasing him in a cocoon of living electricity.

And then—

BOOM.

The light vanished.

Vincent was gone.

The chamber quaked. Stones rained down in soft clatters. The newly enhanced soldiers stood still.

The Virus dropped to one knee.

His form was broken now. A god-machine drained of its fire, teetering on the edge of extinction.

But his eyes, dim though they burned, still held more than rage.

They held purpose.

He turned toward the mouth of the cave, where the storm of war awaited.

And whispered. Not with fear, but with promise:

"Let them come."

#

The wind howled across the charred cliffs of Ashenfell, shrieking through jagged rock like a warning. The aircraft's engines powered down with a mechanical groan, and the rear ramp descended into smoke and silence. Four silhouettes emerged.

Alex led the way, his ash-streaked cloak flaring behind him like the tail of a dying comet. Laura and Nikki followed close, each with eyes fixed on the cave ahead, its mouth aglow with a red pulsing light. It throbbed like the slow, rhythmic heartbeat of something ancient and hungry.

Before joining them, Connor had introduced Jenna to the computer system so that she could help the team from afar.

"The ship has got the most advanced technology the Task Force has to offer," he explained. "The system is hooked up to our body cams. From here, you'll be able to monitor our every move. The system will work to monitor and learn any patterns and weak spots from our enemies. Your only job is to stay safe and call out the best attack points."

"Great," Jenna replied, sitting at the monitors. "No pressure..."

Connor smirked.

"You've got this."

Without wasting another second, he ran down the ramp.

The group stood in a tense silence as the ramp hissed closed. Ahead, they could see a dim red glow approaching.

Two monstrous shapes emerged from the cavern, grotesque silhouettes forged from flesh and horror. They had once been men. Now, sinewed limbs jutted from armorlike plating, their skin stretched thin over glowing veins that pulsed like molten lava. Fingers had become blades. Eyes, flickering red lenses of hatred.

Behind them came the Virus.

He moved like a phantom of metal and smoke. His steps dragged, his armor cracked, and his body leaked red mist from every joint. He flickered at the edges, as if he was unraveling, but even now, his eyes burned like twin embers in a dying furnace. Not bright, but endless.

"He's weak," Alex said, narrowing his gaze. "He must have spent everything to strengthen them."

"If that's him weak, I'd hate to see him at full power," Connor muttered.

"The soldiers' joints are under massive strain," Jenna's voice echoed through their comms. "Look for instability. Hips, knees, lower spine. Hit them hard enough and they'll collapse."

"The great Protector of Midtown," the Virus called out. "I suppose I should be honored."

"I'd offer a chance to return to whatever hellhole you crawled out of," Alex replied, "but considering the number of lives you've cost, I don't think you deserve it."

"Only a fraction of what's to come," the Virus said. "Turn back or join the fallen."

Alex clenched his fists, taking a few steps forward.

"Very well."

The Virus raised his hand and snapped his fingers.

His soldiers charged.

The first enemy moved like a cannonball, smashing toward Connor, who dove and opened fire. Laura followed with precision bursts from her rifle, her shots riddling the ground with sparks. Nikki vanished in a haze of violet smoke, reappearing above the second creature and striking down with her scythes. One blade sliced deep, sparks and black fluid spilling, but the creature howled and retaliated, slamming her with a clawed arm.

"They're adapting!" Jenna warned. "Predicting your movements. Switch your rhythms!"

One soldier tackled Alex, driving him into the stone with the force of a freight train. The other turned on Nikki, but she blinked out midswipe, reappearing behind it with her blades already midswing. One scythe tore through the back of its knee. It buckled.

Alex erupted from the dust, grappling his attacker and slamming it to the ground hard enough to shake the cliffside. He rolled and drove his fist into its exposed spine. Bones cracked. The thing screamed.

"Headshots don't work!" Connor shouted, diving for cover. "Just piss 'em off!"

Nikki rejoined Alex. Together, they moved like a current, fluid and fast. Nikki ducked beneath a clawed swing and teleported behind the enemy, her blade slicing its side. Alex followed with a crushing blow to the chest that launched the beast backward.

Laura finished it. A bullet to the unstable joint in the spine dropped it midlunge.

The last soldier snarled, and Nikki caught it with a scythe beneath the ribs while Alex struck high. It slumped. Dead. Finally.

Then…silence.

Only the Virus remained.

He stepped forward slowly, his form pulsing and frayed, sparks trailing from his armor.

He clapped once. Mocking.

"They weren't even the strongest I've made," he rasped. "And already, you bleed. You pant. You falter."

Alex stepped forward, hands clenched.

"You think that was our best?" he asked.

The Virus tilted his head.

And then he lunged.

The impact shattered the stone beneath them. Alex met him midcharge, their clash creating a shockwave that split the cliff face. Sparks flew. Metal ground against enhanced flesh. Every strike carved gashes in the earth.

Nikki joined, teleporting behind the Virus and slashing his lower back, but the Virus twisted unnaturally, catching her arm and flinging her across the battlefield. She struck a jagged outcrop hard, gritting through the pain as blood trickled down her temple.

"He's diverting energy to absorb attacks," Jenna said urgently. "His defenses shift. Focus on his left! There's a lag there!"

Alex feinted high. Nikki, limping, blinked behind and slashed low at the Virus's left leg. He buckled.

Alex slammed into him full force, lifting the Virus off the ground and pinning him into the dirt.

But it wasn't enough.

The Virus roared, energy flaring. He exploded outward, sending Alex flying and slamming Nikki hard into the stone once more. She lay still for a beat, then coughed, forcing herself to rise. Blood smeared her lips. Her mask was torn.

Alex grunted and pushed up. He stumbled toward the Virus, grabbed a shattered piece of armor jutting from his chest, and ripped it free.

The Virus screamed.

"You're finished," Alex said, breath heaving.

The Virus's eyes gleamed.

"Finished?" he asked, a grim smirk appearing on his face. "We're just getting started."

His chest began to glow.

A deep, pulsing red, growing brighter.

"He's going to self-destruct!" Jenna shouted.

"Get back!" Alex barked.

Then he moved.

In a blur of ash and light, Alex wrapped his arms around the Virus and launched skyward. His cloak snapped in the wind, the two of them vanishing into the clouds like a flare of burning vengeance.

The Virus laughed, high and hollow.

Then—

BOOM.

A colossal fireball exploded in the sky, red and black light blooming across the heavens. The earth screamed beneath it. Shockwaves split the rock. Wind and flame howled across Ashenfell's cliffs.

A figure fell.

Alex struck the ground with a thunderous impact, cratering the stone. Smoke hissed from his body.

Nikki was at his side in a flash, mask shattered, eyes wide. "Dad!"

She slowly and carefully propped him up.

"Still here…" Alex replied, his voice rasped.

Connor and Laura rushed to them.

"Is he gone?" Connor asked.

Alex looked toward the raining debris, smoke curling in the air.

"No," he said. "That wasn't a fight…"
He looked to the crater burning at the heart of the mountain.
"It was his warning shot."

13

In Control

The warehouse was still.

No sirens. No fire. No storm overhead.

Only the dull flicker of dying lights and the mechanical hum of breathless machinery, constant. Like a weak heartbeat refusing to fade. Shadows pooled in every corner like rot.

Vincent staggered through the entrance, half-collapsed, one arm clutching a scorched satchel to his ribs. His coat was torn, soaked with sweat and ash. His face was a ruin of panic, smeared with soot, eyes glassy from strain.

He dropped to his knees. The bag slid from his shoulder and spilled open across the cracked floor. Obsidian crystals tumbled free like blackened teeth from a shattered jaw. Instantly, the room recoiled. Lights dimmed, wires twitched, heat warped the air into shimmering sheets.

Vincent doubled over and vomited.

Bile and acid burned his throat.

He wiped his mouth with the back of his hand, trembling, and forced himself to gather the crystals. One by one, he stuffed them back into the satchel, his fingers twitching at each contact. They pulsed now. Watched. Whispered. Each shard hummed, its voice just beneath hearing, like a frequency meant only for madness.

He turned to his workbench, staggering like a man walking underwater.

He dropped the bag onto the steel surface and braced himself.

"Where do I begin...?" he rasped.

His skin crawled with fever. His temples throbbed. The sickness inside him was no longer physical; it was a presence, a pressure, a voice just waiting to become louder.

Then—

Silence.

The hum vanished.

The light died.

Vincent turned, and the warehouse was gone.

He stood in a void.

A black chamber, vast beyond comprehension. No floor. No ceiling. No horizon. Only smoke layered atop shadow, stacked like old prayers in a godless cathedral. The air reeked of rust and rotted circuitry.

A heartbeat echoed in the distance. Slow, mechanical, eternal.

A voice came, low and laced with contempt.

"You should not be here. You do not belong."

Vincent stumbled back, but shadows caught him. Fingers of smoke, cold and unyielding. They held him upright. Refused to let him fall.

Then the dark shifted.

A shape slithered forth, towering, inhuman, formless, but

watching. Red eyes opened one by one across its surface like blooming sores. Dim. Timeless. Ravenous.

"I see," the creature murmured. *"You are not alone in your mind."*

A second voice answered.

"No."

Vincent turned.

The Virus.

Not the broken shell from Ashenfell, but something older. Something deeper. He was fire now, coiled in shadow. His form shimmered like a ghost caught between frequencies. Flickering. Fading. But still powerful.

"He is here because I allow it," said the Virus.

The tall figure snarled, its voice like static ripping through steel.

"You let them destroy your vessel. You squandered the breach. And now you bring this mortal into our domain?"

"Please…I only want to assist—" Vincent tried to speak, tried to explain, but the shadows squeezed his chest like iron bands. He screamed.

"Silence," the entity boomed. *"You breathe only because I allow it."*

The Virus stepped forward, his silhouette pulsing faintly with red light.

"He serves as my architect," he said. "He holds the crystals. He will rebuild what was lost. The portal will open again."

Silence.

The void pulsed.

Then the figure moved.

It glided toward Vincent, its shape shivering like a cloak made of teeth, and when it spoke again, its voice was colder.

"One last chance. That is all I will grant. You will not fail again."

Above Vincent's chest, a shard of red light materialized—glowing, humming, hungry.

And then—

SHUNK.

It plunged into him.

Vincent screamed.

A raw, hollow sound, ripped from the depths of him.

The light seared through skin, through bone, branding itself deeper than flesh, into memory, into soul.

He woke.

Gasping.

Clutching his chest.

Sweat falling like rain from his brow.

The warehouse flickered back into being. Pale light buzzed above. Machines hummed again.

But Vincent was not the same.

He could feel it. The shard, lodged inside him. Thrumming like a second heart. The crystals on the bench pulsed in rhythm.

And then, from inside his skull, a whisper:

"Free Frederick. He will give you the strength. He will help you complete the portal."

Vincent stood.

His limbs burned. His breath shook.

But he obeyed.

He threw on his coat, grabbed the satchel, and disappeared into the night, his eyes now faintly glowing red.

#

The lights buzzed overhead with a waspish, anxious drone. The interrogation room was a tomb of concrete and steel—no windows, no clock, no sound beyond the flickering fluorescent bulb. Just a surveillance camera in the corner, blinking like a bored god.

Frederick sat shackled to the table, wrists locked in reinforced cuffs. His knuckles were crusted with dried blood, the result of hours spent wrenching, twisting, fighting. The restraints hadn't broken. But he'd made sure they'd remember him.

And then—

BOOM.

The world convulsed. A concussive blast rang down the hallway beyond the door. Dust cascaded from the ceiling. The lights spasmed, casting the room in strobed chaos—like lightning had struck indoors.

Frederick's head snapped up.

Footsteps.

Slow. Heavy. Deliberate.

The door didn't open. It detonated.

Steel flew inward, hinges torn loose with a shriek of surrender. The frame groaned. Smoke filled the doorway.

And from it stepped Vincent.

Or something that wore his body like a suit.

His coat flared with each step, trailing soot and silence. His eyes glowed—not merely lit, but burning, red and inhuman. Something inside him pulsed. Alive. Ancient.

Frederick's eyes narrowed, jaw flexing.

"You?" he muttered. "The big guy couldn't bother coming himself?"

Vincent didn't respond.

He raised his hand.

The cuffs shrieked—and shattered. Metal curled inward like melted wax, then dropped to the floor in whimpering shards.

Frederick rubbed his wrists as if annoyed more than relieved.

"Let me guess," he drawled, rising. "The Virus powered you up now?"

Vincent's mouth opened.

But the voice that came wasn't his.

"*You gave me up*," the voice rasped—low, ragged, echoing like a curse whispered in a cathedral. The Virus, speaking *through* him.

Frederick arched an eyebrow.

"So you did come," he said coolly. "I gave you a chance. You knew they were coming. Whatever happened next was on you."

Vincent's hand snapped upward.

Frederick *slammed* into the wall—lifted clean off the ground, pinned by unseen pressure. The impact cracked the concrete. The breath was wrenched from his lungs.

Still, he smiled.

"Admit it, pal," he gasped, blood sliding from his lip, "you need me more than I need you, and you know it."

Vincent stepped forward, red light flaring around his form like a halo warped by hellfire.

"The only reason you're alive," the Virus snarled, "is because you still serve a purpose. The portal must be rebuilt. I need more soldiers."

Frederick's fingers curled, not in fear—but defiance.

"You want soldiers?" He wheezed. "Go do your little mind

trick."

The pressure tightened.

Frederick's back bowed against the wall. His ribs ached. Something cracked in his chest. Still, he grinned.

"You can't, can you?" he said. "You really *do* need me."

The pressure tightened even more, almost crushing him.

"You kill me now," Frederick hissed, "and *you lose everything.* Your portal. Your leverage."

The Virus hesitated.

Vincent's hand trembled slightly—just enough.

Frederick saw it. And pounced.

"I know how to kill him," he rasped. "The Protector."

The lights above flickered violently.

"You dare lie to me?" the Virus roared, voice vibrating the walls.

"I'm not lying," Frederick said, eyes burning through the pain. "There are weapons—real ones. Ones strong enough to weaken him. Strong enough to *kill* him."

Vincent paused, motionless.

Frederick twisted the knife.

"Only one man has them," he said. "But I know where he is."

"Where?" the Virus asked.

Frederick bared bloody teeth.

"Veilhaven," he said.

A long, seething silence followed.

Then Vincent's hand lowered. The invisible grip dissolved. Frederick dropped—hard—but landed on a knee, catching himself. He spat blood onto the floor, then slowly rose, straightening his jacket with calm, practiced grace.

"I'll go," he said, chest heaving. "I'll bring back the weapons. I'll leave my men here. You'll have what you need for your little science project."

Vincent turned.

And the Virus spoke one last time:

"If you run," he said, voice molten with threat, "I will find you. And you will beg for the mercy of death."

Then he disappeared into the hall, smoke curling in his wake like the breath of something ancient.

Frederick watched him vanish. He didn't move for a while.

Then—slowly—he rolled his neck, wiped the blood from his mouth, and smiled again.

"Veilhaven it is," he whispered.

#

The wind howled across the ridge of Ashenfell, sweeping smoke and ash through jagged cliffs and the hollowed husks of what remained. Below, the remnants of the explosion still smoldered—a crater carved deep into the earth where Alex had fallen from the sky. The atmosphere was heavy, stained in burnt orange and soot, the last breath of battle lingering.

Alex sat hunched on a broken slab of stone, his robe torn and tattered. Every breath came slow and deliberate, each inhale a struggle after the strain of carrying the Virus into the air and surviving the blast. Laura stood beside him, her hand resting on his shoulder—a silent offering of strength and memory.

A few feet away, Jenna stood near the dropship, her brows furrowed as her fingers moved swiftly across the glowing surface of a tablet. Smoke drifted past her boots. The red light from her screen made her look haunted.

Nikki sat at the rim of the crater, legs dangling over the

edge, watching as Connor clambered up from below.

"Come on," Connor grunted, hands scraping at loose gravel. "This isn't funny anymore."

Nikki smirked. With a brief shimmer of violet light, she vanished and reappeared beside him, grabbed his arm, and teleported them both out of the pit in a burst of smoke.

"Ugh…" Connor dry heaved. "I will never get used to that. I think my pancreas flipped upside down."

"You'll live," Nikki said, settling back on the edge, brushing soot from her boots.

Jenna didn't look up.

"We have a problem," she said, voice clipped.

The group turned. Her face was pale.

"Frederick's gone," she said, raising the display. "Broke out less than an hour ago. I just pulled footage from the Task Force surveillance. Some…old man ripped the door off its hinges like it was made of paper."

Laura stepped forward and squinted.

"That's Vincent," she murmured, dread creeping into her voice.

"Who?" Alex asked.

"Our top physicist," Laura said. "Vincent helped design the original portal tech. If anyone could rebuild it—"

"It's him," Connor finished.

Alex stood slowly. Pain shadowed his expression, but his attention sharpened.

"How long ago exactly?"

"Thirty minutes, tops," Jenna replied. "They're probably long gone."

"So how do we find them?" Nikki asked. "There's no telling where they could be by now."

"Actually," Connor cut in, pulling a slim datapad from his jacket, "I thought ahead. Planted a micro-tracker on Frederick right before the interrogation. Figured we might need a backup plan."

He tapped a few keys. A map blinked to life.

"Got him," Connor said, then frowned. "He's moving west—straight toward Veilhaven. If we go now, we can beat him there."

The name struck the group like a gust of cold wind.

"Veilhaven?" Alex repeated. "Why would he go there?"

Laura hesitated. Her mouth opened, then closed.

"Laura," Alex said, voice firmer now. "What aren't you telling me?"

She drew a breath and stepped forward.

"There's a black-market dealer who operates out of Veilhaven," she said. "They call him the Gunsmith. No confirmed sightings. No known location. But he's armed half of the worst criminals in Midtown."

"He's also the one person still obtaining the enhanced weapons you've fought before," Connor added.

"We destroyed what we could," Laura said. "But a few slipped through. If he's still operating, and Frederick reaches him…"

Alex stepped in closer, face-to-face with her.

"You should've told me."

Laura held his gaze. Her voice trembled just slightly—not with fear, but truth.

"I didn't tell you," she said, "because the last time we faced those weapons, you left. I couldn't risk losing you again."

That landed. Quietly. Like a blade.

Alex's eyes softened. His shoulders, however, remained

squared.

Nikki stepped between them.

"We can either sit here and brood," she said, glancing at Alex, "or we can move. Fast. I don't know about you, but I'm not letting Frederick win. Not after everything we've done."

Alex looked to her. Then to the rest of the group—worn, bruised, but standing.

He nodded once.

"Then we don't wait," he said.

He stepped aboard, the others at his heels, smoke curling around their boots as the dropship rose into the ash-laced sky.

Beneath them, Ashenfell smoldered. Ahead, Veilhaven waited—armed, hidden, and already listening.

14

Veilhaven

The aircraft descended through a heavy shroud of cloud, its shadow slicing through the mist like a blade. Below, Veilhaven emerged from the fog— less a city than a scar carved deep into the earth. Its sprawl was chaotic and unnatural, like the skeleton of a long-dead machine. Buildings leaned at odd angles. Rooftops were piled with antennas, rusted solar panels, and black-market tech scavenged from other cities. Streets curved like veins through the decay, as if the city had been folded and bent by paranoia itself.

Inside the ship, Alex stood at the window, arms crossed, eyes narrowed.

"Why don't I remember this place looking so…ruined?" he asked, watching the rust-colored skyline unfurl beneath them.

"Because it wasn't," Connor replied, adjusting the nav systems. "After you left, everything spiraled. Veilhaven turned into a literal haven for fringe tech, conspiracy nuts, and weapon smugglers. You name it, it's here—and probably aimed at someone."

The aircraft dipped lower, settling onto the roof of a long-abandoned high-rise at the city's edge. The rooftop groaned under its weight as the landing ramp hissed open, a gust of sulfur-tinged air flooding the cabin.

The team gathered their gear. As Alex started forward, Laura stopped him, holding out a folded hoodie and a black cloth mask.

"Wait," she said. "You'll need these."

He raised an eyebrow.

"This city's obsessed with conspiracies," she explained. "Half of them are about you. If someone recognizes the Protector of Midtown walking around, we'll have every unhinged faction in the city on our trail."

Alex stared at the bundle like it had personally offended him. Then, with a sigh, he tugged the sweatshirt over his shoulders and tied the mask across his face.

"Happy?" he muttered.

"Better than the dumb robe," Nikki said, passing by with a smirk.

Laura masked up as well. Connor slung on his jacket and glanced around.

"I don't get a disguise?" he asked.

"I honestly doubt anyone will recognize the Task Force's second-in-command," Laura said flatly. "No offense."

"Wow," he muttered. "Mark me as crushed."

Jenna stepped forward, her small tech kit already open and humming softly. She had the layout of Veilhaven's sectors projected in front of her on a glowing screen.

"Let me help," she said. "I've got cams, audio links, facial scanners—I can sweep crowd density, tap into abandoned surveillance grids. I can guide you."

Nikki paused, considering her.

"You've already done more than enough," she said gently. "But this city's different. It's unstable. People here don't fight fair, and the weapons floating around aren't like the ones we've seen."

"I know the risks," Jenna said. "But I want to help."

"I trust you," Nikki said. "That's why I need you up here. If something goes wrong, I need eyes in the sky. Someone watching every feed. Someone who can warn us before we're in too deep."

Jenna hesitated, then nodded.

"I'll keep my comms in," she said. "If things get ugly…just call."

"Thanks," Nikki said with a small, genuine smile. "We'll come back in one piece."

Alex turned toward the exit, tightening the hood over his head.

"Let's move," he said. "The longer we wait, the more ground Frederick gains."

"Agreed," Laura said. "Let's split up. Nikki and I will take the north side. You and Connor hit the south. Powered on both ends. Balance and backup."

Alex glanced her way.

"Wait," he said, "why am I stuck with him?"

"Because two people in hoods asking questions together is a red flag," Laura explained. "You need a buffer. Someone who doesn't look like he walked out of a medieval prophecy."

Connor clapped a hand on Alex's shoulder.

"Let's call it a bonding exercise."

Alex stared at him.

"Let's call it over quickly."

The team descended the ramp. Boots struck rusted steel, swallowed by fog. Above them, the smog thickened, blotting out the last traces of daylight. Behind them, the aircraft sealed shut with a hiss.

Inside, Jenna sat alone at the command deck, eyes darting between live feeds and flashing alerts. Her fingers hovered above the controls, already searching for the next threat.

Beyond the rooftop, Veilhaven waited—twisted, watching, and armed.

#

Veilhaven's streets spread like veins through rusted scaffolding and flickering neon. In the southern district, faulty generators buzzed beneath balconies laced with wire and smoke. Shouts echoed from far-off alleys, blending with static-laced music and the low rumble of underground trade. Markets lined the walkways—crowded, chaotic—vendors shouting over one another as they hawked black-market tech beneath sagging tarps.

Alex moved like a shadow beneath his hood, cloth mask stretched tight across his jaw. His eyes flicked over every crumbling façade, every whisper behind broken windows. Beside him, Connor walked with practiced ease, hands deep in his coat pockets, like he'd always belonged in the city's decay.

"For someone who trained five years to be more disciplined," Connor said, glancing sideways, "you're terrible at looking casual."

"Maybe that's because I didn't spend five years loitering in hellholes," Alex muttered.

Connor smirked.

"And your people skills? Still world class."

They passed under a neon sign twitching in and out of existence, its glow washing over a web of makeshift stalls. Power cells sparked and groaned where they were stacked beside crates of old drones and copper wiring. Behind one, a vendor with grime-fogged goggles looked up.

"We're looking for someone," Connor said, leaning in casually. "The Gunsmith. Know where we can find him?"

The vendor let out a rasp of a laugh—more smoker's wheeze than amusement.

"You and every other lunatic in Veilhaven," he said. "The Gunsmith's a ghost. You don't find him. He finds you. Usually when it's already too late."

"We don't have time for riddles," Alex growled. "Where is he?"

The man tilted his head.

"Even if I knew, why would I tell a masked narc? Asking around here gets people dead. Word of advice—get out while you still can."

Alex stepped forward, jaw tightening, but Connor grabbed his arm, pulling him back into the crowd.

They moved through tight corridors where cracked pavement gave way to sagging fire escapes. Overhead, graffiti-covered balconies leaned low, and electrical cables hung like vines. Around them, whispers spiraled like smoke. Some spoke of the quake. Others claimed a god had risen from the ash. A few swore the Protector himself had returned. Alex tugged his mask tighter.

"Hey!" a voice called behind them.

They turned. In the shadows of a narrow alley, a figure

motioned them closer with two fingers.

"We really doing this?" Connor asked, brow raised.

Alex didn't answer. They moved forward.

The man was rail thin, swaddled in layers of mismatched fabric. Scraggly hair jutted out from beneath a shredded hood, his face streaked with soot and years of street living.

Connor blinked.

"You've gotta be kidding."

"Name's Crusty," the man said with a crooked grin. "Been tailing you since you landed. Like to keep tabs on newcomers."

"I'm sorry," Connor said. "Did you say…Crusty?"

"I know things—people, places, backdoors and bolt holes. You want the Gunsmith? I'm your guy."

"No offense," Alex said flatly, "but trusting some alley-wraith named Crusty isn't high on my to-do list."

"You'll have to excuse my friend," Connor added smoothly. "He's allergic to grime. But sure—let's hear what you got."

Crusty's eyes lit up like a control panel.

"Help doesn't come free in Veilhaven," he said.

Alex stepped forward, irritation rising, but again Connor raised a hand.

"How's five hundred sound?" he said.

Crusty's eyes widened. He clapped his grimy hands together.

"You got yourself a deal."

He offered a hand—filthy, cracked, and questionably moist.

Connor hesitated, then gave the world's most reluctant handshake.

"Right this way, gentlemen," Crusty said, turning and waddling deeper into the city's smoke-stained arteries.

They followed him through narrow alleys, past burning

barrels and slumped bodies curled in doorways. The deeper they went, the more the noise faded—replaced by a hush. The air thickened. The mood shifted.

"You know," Connor said, lowering his voice, "it's kinda messed up."

Alex glanced over. "What is?"

"That you just showed up," Connor said. "And expected everything to fall in line. Like we're supposed to praise you for being the hero again."

"I didn't come back to be praised," Alex said.

"No, you came back and started barking orders," Connor replied. "Like you never left. But you did. While you were off in the mountains meditating or punching waterfalls or whatever, Laura was holding the Task Force together with blood and duct tape."

Alex's pace slowed.

"And Nikki?" Connor continued. "She stepped into your shadow because it was the only thing she had left. She didn't ask for your legacy, but she's been killing herself trying to live up to it."

Alex stopped walking. His eyes lowered.

"I didn't leave to hurt them," he said. "I thought if I stayed, I'd only put them in danger."

Connor stopped too. Looked at him.

"Maybe they didn't need the Protector," he said. "Maybe they just needed *you*."

The silence that followed was sharp and bitter.

Alex finally nodded.

"Thanks," he said quietly. "For being there. For them."

Connor blinked. Then nodded back.

"They're my family too," he said.

"Oi!" Crusty's voice echoed from around the corner. "Let's go, lovebirds! The trail's not gonna follow itself!"

Alex and Connor shared a look, then kept walking.

Veilhaven swallowed them whole.

#

On the other side of Veilhaven, a half-dead sign buzzed with a blue flicker and cast a sickly light as Laura and Nikki moved beneath it, their steps muted but purposeful.

"You said this side was safer?" Nikki muttered, skeptical.

Laura's eyes scanned the path ahead, quick and clinical. At the alley's bend, a small cluster of men huddled around a barrel fire, shadows flickering across their hollow faces as the flames snapped in defiance of the cold.

"Not safer," Laura replied, "just louder. People talk more when they're desperate."

They approached slowly. Heat licked against Laura's gloves. The air reeked of burnt plastic and synthetic cloth. One man spoke with near-religious urgency, arms slicing smoke as he ranted to the group.

"The quake was a warning," he cried. "The Protector has returned—and the veil's tearing open! He's brought the end with him!"

"I saw it too," rasped another. "The sky cracked. Something was crawling through."

Laura stepped closer, keeping her coat tight, her badge hidden deep inside.

"Evening, gentlemen," she said, voice calm but clipped. "We're looking for someone. Goes by the name the Gunsmith. You know him?"

The moment the name left her mouth, the group tensed. Eyes turned—sharp, hungry, unreadable.

A tall man stepped forward. His arms were wrapped in faded tattoos: old gang markings, prison codes, relics of forgotten cults. His lip curled.

"The Gunsmith?" he echoed, slow and dangerous. "That's not a name you toss around. Not unless you've got a death wish."

"We're not here for trouble," Laura said evenly. "Just looking to buy."

His eyes flicked to Nikki—half a step behind, poised, one hand brushing near her hip.

"You don't look like buyers," the man sneered. "She's too clean. Too steady. Like she's been trained."

Another man stepped into the glow, grinning crookedly. "They're Task Force. Smells like government and lies."

The energy shifted—snapped tight like a tripwire. One of the men drew a rusted blade. Another palmed a brick. Others reached for pipes or sharpened scrap.

Nikki's fingers twitched. But Laura raised a hand.

"Look," she said, voice still cool, "you don't want this. We're not here to bust anyone. If you don't know where he is, we'll go bother someone else."

"That's the problem," the tattooed man growled, drawing a machete. "Veilhaven doesn't want to be bothered."

Laura stepped into him with no hesitation. One brutal elbow to the ribs—and the machete clattered to the ground. Nikki surged forward, a blur of motion. She dropped the second man with a punch to the throat. He crumpled, gasping.

A third charged from behind—but Laura pivoted, caught his wrist, and slammed him against the wall with surgical precision. His head struck brick and he slumped.

The rest bolted, vanishing into smoke and shadow.

Laura didn't release the final man. She kept him pinned, arm twisted, face scraping against stone.

"The Gunsmith," she said, voice like cut steel. "Where?"

"I—I don't know!" he stammered. "He moves around! Underground. Masked. Guarded. Only deals direct—and only with a few! Nobody knows his base!"

Laura studied him, then shoved him back. He stumbled and ran without another word.

A low rumble split the sky.

Nikki and Laura both looked up as a helicopter tore through the smog—angular, black, unmistakable.

Task Force model.

"I'm guessing that's not one of ours?" Nikki asked.

"No," Laura said, her eyes narrowing. "That's Frederick."

She turned sharply.

"If he's here, he's headed to the Gunsmith. We follow him—we find the base."

Nikki was already moving.

"Finally. A real lead."

The barrel fire cracked behind them. Smoke spiraled upward. Shadows twisted along the walls like watching eyes.

#

The crooked veins of Veilhaven tightened into a knotwork of alleys and rusted scaffolding. Dust and suspicion clung to the air as Crusty led the way, his uneven gait stirring grime with every step.

Alex scanned the shadows, jaw clenched.

"How long is this going to take?" he asked, eyeing the silent locals whose stares lingered too long.

"Not long," Crusty said. "I've got something that'll speed things up. Stay here."

Before either could argue, Crusty vanished down a narrow alley—swallowed by smoke like a greased rat diving for cover.

"This was a terrible idea," Alex muttered.

"Hey," Connor said, "beats wandering around blind."

Then—a low, thunderous thrum.

Both men looked skyward as a matte black helicopter sliced through the smog-choked sky.

"That's one of ours," Connor said, squinting.

"No," Alex replied, voice stiffening. "That's Frederick."

"There's no way we catch up on foot," Connor replied.

"You won't be on foot," Crusty called, suddenly behind them.

They turned—and froze.

He was now seated on a rickety pedicab: bent wheels, rusted frame, and a wire basket strapped to the front like a last-minute miracle. He wore a dented helmet three sizes too small.

"You've got to be kidding," Alex said.

"No time!" Connor shouted, already climbing in.

Alex groaned and followed.

"Hold tight, boys!" Crusty whooped—and launched forward.

The pedicab shot into motion, shrieking as it tore down the warped streets. Vendors dove aside. Children screamed and laughed. Trash spun in their wake like confetti.

"I'm gonna throw up!" Connor yelled, gripping the frame.

Two figures stepped onto the road ahead.

Crusty swerved, nearly flipping the cart.

"Watch it, psycho!" a familiar voice snapped.

Alex blinked. Laura and Nikki stood in the road, weapons raised, eyes wide.

"What the hell are you doing in a pedicab!?" Laura shouted.

"Following the chopper!" Connor shouted back. "You?"

"Same!" Nikki called.

Crusty grinned. "You all know each other? Small world! Hop in!"

Laura and Nikki exchanged a look of exhausted disbelief… then climbed in.

Crusty cackled and rocketed toward the city's edge.

They rolled to a rattling stop at the edge of a collapsed overpass.

Below, the twisted wreckage of an old railyard sprawled like a metal graveyard—freight containers stacked like crumbling bones, cranes frozen midcollapse, vines of rust stretching across shattered steel.

"There," Connor said, pointing down.

A black helicopter sat in a clearing near a gutted control tower, blades still spinning in a slow, deliberate crawl. Frederick stepped out, flanked by soldiers, his coat catching the smoky wind.

Crusty beamed from the pedicab seat.

"Told you I'd get you here. That yard? Gunsmith territory. Secret entrance is underground. I take cash."

Connor shoved a few bills into his hand without looking.

"Who even is this guy?" Nikki muttered.

"Long story," Connor grumbled.

"I'll be right here counting my blessings," Crusty said, already reclining in the pedicab.

The group crept down into the yard, ducking behind a stack

of crates. From their vantage point, they watched Frederick surveying the field.

"We should wait," Laura said. "Scope the place out before rushing in."

"Yeah," Connor agreed. "Frederick's boxed in. When we see the entrance—"

"No," Alex said sharply, standing.

"Alex—" Laura warned, but he was already gone.

Alex blurred into motion.

One heartbeat he was behind the crates—next, he was a streak across the clearing, cloak whipping behind him like a shadow torn loose.

Frederick had just stepped away from the helicopter when Alex struck.

WHAM.

He slammed Frederick hard against the side of the chopper, the metal groaning beneath the impact. Dust and heat kicked up in waves. Frederick grunted—but didn't resist.

A dozen weapons clicked in unison as his soldiers surrounded them, barrels rising like teeth around a wound.

"Stand down!" Laura's voice rang from across the yard, sharp and commanding as she and the others sprinted to the edge of the clearing.

Nikki flanked her mother, already braced to teleport. Connor raised his hands, trying not to escalate the already explosive tableau.

Frederick smiled.

Despite Alex's forearm across his throat and the surrounding guns, he looked amused—like someone watching a chessboard tilt in his favor.

"Fancy seeing you here," he rasped, a bloody grin twisting

his mouth.

Alex growled low in his throat but didn't tighten his grip.

"Back off," Laura warned, stepping closer. "This isn't the time."

Frederick's men shifted—fingers twitching on triggers, breath fogging the air. Tension rippled through the yard like heat from pavement.

Then—a sharp metallic snap.

A silver chain tore through the air and coiled tightly around Alex's right forearm. An emerald mist steamed off it. In an instant, it yanked him backward, dragging him off his feet.

WHIP—CRASH!

Alex hit the ground hard, skidding in dust, cloak tangled. He spun and rolled to one knee, instinct already pushing him upright—

And then he froze.

Standing near the edge of the train yard, silhouetted by smoke and rising steam, was a tall figure in a black leather coat and a wide-brimmed hat. His face was concealed behind a reinforced steel mask, dark glass hiding his eyes. His stance was calm, almost casual—but the chain in his hand crackled with coiled energy.

Laura swore under her breath.

Alex looked at the length of chain wrapped around his arm— and his expression shifted.

Recognition.

Not fear.

Not anger.

But something deeper. Older.

"Jacob," he whispered.

The man didn't respond, just reeled the chain in with one

hand, silent and slow.

Frederick straightened his jacket and stepped away from the chopper.

"Well," he muttered, brushing dirt off his coat, "this just got interesting."

"Who is he?" Nikki asked.

The Gunsmith finally spoke, his voice mechanical and distant beneath the mask.

"This territory is mine. You dare bring war to my doorstep. I'll give you one chance—all of you—to walk away."

"We don't want any trouble," Laura said. "We're here to stop him."

She pointed at Frederick.

Frederick laughed again.

"Stop me from what?" he asked. "I'm just visiting a friend."

The Gunsmith raised a hand. His chain uncoiled from Alex's arm and returned to him.

"This is your last chance," the Gunsmith said.

"We aren't leaving without him," Alex said, gesturing toward Frederick.

"Good luck with that," Frederick said. "My men and I will get out of your hair…just as soon as we get the weapons."

"So be it," the Gunsmith said. His fists clenched and his chain widened, stretching around both of his forearms, the emerald mist growing thicker.

Alex stood tall, loosening his shoulders.

Nobody backed down.

#

Alex didn't wait for another word. He lunged.

They collided in an explosion of kinetic force. Chain met fist, power clashed against precision. The Gunsmith's constructs whipped through the air like vipers, striking with lethal intent. Alex ducked and parried, hammering the Gunsmith with brutal counters. He drove him back with a shoulder slam that sent sparks flying.

The Gunsmith retaliated, snaring Alex's wrist with a chain and swinging him into a stack of crates. The steel buckled under the impact. Alex hit the floor and rolled to his feet.

As he stood,

The chain around Alex's arm crackled as it tightened.

For a beat, everything was still.

Then—chaos.

Gunfire erupted from every direction.

Laura and Connor, from behind freight containers, fired with brutal precision.

Frederick's men ducked and returned fire, unleashing crackling bolts from customized weapons.

Alex ripped the chain free with a shout and launched himself into the fray.

Nikki blinked through a violet burst and slammed two of Frederick's soldiers aside. Laura flanked to the left, leading with disciplined shots from a rifle. Connor moved low and fast, drawing fire away from the others.

The Gunsmith raised both arms. Chains spiraled around him, lashing outward. They snared weapons, tripped fighters, and tore metal from nearby crates.

He was a storm—and Alex charged straight through it.

They collided midfield, powers clashing like gods of old. Brute force against honed technique. Jacob wrapped a loop around Alex's leg, trying to drag him down—but Alex flipped forward and slammed both boots into his chest, sending Jacob flying back.

Across the battlefield, Frederick moved fast.

"Cover me!" he barked, sprinting toward the hidden entrance now exposed beneath the broken tower. His men laid down suppressing fire, keeping Laura and Connor pinned behind debris.

"We can't let him get those weapons!" Nikki shouted, teleporting from one shadow to the next, knocking a soldier unconscious before vanishing again.

Frederick reached the open hatch and punched a code into the panel. The steel doors yawned wider. He disappeared inside, two of his men following.

Laura gritted her teeth.

"He's in," she said. "He's going for the cache."

"I'll go!" Connor called, sprinting toward the base.

The Gunsmith cracked his whip of chains and launched it toward Connor—but Alex caught it midair and yanked, dragging the Gunsmith back into the fight.

"You used to be better than this" Alex growled.

"You never were," the Gunsmith snapped, slamming a fist into Alex's ribs.

Meanwhile, Frederick re-emerged with two men—hauling a massive reinforced crate between them. The case thrummed with unstable energy, marked with Task Force warnings.

The Gunsmith turned sharply, fury building behind his mask. He raised a hand and a chain shot out.

But it never reached its target.

Alex tackled him from behind, pinning him to the ground.

"No!" the Gunsmith bellowed. "They'll escape!"

Frederick and his men bolted toward the chopper.

"Cover fire!" one of them screamed.

Gunfire blazed as the soldiers laid down their final barrage.

Nikki teleported forward—too late.

Frederick climbed aboard the helicopter, dragging the case inside. The two men leapt in after him.

The rotors spun.

Blades roared.

They lifted off.

"NO!" the Gunsmith shouted, shoving Alex off with a surge of strength.

He stumbled to his feet as the helicopter vanished into the smoke-soaked sky, its silhouette shrinking into a speck of shadow.

"You let him GO!" he roared at Alex, voice shaking with rage. "Do you have *any* idea what he just took?!"

Alex stepped forward, chest heaving.

"You want to blame me?" he said. "You've been hiding, running weapons, playing king of the shadows. This is on you."

The Gunsmith removed his mask, revealing Jacob's weathered face.

Alex's eyes burned.

"Talk," he said, his voice tight with betrayal. "Now."

15

Edge of Trust

The air inside was colder than it should've been. Not the cold of weather, but the kind that settles after violence—damp, metallic, and still. The scent of rust and gunpowder lingered like ghosts in the walls. Pipes crisscrossed the low ceiling like ribs exposed in an autopsy, their slow, irregular drips echoing through the silence. The cracked concrete floor shimmered in places where shallow puddles reflected flickering bulbs. The lights buzzed. Flickered. Faded. Dying, like the city above.

Shadows clung to the corners. They didn't move—but they felt like they wanted to.

Alex stood at the front of the group, his body wound tight. Every instinct in him was on edge. The torn sleeve of his coat hung in tatters, dried blood crusted along the fabric. His chest rose and fell with careful breath. His gaze didn't waver.

It was fixed on Jacob.

The man stood a few paces ahead, his palms raised in a slow, unthreatening gesture. His long coat hung like drapery around his frame, and beneath the wide brim of his weathered hat, a faint smirk tugged at the corner of his mouth.

"I've told you," Jacob said, his voice low and gravel rough. "I'm not the Gunsmith. Not really."

The tension was thick enough to suffocate. Behind Alex, Nikki shifted her stance, sparks crawling across her knuckles like restless fireflies. Her stare locked onto Jacob, unblinking.

Laura stepped forward. Her posture was all steel—back straight, boots planted.

"You've been running his base," she said sharply. "His soldiers. Selling his weapons. Why should we believe a word you say?"

Jacob chuckled—soft, almost amused.

"You're the director of the Task Force," he said. "Tell me you haven't noticed something off. The shipments I've 'sold'? Faulty. Jammed parts. Weak casings. Useless after a few shots. I've been feeding the dealers trash."

He slowly lowered his hands. Laura glanced at Connor, both registering the truth in his words.

"I've been sabotaging the operation from the inside," Jacob continued. "Didn't have much of a choice. When I got to Veilhaven, the real Gunsmith had already vanished. No trail. No name. Just rumors and wreckage. So I stepped in. Took up the mantle. His soldiers followed without question. Thought I was him. I ran with it—long enough to bury the network from within."

"And what about the weapons Frederick took?" Laura pressed. "Those weren't faulty, were they?"

Jacob's jaw tightened.

"No," he said. "That crate was real. The last batch I hadn't tampered with."

"So now they're in his hands," Nikki muttered. "Perfect."

"I didn't expect him to show up," Jacob said. "And I sure as hell didn't expect him to be working with something from another realm."

"He is," Alex said, voice flat. "And it's worse than you think. If we don't stop him, none of this will matter. Midtown. Veilhaven. The Task Force. It all burns."

The silence that followed was heavy. Even the leaking pipes seemed to hold their breath.

Nikki stepped forward, voice low.

"Then we need to fight back. If they're going to use enhanced weapons, we should too. Can't we build more?"

"That would be ideal," Laura said, crossing her arms, "except the man who built them is dead."

"His workshop still exists, though," Connor added. "Everything inside should still be intact. It's Task Force property."

Jacob nodded slowly.

"Then get me there," he said. "If the tools and materials are still usable…I might be able to recreate them."

Alex took a step closer, eyes narrowing.

"And why should we believe you now?" he asked.

"Because you don't have much of a choice," Jacob answered. "If things are as bad as you're making them seem…it sounds like you need me."

Alex didn't reply. His jaw clenched. His fist twitched at his side.

Laura placed a hand on his shoulder.

"He's right," she said softly. "He's all we've got."

Alex exhaled through his nose. The moment stretched.

"Don't let us down."

#

The warehouse creaked like old bones settling. The heat inside was suffocating, heavy with static and the metallic tang of ozone. Outside, Halvade lay in uneasy silence. Streets empty. Lights flickering. A false peace hung over the ruin.

At the center of the chamber, a crude, makeshift portal frame had been assembled from salvaged wiring, scorched plating, and rust-streaked steel. It looked like a dead god's rib cage straining to breathe again. Frederick's men had welded all night under Vincent's direction, forging the bones of something they didn't understand.

Frederick's boots echoed as he marched in, followed by two soldiers hauling a crate marked with the black cougar insignia—the Gunsmith's legacy. The weapons inside shimmered faintly, pulsing with unstable heat and energy. Even the most hardened of Frederick's men gripped the edges like they were handling a ticking bomb.

They set it down in front of Vincent.

Frederick stopped short.

The man who had once been a brilliant professor was now a shadow—hair damp and stringy, skin pallid with fever, fingers twitching uncontrollably over a cracked keyboard. His shirt was soaked through with sweat. His lips moved constantly, mumbling the same fragments on repeat, a mantra or maybe a warning. His eyes never stopped moving—tracking things no one else could see.

Frederick raised an eyebrow.

"You look worse every time I see you, doc."

Vincent didn't turn.

"The portal...almost ready," he muttered hoarsely. "But power...we're low. Not stable. Not enough juice to hold it long."

Frederick nudged the crate with his foot.

"I brought the weapons," he said. "Problem is, it's sealed—some kind of lock on the thing. Can't crack it."

Without speaking, Vincent turned. He placed one hand on the lid…then ripped it open with sudden violence. The lid flew across the warehouse, clattering into shadow.

"Well…" Frederick said, caught off guard. "That works."

Vincent knelt and studied the contents—sleek weapons of black alloy, each laced with glowing red circuitry down the barrel. Energy thrummed through the crate like a pulse.

"How do they work?" Vincent asked, voice beginning to shift—deeper now. Edged with something…*inhuman*.

Frederick shrugged.

"Hell if I know," he said. "Can't be that hard. Point and shoot."

Without hesitation, Vincent grabbed one of the rifles, turned, and fired.

A soldier crumpled midstep, body thrown violently against the far wall. The impact left a black smear on the concrete. Smoke hissed from the ruin of his chest.

Frederick stepped back, stunned.

"What the hell—!?"

Vincent handed him the rifle with eerie calm.

"You were correct. Point and shoot."

He returned to the terminal, fingers jittering across the keys. The machine chirped. Then screamed.

The portal frame groaned as it surged with red light. Sparks danced along its rim. Wires snapped and recoiled like striking serpents. The air trembled with heat and static as the glow pulsed—red, then deeper red, then *corrupted* red.

"What the hell are you doing?" Frederick shouted over the

roar. "Shut it off!"

Vincent's voice cracked.

"I—I can't stop it. It's taking the power on its own…"

The room shook. The floor vibrated beneath them.

The ring shrieked like a banshee.

Then a boot stepped through.

Massive. Metallic. Unmistakable.

Frederick backed away, rifle raised.

"No way…"

The figure emerged from the swirl of light—towering, humanoid, monstrous.

The Virus.

His new form gleamed with obsidian armor, smooth and cold as glass. Red wires snaked beneath his plating like veins, pulsing with dark energy. His face was sculpted, almost human—sharp cheekbones, a cruel smirk. But the eyes ruined it. Two red orbs flickering with code, glowing brighter than fire. He was nearly twice the size he'd been before—sleek, perfect, and terrifying.

Frederick kept his weapon trained.

"Is…is that you?" he asked.

The Virus turned his head. His voice rumbled like a machine breathing.

"I have returned."

The portal sputtered behind him, its power fading.

Vincent rushed to the terminal, frantic.

"No—no, no, no!" he shouted. "There's not enough power to keep it open!"

The Virus didn't move. He raised one hand.

A weapon materialized behind him—a crimson spear formed from pure, glitched data. It hovered midair.

It's form glitched, as if crafted from code.

Then the Virus clenched his fist and the spear whirred behind him like a bullet, straight into Vincent's body.

Frederick stood quickly, gripping his rifle.

"Hey!" Frederick screamed.

Vincent gasped as it drove through his back, piercing his chest. He dropped to his knees. Breath hitched. Then stopped.

The spear shattered into particles. Vincent's body collapsed.

Frederick stared.

"What the hell did you do that for?!" he roared. "He was the only one who could fix that damn thing!"

The Virus looked down at the body with indifference.

"He has served his purpose," he said. "We will not rely on fragile things again. We will power it ourselves."

"And how do you plan on doing that?" Frederick snapped. "You heard him. We don't have the power."

The Virus stepped forward.

"Then we'll take it."

Frederick lowered the rifle slightly, uneasy.

"From where?" he asked, his grip not loosening.

The Virus turned, eyes glowing brighter.

"The Task Force."

#

The aircraft rattled as it soared through thick gray skies, each gust of turbulence groaning through the steel frame. Inside the dimly lit cabin, the air was tight with silence and suspicion.

Nikki sat stiffly, her gaze locked on Jacob, who was sitting across from her.

He hadn't spoken a word since takeoff. One boot rested

across his knee, arms folded tightly over his chest. His long coat was draped over his lap, and the brim of his weatherworn hat kept his face half-shrouded in shadow. But even without words, there was something…electric about him. Not in the way Nikki's powers sparked and flashed. No. His presence carried weight. Stillness that suggested danger.

Another superpowered person. Just like her. Just like her dad.

But why now? Why *him*?

She glanced toward Alex, standing on the far side of the cabin, arms crossed, jaw set.

Before she could speak, Jenna's voice cut through the tension like a blade.

"Okay," she said, pulling off her headset and looking around the cabin. "I have to ask. Who is this guy and why is he sitting in here like he's suddenly part of the team?"

Connor looked up from a monitor but didn't respond. His silence said plenty.

Jacob finally moved, just slightly. He turned his head, and the shadow beneath his hat receded.

"Do you always talk this much?" he asked, voice low and sandpaper rough.

Jenna blinked.

"Only when I'm nervous…"

"Then maybe you should pick your words more carefully," he said.

"Yeah…" Jenna said, turning back around. "Got it. Less words. Much…much less words."

Nikki crossed the cabin to her father, dropping her voice to a whisper as she stood beside him.

"You need to tell me the truth," she said. "Who is he? And

why does he have powers? I thought it was just supposed to be the protector who had abilities. That's what you told me."

Alex exhaled through his nose, rubbing the back of his neck like the weight of old memories had landed all at once.

"It's…complicated," he said. "Jacob and I go back a long way. Before the Task Force. Before your mother."

Nikki raised an eyebrow.

"So, what? He's some kind of ancient war buddy?" she asked.

"Something like that," Alex said. "We trained together a lifetime ago. But even then, he kept things close to the chest. I don't know much about his past—barely anything, really. He vanished after one of our last missions. No warning. No goodbyes. Just gone."

She studied Jacob again, her expression narrowing.

"Has he always been that weird?" she asked, watching him closely.

"Always," Alex replied. "Closed off. Sharp. That's the type of person he is. He's got walls built around himself. Even when I first met him, when we would train together, he wouldn't tell me much about himself. I barely know anything about his past."

Alex looked over his shoulder, toward Jacob.

"But I believe him," he continued. "He sabotaged those weapons. He fought to stop Frederick. Whatever his past is…I trust him."

There was a pause.

Nikki let out a soft sigh and nodded.

"If you trust him, so do I."

The ship jolted slightly as it dropped below the clouds.

Through the narrow side window, the city of Wolfridge

emerged from the mist—gray, low-slung, and braced for survival. The streets were narrow and cracked, flanked by iron fences and blocky warehouses. Scattered damage from the quake marred some rooftops, but the city had weathered worse.

Smokestacks pierced the horizon like jagged spires, belching smoke into the ash-streaked sky. Steel and concrete hunched low beneath the hills. It was a place built to endure.

Laura approached them, datapad in hand.

"The workshop's on the far edge of the scrapyard district," she said. "Hasn't been touched since Karsten's death. But most of the equipment should still be usable."

The aircraft groaned as it descended. Landing struts extended with a hydraulic hiss.

The ramp unsealed with a mechanical shudder and began to lower.

Jacob rose slowly. His boots thudded against the steel floor as he walked toward the exit. He stopped just before the ramp.

"Get me inside," he said. "If the tools are there…I'll do what I can."

No one argued.

The group followed him into the heart of Wolfridge.

The forge of what would come next.

16

The Workshop

Scorched metal clung to the walls like soot-stained memories. Shafts of dusty light filtered through cracked skylights, casting golden bars across rusted machinery and splintered shelves. The scent of smoke—old but not forgotten—hung in the air like something waiting to reignite. Faded Task Force insignias peeked through grime on crates and tool cabinets. The concrete floor bore blackened scars from the fire, and oily trails marked where machines had been dragged and left to rot.

Jacob stepped in first. His boots crunched over broken glass and debris, his gaze sweeping the room with a strange reverence. It was like stepping into a cathedral of lost invention.

Behind him, Laura, Nikki, Connor, Alex, and Jenna entered in a loose, cautious group.

"This place is giving haunted hospital vibes," Jenna muttered, brushing cobwebs from her sleeve. "Like we're about to find a chainsaw with our names on it."

"Quiet," Jacob said, already moving deeper into the workshop. "Start searching. Look for metal casings, prototype cores, anything unusual. He must've had some kind of custom energy source to power those weapons."

"You think he had that kind of power?" Nikki asked, eyeing a shelf stacked with shattered components.

"He did," Laura answered, crouching beside a crate. She brushed away a thick layer of dust to reveal a box packed with smooth, metallic parts—copper-lined plates and synthetic wiring coiled like vines. "He was one of our black ops engineers. Off the record. Brilliant. Paranoid. Built things no one else could."

"So what happened to him?" Nikki asked.

"He died," Laura said softly. "Four years ago. This place went up in flames. They found a body—burned beyond recognition. DNA said it was him."

"At least his work survived," Jacob murmured. He dragged a heavy crate onto the worktable and pried it open. Inside were disassembled weapon frames, scorched blueprints, and a handful of handmade energy cells the size of shotgun shells.

"Found it," he said, holding one up between two fingers. "These are the cores."

He bent down, pulling another crate closer—

A sharp metallic scrape echoed from the far end of the room. Everyone froze.

The sound came again—slow, deliberate. Like steel boots over a metal grating.

Then a voice.

"Put those down."

Low. Calm. With an edge like a trigger half-pulled.

Connor instinctively stepped in front of Jenna, hand drifting toward his holster.

"I wouldn't," the voice called. "Not unless you're ready to lose that hand."

From the shadows at the far end of the workshop, a figure emerged.

A tall, lean man clad in a long black coat streaked with soot and burn marks emerged. His boots were scuffed, his skin roughened by ash and time. A welding harness dangled from his belt, and in his hand was a pistol unlike any of theirs—sleek, custom, glowing faintly with blue heat.

Jacob stepped back from the crates, slow and cautious.

Alex stepped forward, tense, his fists clenching at his sides.

"Who are you?" he asked.

The man cocked his head slightly, then holstered his weapon.

"I'm the guy who owns this place," he said, voice dry. "And I'll be damned if I let a bunch of scavengers walk off with my legacy."

Laura moved to get a better look, her eyes narrowing.

"Karsten?" she breathed.

The man met her gaze, unblinking.

Laura's breath caught.

"You're supposed to be dead."

#

The Virus stood in the warehouse. He observed as Frederick's men prepared to head out, all brandishing their new enhanced weaponry.

The Virus stood motionless in the center of the warehouse.

The walls hummed faintly, warped by the energy that still pulsed from the failed portal. Red light flickered across the floor, glowing from the enhanced weapons now carried by Frederick's men. The air smelled of ozone and scorched steel.

They were ready—lined up and waiting. Two of Frederick's largest men were armed with the deadly inventions pulled from the Gunsmith's vault. Each weapon buzzed with unstable energy, whispering threats beneath their hum. Even the soldiers, hardened and loyal, held them with silent unease.

Frederick approached, also carrying a powerful weapon. His voice was low with caution.

"You sure about this, big guy?" he asked. "The Task Force won't go down easy."

"They can fight," the Virus replied, his voice like gravel ground underfoot. "It won't matter. They've already lost."

Without another word, the Virus turned and walked toward the back of the warehouse, where shadows bled deeper than they should.

"Leave me," he said. "I must prepare."

Frederick lingered for half a breath, then nodded.

"Right," he muttered, stepping away as the others followed.

The warehouse dimmed.

The floor beneath the Virus's feet cracked—no sound, no tremor, just absence. And then, in a blink, the world changed.

The warehouse peeled away, unraveling like old cloth. Darkness swallowed everything.

Now he stood in the in-between—a realm of void and silence, where even thought echoed like thunder.

A cold wind curled through the emptiness. And from that stillness, his master came.

He did not walk. He *formed*, bleeding from the black like infection. Massive. Cloaked in layers of churning smoke and tattered red mist. His size dwarfed the Virus. His face—if it was a face—was a suggestion more than a shape, ever-shifting beneath the haze.

"You wear the gifts I gave you," the master said. His voice was layered, a hundred whispers bound into one.

The Virus bowed—not low, but enough.

"Thank you, master," he said. "You rebuilt me...made me more than I was. I feel it—power, purpose. I am stronger than before."

"Do not mistake this for favor," the master said. *"You are not a prince. You are a tool. Sharpened and reforged for a singular task. A task you've already failed once."*

The Virus's fingers twitched. Red lightning crackled faintly in his palm.

"That was before," he said quietly. "Before I understood. This time, I will finish what I started. I will hold the portal. I will tear down the walls between our realms."

The master loomed closer. Tendrils of red mist curled around the Virus's legs like chains.

"The army waits," the master said. *"Every moment they are caged is a risk. The cracks in this world grow wider. You will open the path."*

"I will," the Virus vowed. "This time...I will not fail."

The void quivered. A hiss tore through the silence like metal shearing apart.

"See that you don't."

The master's form began to retreat, not vanishing but folding back into the dark—like something too large to be perceived fully, withdrawing behind a curtain of reality.

A final warning drifted after him, slow and cold:

"Because if you fail me again..."

The air bent. A low rumble passed through the nothing.

"...you will not be rebuilt."
And then—
Light.
The flicker of a buzzing overhead bulb. The scorched scent of metal and ash. The groan of an old pipe in the ceiling.
The Virus stood once more in the warehouse.
Alone.
Vincent's body still lay where it had fallen—crumpled, charred, his mouth frozen midbreath. The embers around him hissed softly, pulsing with the last remnants of portal energy.
The Virus lifted a hand.
The corpse rose into the air like a marionette. With a flick of his wrist, it disintegrated into red ash, scattering into the dark like dust on the wind.
"No more mistakes," he whispered.
And with that, he turned and walked into the shadows.

#

The group surrounded Karsten, their expressions caught somewhere between disbelief and unease. The man who was supposed to be dead leaned against his workbench like he'd never left it—dust on his shoulders, soot on his sleeves, but alive.
Laura stepped forward slowly, her voice edged with suspicion.
"How?" she asked. "How are you alive?"
Karsten gave a dry chuckle. His arms folded across his chest.
"It's a long story," he said.
"I'm not in the mood for long stories," Laura snapped. "Your

body was found. The DNA matched. You were *dead*."

Karsten scratched at the edge of his stubbled jaw and shrugged.

Connor's brow furrowed.

"You faked your own death?"

"Call it a tactical exit," Karsten replied. "There are some things even your precious Task Force isn't meant to know. I'll give you the whole truth eventually. But not now."

He glanced around the workshop. Crates had been opened. His tools moved. Supplies scattered. His mood shifted visibly.

"Now, while we're throwing questions around," he said, gesturing broadly, "what the hell are all of *you* doing in my shop? And is that"—he pointed toward Alex—"the Protector? Midtown's ghost in the flesh?"

Alex stepped forward.

"Our world's unraveling," he said. "We're under siege by something far worse than we've ever faced. We came here looking for your weapons—specifically, the enhanced ones. We thought we might be able to finish what you started."

Karsten raised an eyebrow, half-amused.

"You thought you could just stroll into my grave and reverse engineer my tech?" He scoffed. "You could throw a thousand Task Force engineers at my designs and still end up with a grenade that heats your tea."

"Then help us," Laura said. "We're running out of time. We need those weapons, Karsten."

"Mr. K," he replied.

"What?" Laura asked.

"Mr. K," he repeated. "You keep calling me Karsten. It's Mr. K. It's the name I adopted so nobody would find me."

The group was silent for a moment.

"Are you sure this is the guy?" Alex asked.

Laura sighed and gave an annoyed nod.

"Okay…Mr. K," she said. "Can you help us?"

He looked over the mismatched group: the protector, a soldier, a vigilante, a green-haired hacker, and an old friend in a wide-brimmed hat. Definitely not a Task Force unit. More like a last hope.

"Lucky for you, I've been busy," Mr. K said, smirking.

He went back into the room he had come from. A moment later, he returned, dragging a crate full of weapons.

"There is one problem, though," he said. "As much as I'd love to play knight with the misfit brigade, this place is a ruin. The fire destroyed everything. These weapons aren't finalized. And I don't have the tools to do it."

Jacob stepped forward, his voice even.

"I brought tools," he said. "Straight from the Gunsmith's vault. Everything we need to finish your designs is sitting on our ship."

Mr. K stared for a beat, then let out a slow, impressed exhale.

"Well," he muttered. "Guess I picked a good day to come back from the dead."

"So…" Laura said, "can you do it?"

"With those tools and my blueprints?" he asked, already moving toward the crates. "Give me a few hours. I can finish what I started."

Just then, a sharp chime echoed from Jenna's tablet. She stepped aside, brows pinched as she scanned the incoming feed.

Her voice cut through the moment.

"Guys," she called. "You need to see this."

She returned to the group and flipped the device around.

A grainy live feed showed Capital City's skyline, curled in smoke. Not ordinary smoke, but red and alive, like it was bleeding from the sky itself. Through it marched an army, black silhouettes beneath a crimson fog. At the front: Frederick. And beside him—the Virus.

"This was just recorded twenty minutes ago," she said.

Silence fell.

Nikki stepped forward, her voice low and steady.

"He's back."

Alex's jaw clenched.

"We're out of time," Laura said.

Jacob looked from the screen to the crates beside Mr. K.

"Then what are we waiting for?" he asked. "Let's get these weapons on the ship and get moving."

He turned to Mr. K.

"Will we be able to do this on an aircraft?"

Mr. K took a second to think. Then he nodded.

"We can do it," he said. "We just can't be interrupted."

"We'll hold them off," Alex said.

"Perfect," Mr. K replied, a smirk on his face. "Then let's get a move on."

17

Shattered Lines

The ship cut through thick cloud cover, a dark shape soaring toward the heart of a dying city.

Inside the main cabin, the group stood in tense silence. The whine of the engines was constant, but it was the sound beneath it—the distant rumble of collapsing buildings, the echo of gunfire, the low hiss of burning metal—that turned the silence into dread.

Capital City appeared ahead like the edge of an inferno: skyscrapers buckled and broken, streets swallowed by flame. Red smoke twisted through the air like veins of blood in water. And at the center of it all—the shattered remains of Task Force Headquarters, now barely recognizable. Its once-proud spires sagged, cracked and flickering with failing lights. The stronghold of order, overrun.

Nikki stood near the window, her face pale in the reflected firelight. Her fists were clenched, her jaw tight.

"It's worse than I imagined," she whispered.

Beside her, Alex stood unmoving. The glow beneath his skin had returned, faint but steady, like embers waiting to ignite. His eyes scanned the chaos below, cataloging every detail with calm precision.

Connor entered from the cockpit, holding a tablet synced to Task Force systems.

"The main tower's grid is still responding," he said. "If we can get inside and trigger the emergency lockdown, we can cut off power to the building and override the backup systems. That'll stop the Virus from starting his portal."

"How do we even get in there?" Nikki asked. "There's a whole warzone between us and that building."

"We won't all go," Laura said, stepping forward. "Connor and I will infiltrate the tower through the east entrance. If it hasn't collapsed yet, we can slip in and reach the control room."

"Just the two of you?" Nikki asked, turning to her.

"I can get us inside," Laura replied. "It's what I trained for."

"And what about us?" Nikki asked.

Alex's voice was steady.

"We'll be the distraction."

He turned toward the viewing window again, gaze fixed on the burning skyline.

"We drop in hard," Alex continued. "Create chaos. Pull their attention away from the tower."

He and Laura shared a glance.

"How long do you need?" he asked her.

She glanced at Connor, then back at Alex.

"Fifteen minutes. Maybe twenty."

"We'll give you more," Alex said. He looked to Nikki. "We've got this."

She nodded.

At the rear of the cabin, Jacob and Mr. K worked at a

makeshift station—tools from the Gunsmith's arsenal laid out in precise rows. Sparks lit the space as Mr. K welded another weapon into form, his expression locked in tight focus.

"We're going to do our best to keep the crowd's attention away from the ship," Alex said. "Make sure they're ready when we get back."

Mr. K gave a distracted thumbs-up without looking away from his work.

"Jenna," Connor said, approaching her at the controls, "you're gonna need to keep the ship steady overhead, while also providing cover fire. It's going to be difficult, but we need all the help we can get."

Jenna nodded and hugged him tight.

"Come back in one piece," she said.

He hugged her back.

The ship began its descent, engines roaring louder as the city below opened like a wound. The rear hatch unlocked with a hiss, and heat rushed in—thick with smoke and the stench of war.

Flames crawled across rooftops. Sirens wailed in the distance, lost under the sound of marching boots and distant metallic howls.

Alex turned to the group, his voice the calm before the storm.

"Let's move."

#

Alex stepped off the loading ramp first. His boots struck cracked pavement as smoke twisted through the air, heavy with ash and oil.

Capital City was unrecognizable.

Fires crawled up buildings like claws. Streets were shattered, cratered from endless blasts. Burned-out vehicles sat like bones at twisted intersections. And at the head of the chaos—marching like a dark tide toward Task Force Headquarters—was the Virus.

Towering. Silent. Leading Frederick and a swarm of black-armored mercenaries, all armed with the new enhanced weapons.

Nikki landed beside Alex, her fingers twitching with violet energy. She adjusted her mask with trembling hands, trying to slow her breathing.

Connor and Laura rushed up behind them.

"Those guns…" Connor breathed. "You really think you can hold them off?"

"There's no other choice," Alex replied.

Above, the ship banked sharply.

"We're airborne," Jenna's voice crackled through the comms. "I'll draw their fire as best I can—keep their attention away from the tower."

Laura checked her sidearm, slid the mag back in with a click. She exhaled slowly.

"Once we're inside HQ, we need to reach the command floor," she said. "If the controls are intact, we can trigger the emergency lockdown. That'll cut power across the entire grid."

"And once that's done…" Alex began.

"We take him down," Laura finished.

Connor rubbed the back of his neck.

"This is suicide."

"It's our job," Laura said, giving him a sharp look.

Alex turned to Nikki.

"Teleport us as close as you can without draining yourself. I need you in this fight."

"I can get us to the front lot," she said. "Maybe a few feet from the main doors."

"It'll have to do," Alex said.

He rested a hand on her shoulder.

"You ready?" he asked.

Nikki nodded. "Let's go."

She grabbed Laura and Connor by the arms.

"Oh great," Connor muttered. "I hate—"

POOF.

They vanished.

They reappeared in a blast of violet smoke—midway across the cracked HQ parking lot. Gunfire echoed in the distance.

"—this," Connor finished, staggering.

Nikki grabbed her mom's arms, eyes locking with hers.

"Please," she said. "Come back."

Laura smiled softly and brushed a hand across Nikki's cheek.

"I still have a promise to keep," she replied.

Then, without another word, she pulled Connor, hurrying toward the building.

Nikki watched them go—just for a moment—then turned and joined Alex.

Together, they stepped into the street.

Across from them, atop the ruined rise of a collapsed intersection, stood the Virus. Towering, motionless. A conqueror of ash. Red code pulsed beneath his skin, and beside him stood Frederick—grinning, relaxed, his enhanced rifle slung over his shoulder.

The Virus raised a single hand. The red glow warped the air around him.

His voice boomed across the battlefield—layered, glitching, massive.

"Give up."

The word hit like a drumbeat.

"You've already lost your city. Your people. Your defenses. You stand in the aftermath of your own failure."

His eyes locked on Alex, who stood tall near the burning wreck of a convoy truck, Nikki at his side.

"I offer you mercy," the Virus said, voice lower now, almost a whisper—but one that filled the world. "Don't make me take more."

Alex stepped forward, flames flickering in the wind around him.

"You'll never take this realm," he said. "Not while I'm breathing."

The Virus tilted his head, a flicker of amusement in the motion. Something mechanical. Calculated.

"Then I'll have to fix that," he replied.

He turned to Frederick and nodded once.

Frederick raised his arm.

"Kill them."

The ground exploded with movement. Frederick's soldiers surged forward, and the two with their enhanced rifles fired red-hot energy bolts that lit the air like plasma.

Overhead, the airship screamed into position. Its cannons fired—huge rounds thundering into the enemy ranks, blowing chunks of earth and men skyward.

Alex launched into motion.

He slammed into the first wave of soldiers, tearing through

them like a wrecking ball. His fists shattered ribs, snapped arms, and sent men flying into nearby vehicles.

Nikki teleported midair and dropped hard onto a soldier's chest, crumpling him. Her scythes flashed into her hands as she spun, slicing two more down in a blur of violet arcs.

Red bolts cut through the smoke. A few struck Alex and Nikki—glancing, but hard. Alex reeled, breath hitched. Nikki stumbled.

Frederick leveled his weapon.

A bolt ripped into Alex's chest, sending him to one knee.

Nikki's eyes blazed. She teleported again—straight toward Frederick—scythe arcing down.

CLANG.

He blocked it with his rifle, sparks flying. He twisted and slammed a boot into her gut, knocking her back.

Before she could recover, a chunk of stone—wreathed in red, glitching energy—slammed into her ribs. She hit the pavement hard, coughing.

Above her, the Virus descended from the rise. Slow. Inevitable.

Alex surged forward, trying to reach her—but another bolt caught him in the back, sending him sprawling.

"Stop him!" he shouted.

The ship's guns adjusted, targeting the Virus directly. The cannons roared—rounds slamming into him like meteors.

The Virus jolted, staggering slightly under the barrage. Smoke hissed from his frame—but he didn't fall.

Instead, he raised his arm toward the ship, palm open.

A red mist poured from his hand. Thick. Pulsing. Alive.

It rose like smoke, but it *moved* like something sentient—seeking.

Nikki watched from the ground, dazed, as the mist curled upward toward the ship.

#

The red mist scraped against the windshield like smoke with claws, dragging threads of itself across the glass. Inside the cockpit, Jenna sat frozen at the controls—eyes wide, lips parted, breath caught in her throat.

As the mist entered the cockpit, it made its way into her body.

For a moment, everything went still.

And then, she heard him.

A voice. Deep and layered. Familiar now.

It slithered through her ears, bypassing thought, curling around her brain like barbed wire.

"They don't need you, Jenna."

She gripped the flight stick tighter.

"They never did."

The voice echoed in a space beyond the cabin—a whisper just behind her eyes.

"She leaves you behind. Every time. Because you slow her down. You're the weak link. The spare part."

"No," Jenna whispered.

She reached for the comms switch—but her hand trembled violently. Her vision shimmered, warping at the edges. She blinked. The ship's lights dimmed. Her reflection in the glass pulsed red.

"She's a warrior. A protector. A chosen one."

Jenna's chest rose in shallow gasps.

"And what are you?"

A flicker in her mind—a memory—Nikki hugging her, laughing, thanking her for helping decode the maps back in Veilhaven.

But the voice tore through it.

"You're the girl behind the desk. You sit safely in the sky while they bleed on the ground."

Her knuckles whitened as her grip spasmed. Tears welled in her eyes.

"You're not a hero, Jenna. You're a burden."

The red mist seeped into the cracks of the windshield. The controls buzzed, then twitched.

Jenna clutched at her headset.

"I—I can't—" she gasped. "Get out of my head—"

The voice grew louder.

"You couldn't even save your mother."

And with that, the world tilted.

The airship veered sharply, its engines screaming. The nose of the craft dipped low as the left stabilizer lost control.

Alarms blared in the cabin.

Tools and weapons scattered as the ship jolted. Jacob stumbled, catching himself on a metal railing. Sparks erupted from a wall panel.

He looked up toward the cockpit, eyes narrowing.

"Jenna?!" he shouted.

No response.

Mr. K struggled to keep the tools on the workstation.

"Get it under control, Jacob!" he yelled. "Before we go down!"

Jacob sprinted forward, crashing through the cockpit door.

Jenna sat rigid in the pilot seat, shaking, eyes glassy. Her hands hovered inches above the controls, not moving.

"Hey—hey!" Jacob shouted, grabbing her shoulders. "Jenna! Look at me!"

Her eyes were pale, almost a full white.

"They don't need me…" she muttered quietly. "I'm useless… I can't help…"

Jacob cursed, lunging for the controls. The ship groaned beneath them, another engine flashing red on the dashboard.

He forced the flight stick up, the ship jerking hard in response.

"Come on…come on, stay with me…" Jacob muttered.

Jenna collapsed sideways into his arms, unconscious.

Below them, the battlefield raged on—but the ship steadied…just barely.

Jacob clenched his jaw, guiding the ship toward a safer altitude.

He looked down at Jenna—sweating, pale, tears streaked down her face.

Struggling to find a way to snap her back to reality, he held her close.

"I've got you," he whispered. "You're not useless."

As he held her, she slowly came back to.

She held on to him and let out a heavy exhale.

Jacob took a step back and looked into her eyes.

"Hey, hey," he said. "It's okay. Are you okay?"

Jenna nodded weakly. She gripped the flight stick.

"I've got it," she said. "I'm good."

"If you two are done screwing around over there, I could use some help," Mr. K called from the workstation.

#

Back on the battlefield, Alex soared straight into the air. Then he turned and flew straight down, aiming for the Virus like a meteor.

He slammed into him with the force of a missile, throwing a flurry of punches.

The Virus barely budged. He responded with his own brutal strikes, hammering Alex with blows that cracked the pavement beneath them.

Nikki leapt back into action, her scythes slicing through the air as she slashed at the Virus's side.

Alex shook off the attack and rejoined her. Together, they battered the Virus, pushing him to one knee.

But then—*CRACK!*

A bolt from Frederick's enhanced rifle shot through the chaos, blasting them both off their feet.

Alex rolled, already scrambling back up as more of Frederick's men closed in. He launched himself forward, tearing through them with raw, explosive force.

Ahead, the Virus had turned. His glowing gaze had shifted. Laura.

In a single, glitching blink, he blurred forward—appearing at the HQ entrance before Laura and Connor could react.

Laura raised her weapon.

Too slow.

A red energy wave burst from the Virus's palm, sending Connor flying like a rag doll into the wreckage.

"CONNOR!" Laura cried out.

Nikki and Alex turned, panic rising—but before they could move, another shot from Frederick struck them, knocking them down again.

The Virus lifted a hand, and Laura's body rose into the air.

She strained to lift her gun and fired—once, twice. The bullets hit his chest and dissolved like raindrops in flame.

"Pathetic," he said.

Laura's eyes found Nikki's. She shared her last glance with her daughter.

Then the Virus closed his fist.

In the blink of an eye, Laura vanished—no body, no scream—just a burst of red static where she had been.

Alex and Nikki froze.

She was gone.

Nikki's scream split the battlefield.

Something inside her cracked—and detonated.

The world blurred into a swirling vortex of violet energy.

A shockwave exploded out of her body, ripping apart the ground. Concrete shattered. Cars flipped. Soldiers were hurled like rag dolls into walls, through flames, across streets.

Her eyes burned with unnatural violet light. Glowing veins crawled across her arms and neck. Tears streamed down her face—but they evaporated in the searing heat radiating from her.

"NIKKI!" Alex shouted, plowing through enemy fire, sprinting to reach her.

She didn't hear him.

Nikki vanished in a flash—then reappeared in front of the Virus, slamming both scythes into his chest with a devastating shriek. The blow threw him back several yards.

The Virus stumbled to a stop, surprised. He blinked. For the first time, he looked...unprepared.

"Interesting..." he murmured, eyes narrowing as Nikki flashed forward again.

She yelled as she attacked, one strike after another after

another. Every impact cracked the street. Windows shattered. The air screamed around them.

The Virus raised a glitching hardlight shield.

Nikki shattered through it.

She teleported again—this time from above—crashing down with both blades into his shoulder.

He roared. Sparks burst from the wound.

"Nikki, STOP!" Alex bellowed, punching his way through soldiers to reach her.

Connor, bloodied and limping, pulled himself from the rubble.

"We have to go—*now!*" he called out.

Over the comms, Jenna's panicked voice screamed: "Nikki! You're surrounded! If you don't leave, you're all dead!"

There was no response.

Her violet energy flared, uncontrolled. Her body trembled, cracking with light. Her pulse hammered in her ears like war drums.

Then—arms wrapped around her.

Alex.

He grabbed her, trying to drag her back as rounds struck his body. He grunted through the pain.

She didn't stop.

Connor lunged in too, grappling her arm.

"Nikki! *We have to go!*" Alex shouted, voice ragged, desperate.

Nikki turned, her eyes locking with her father's.

Her whole body trembled—rage, grief, exhaustion tore through her like fire.

More soldiers closed in, their weapons trained on her.

And then—she let out one final, broken scream.

They vanished in a blast of smoke.

POOF!

Alex, Nikki, and Connor reappeared on the ramp of the airship.

The ramp hissed shut behind them as the ship rose once again.

Below, through the thick glass, the Virus stood alone in the street—watching, smirking.

The engines roared.

The ship banked hard, lifting toward the clouds.

Inside the cabin—silence.

Nikki collapsed, shaking, sobbing so violently she couldn't breathe.

Alex sank beside her, arms shaking, his hands stained with blood.

Connor leaned against the wall, gasping, covered in dust and ash.

At the front of the ship, Jenna sat at the controls—face pale, eyes wide. Her hands trembled as she guided the ship skyward.

Behind her, Jacob paced, one hand gripping a support beam, his chest heaving.

Mister K, stained with oil, slowly lowered a pair of sparking tools, staring out the window.

No one spoke.

No one needed to.

They had escaped.

But Capital City had fallen.

And Laura was gone.

18

Embers

The inside of the dropship was silent.

Not the tense, charged kind of silence that came before a mission—but the brittle, hollow quiet that followed loss. The kind that settled in the bones. The kind that refused to leave.

The air felt thinner, like grief itself had drained the oxygen. Every breath took effort.

Nikki sat curled by the rear hatch, arms around her knees, her face streaked with tears that had long since dried. Her mask dangled from limp fingers. Every so often, a flicker of violet energy pulsed along her skin—faint, involuntary. Like her powers didn't know how to shut off anymore. Like they were grieving too.

Connor sat across from her, strapped into a jump seat, elbows on his knees. His head hung low, fists clenched tight enough to make his knuckles go pale. He hadn't moved in minutes. Maybe longer.

At the controls, Jenna sat motionless. Her gaze drifted from console to console, but she wasn't really looking at anything.

Her jaw was tight. Her hands didn't tremble—but her eyes did.

Mr. K and Jacob were at the workstation. They worked in silence, tools in hand, movements mechanical. Jacob's brow was furrowed in concentration. Mr. K's hands shook.

And Alex stood at the front viewport, still as stone. One hand rested on the frame. His coat was torn at the sleeve. He hadn't looked away from the ruined skyline since they'd lifted off. He didn't blink.

No one spoke.

No one could.

Only the soft hum of the engines and the slow exhale of hydraulic lines filled the silence. A machine still breathing— while they barely could.

Then—metal slammed.

Mr. K slapped a wrench down onto the table.

"There," he said, voice hoarse. "The weapons are done. Let's load up and turn back. We can end this."

"No," Alex said.

Flat. Final.

Everyone turned.

"What do you mean, *no?*" Nikki's voice cracked, brittle with disbelief. Her face flushed with fresh tears. "We can't just sit here! I was *hurting* him. I felt it. He was slowing down. I was winning—"

"You weren't hurting him," Alex said, turning to face her. His expression was carved from granite. "You were pushing him. There's a difference."

He stepped forward, slow.

"You pushed him just enough to make him take you seriously. And next time..." His voice dropped. "He won't hold back."

Nikki's entire body trembled. The flickers of violet light surged again—then vanished.

"So what?" she said, her voice rising. "We just let him keep taking everything? We do nothing?"

"If we hadn't left," Alex said quietly, "we'd all be dead."

Connor looked up sharply.

"So what's the plan, then?" he said. "Let him keep the city? Let him burn what's left of the world?"

"I didn't say that."

"You're not saying *anything*!" Connor stood. "You've been gone for years. Maybe you've forgotten what it's like to lose people—but I haven't. She was my friend. My *best friend*."

Alex stepped toward him.

"I loved her," he said.

"So did I!"

They were inches apart now—rage clashing with grief. Neither flinching.

Jacob stood and got between them, placing one firm hand on each of their chests.

"Enough," he said, his voice like flint. "We don't win this by tearing each other apart."

They froze, breathing hard. But they stepped back.

Nikki's voice broke the silence again. Softer this time. Fragile.

"He didn't even *try*," she said. "He just looked at her—and she was gone. How do we fight that?"

No one answered right away.

Then Alex turned toward the cockpit.

"We're going to do something," he said.

He leaned toward Jenna, his voice low but clear.

"I need you to take us somewhere. Somewhere far."

He turned back, eyes locking onto Nikki.

"We can't win. Not like this. We're not ready. And I'm done losing people."

No one argued.

Even Mr. K had gone still.

Jenna nodded faintly, then reached for the throttle.

"Where to?" she asked.

"The mountains," Alex said.

The ship banked east, away from the wreckage, rising high above the clouds. Below them, Capital City burned—its towers cracked, its sky veiled in smoke and floodlight.

They didn't look back.

#

The air inside Task Force Headquarters had twisted into something…wrong.

What was once a sanctuary of order and steel discipline had rotted into a cathedral of corruption. The sterile hum of fluorescent lights had become a twitching, strobe-lit nightmare—ceiling panels sputtered violently overhead, casting the war-scarred corridors in disorienting flashes of icy blue and hell red. The polished floors were fractured, scorched black, and smeared with streaks of dried blood and oily residue.

And at the heart of it all—beneath the shattered central atrium where briefings once rallied armies—stood the portal.

A grotesque monument.

A spine of hacked steel and sparking cable, twisted into unnatural shapes. It had been fused to the building's power grid like a parasite latching onto a dying host. Thick cords ran through the floor and walls like diseased arteries, pulsing with stolen energy. Broken control panels blinked nonsense warnings in foreign symbols—code that no Task Force system had ever recognized or written.

The Virus stood at the core, his frame casting a long, crimson shadow across the wreckage. His body pulsed with slow, rhythmic waves of red light—like a machine breathing. Each pulse shivered through the walls, making steel groan and lights buzz in protest.

Frederick stood a few paces behind, arms crossed tight. His enhanced rifle was slung across his chest, his trigger finger flexing—but he kept his distance. From the portal. From the Virus. From the thing he'd agreed to help but no longer understood.

"This thing gonna work?" Frederick muttered, eyeing the flickering ring of the half-born portal. Sparks danced across its surface like insects caught in a magnetic storm.

"It will," the Virus said.

His voice had become even more distorted—lower, deeper, warped like corrupted audio. Every word vibrated in the air. It scraped the inside of the skull, left a metallic tang on the tongue.

"I've reinforced the sequence," he said. "Corrected what Vincent failed to complete."

He raised one metallic hand and touched the control core.

The lights in the building dimmed…then flared. A blinding surge.

Generators howled to life beneath the floors. Ceiling tiles rattled loose. Wall-mounted monitors exploded in static. And deep within the walls—something began to hum. Not power. Something older. Hungrier.

Frederick's skin prickled. The hair on his arms stood

upright, as if the air itself had grown teeth.

The ring of the portal bloomed.

What had once been a hollow arch of metal was now a trembling wound in reality. A faint red shimmer appeared in the center—then deepened, developing like a bruise across space. Symbols crawled across the arch's edges in twitching patterns, neither digital nor arcane, as if the portal was translating a language no human was meant to hear.

Frederick took a step back without realizing it.

"Geez," he whispered. "What's on the other side of that?"

The Virus turned toward him slowly, his red-lit eyes glitching like dying stars.

"Reinforcements."

Then—it tore open.

The portal screamed.

Not a sound, but a *pressure*. A shriek that came from *inside* the air, as though reality were being peeled apart like a rotting scab. The center twisted inward, folding space with it. A hiss of red mist leaked through the rupture, spreading across the marble like smoke from a burning dream.

And from that mist—something emerged.

The first of them.

A creature.

Its silhouette limped forward, all bone and blade and blasphemy. Its body was stretched and shattered—limbs too long, spine bowed backward in a sickening arc. Its eyes burned a steady, solid red. Its jaw split in two, unhinging like a serpent's to reveal rows of saw-toothed fangs that clicked and jittered with anticipation. Metal plating jutted from beneath its skin, as if fused to muscle and bone by fire and violence.

One arm was a massive club of calcified steel. The other

twitched, fingers spasming like broken antennae.

Frederick staggered back.

"What the *hell* is that thing—!?"

Then more came.

Dozens.

Then hundreds.

Some crawled on all fours, their backs split open to reveal pulsating spines. Others galloped like beasts on digitigrade legs, heads lolling as if half-severed. Some had no eyes. Some had too many, blinking in random patterns across their torsos. Some were entirely metal from the waist down. Others had scythe blades for arms, or ribs that opened like cages, revealing thrashing tendrils inside.

The air stank of ozone and rot.

Frederick's men opened fire.

But it didn't matter.

The creatures *moved*. Blurred across the floor. They swarmed the soldiers like insects, tearing through armor and bone. Some fed not on flesh, but on the light of their victims—draining energy, life force, *everything*.

Frederick raised his rifle.

"HEY!" he shouted. "Get off them!"

He aimed.

But before he could fire, the Virus's hand closed over the barrel and forced it down.

"Leave them," he said, voice quiet and final. "They must feed."

Frederick looked on in horror as his men—*his men*—were reduced to twitching husks. Their screams were short-lived. Their bones snapped like twigs.

He didn't move.

He couldn't.

The Virus stepped forward and raised both arms.

From his palms, red energy unfurled like vapor from boiling blood—rising into the air, coiling through the ruins like smoke from a funeral pyre.

"This realm," he whispered, smiling faintly, "is *ours* now."

And the creatures screamed.

A sound like every nightmare collapsing into one. Unified. Deafening.

It shattered what little glass remained in the windows. It shook the ceiling beams. Dust and stone rained from above.

Frederick covered his ears.

But the sound still reached him.

It wasn't just heard.

It was *felt*.

And it was only the beginning.

19

Mountain Forge

The dropship banked low over jagged cliffs, its engines straining as the thin mountain air clawed at the hull. Clouds curled like pale ghosts around the peaks, shrouding the valley in gauzy sheets of mist. Shafts of late-afternoon sun sliced through in fractured beams, painting the stone ridges in strokes of gold and shadow.

Below, nestled in a narrow cradle between two towering cliffs, sat the monastery.

Stone buildings sprawled in uneven clusters—ancient, wind-bitten, half-consumed by creeping moss and tangled ivy. Faded prayer flags clung to splintered poles, trembling in the breeze like forgotten memories. The air was sharp with pine, cold stone, and distant woodsmoke, clean but biting—air that hadn't tasted war in a long time.

At the helm, Jenna eased the ship down onto a cracked landing pad. The landing struts groaned against the rock. A low hiss vented from beneath the hull, the ship settling like a wounded beast finally brought to rest.

Inside the cabin, no one moved.

Nikki sat curled against the wall near the rear hatch, hoodie drawn low, her body small beneath it. Her eyes were puffy and raw, her cheeks stained with salt. Purple static danced around her fingers in erratic flickers—like her grief was short-circuiting the air around her.

Connor sat across from her, hunched forward, arms on his knees. His stare burned a hole in the floor. The muscles in his jaw flexed rhythmically—rage barely held in place.

Mr. K busied himself checking weapon cases, not for utility, but to keep his hands moving. Something—anything—to avoid the weight in the room.

At the front, Jenna sat in silence at the controls, her gaze hollow.

Then Alex stood.

He moved to the ramp controls, his coat still torn, his shoulders still bloodstained.

"We're here," he said, quiet but firm.

The ramp opened with a long, mechanical hiss.

Cold mountain air rushed in—clean and brutal. It cut to the bone, stinging eyes and lungs already brittle from grief. The sunlight hit the stone harshly, as if the mountain itself were daring them to step forward.

They descended in silence.

And there they were.

Dozens of monks stood scattered across the courtyard in earthen robes, their feet bare against the frozen stone. Some were gaunt and ancient, faces carved by time. Others were younger, eyes steeled by discipline, hands calloused from rituals of war and prayer alike.

They did not speak.

They only watched.

Alex scanned the courtyard. Some of the monks he recognized. Most, he didn't. All of them made his skin tighten.

Jacob stepped beside Alex.

"Well," Jacob muttered under his breath, "this is charmingly ominous."

Nikki crossed her arms, her voice sharp and frayed with leftover tears.

"So this is where you ran off to?" she asked. "This is where you hid for five years while we thought you were dead?"

Alex didn't react to the sting. He only nodded.

"Yes," he said softly. "This is where I came. Where I broke. And where I rebuilt."

Alex turned back to the others—Connor, Nikki, Mr. K, Jenna, and Jacob.

"I know how it looks," he said, his voice hardening. "I know how it feels. But we don't have the luxury of blame. The Virus has taken the Task Force. Capital City is burning. If we don't change…we lose everything."

Connor took a step forward, eyes cold.

"So what?" he replied. "You expect us to train in this place and be ready to fight a god? In days?"

"Exactly that," Alex said.

Mr. K let out a weak laugh.

"No offense," he said, "but you had years here. We're supposed to go through your journey in a week?"

Alex didn't blink.

"I didn't come here to ask," he answered. "I came to prepare you. This is where we strip away who we were. And forge what we need to become."

Nikki's fists clenched, and when she spoke, her voice was almost a whisper.

"And if we don't make it?"

Alex's eyes darkened.

"Then we die," he said firmly. "But we die trying. We don't surrender another inch to him."

A wind swept through the courtyard, scattering the prayer flags like whispers from the past.

The monks parted, stepping back as one, revealing the narrow path leading to the main grounds.

Alex turned and walked toward it, not waiting to see if they'd follow.

One by one, they did.

Nikki last. She lingered at the edge of the ship, eyes locked on the valley's shadowed stone, then stepped out into the cold.

Behind them, the last rays of sunlight slipped below the ridgeline.

And the mountain swallowed them whole.

#

The monastery slept.

The stone corridors clung to the cold long after the sun had dropped behind the cliffs. Mountain winds prowled through the eaves, low and restless, like voices that couldn't find peace. Most of the others had retreated to the small, drafty rooms the monks had offered. The silence felt heavy here—not absence, but presence.

Nikki sat alone at the far edge of the yard, perched on a cracked stone ledge overlooking the valley. Her hoodie was drawn tight, knees tucked up, hands pressed against her collarbone as if holding herself together. Purple static still flared in nervous flickers across her fingertips, unable to ground, searching for something to burn.

She stared past the monastery walls, past the black line where mountains met the night sky, past even that—into the kind of darkness that swallowed distance whole.

It didn't feel real.

None of it did.

Her throat still burned from hours of crying, but every so often another sharp hitch of breath ambushed her, the kind that came right before the next wave. She tried to hold it in, but her shoulders shook anyway.

Footsteps scraped across the stone behind her. Slow. Deliberate. Heavy enough she didn't need to turn.

Alex sat beside her without a word. Not close enough to touch, but close enough that his presence pressed against her like a second heartbeat. The weight of him was different now—less father, more shadow of something larger, heavier. His coat shifted as he settled, the coarse fabric rasping against the ledge.

For a while, there was nothing but wind and the distant groan of old timbers.

Nikki's gaze stayed fixed on her trembling hands, on the jagged sparks crawling over her skin.

"You're just…sitting here like none of it matters," she said, her voice cracking.

Alex didn't look at her.

"I don't feel that way," he said quietly. "It matters."

Her throat tightened.

"You're acting like it doesn't," she shot back, louder now. "Like you didn't just watch her die! Your wife! My—"

Her voice broke, falling to a whisper.

"My mother. And you just…You just sit there. Playing

commander. Protector. Whatever the hell you are now. Like she was nothing."

Her words hung in the cold air, brittle and sharp.

"Did you even love her?" she asked, forcing the words out through the tremor in her chest.

Alex's hands stayed still in his lap. His eyes closed slowly, like swallowing something jagged.

"Of course I loved her," he said, softer still. "I still love her. I always will. You think this doesn't touch me? Since the moment it happened, I've felt it every second."

"Then show it!" Nikki's voice broke into a sob. "Because I'm drowning out here, and you're just…sitting there! Acting like it's another mission. Like she didn't matter to you."

Her shoulders shook harder now, tears streaking her face faster than she could wipe them away.

Alex was quiet for a long moment. When he finally spoke, the words dropped heavy.

"I can't."

The two words caught her breath in her chest.

"I can't break," Alex said, his voice steady but ragged at the edges. "Not here. Not now. That's the job. That's the curse. I'm the protector of this realm. I don't get to fall apart."

His fists curled tight in his lap.

"I don't get to scream or collapse, no matter how much I want to. Because if I do…" He turned to her then, and his eyes—storm-gray, bloodshot, exhausted—held hers. "You'll all follow me into that same darkness. And I won't let that happen."

"But I'm not strong enough," Nikki said, her voice falling to a whisper. "I can't…I'm not like you."

Alex reached out—slow, deliberate, as if afraid she might

pull away.

This time, she didn't.

His arms wrapped around her, pulling her in. She clung to him immediately, her fists knotting in the torn fabric of his coat. The sobs came full now, raw and unhidden, echoing through the courtyard like something broken open.

Alex closed his eyes and held her tighter.

For this moment—just this—he let himself be human. Let himself grieve. Let himself hold what was left of his family.

And together, in the shadow of the mountain, they sat in the dark…mourning the woman they had both loved and lost.

#

The world was still wrapped in darkness when Alex stepped into the main hallway.

The air was cold enough to cling to the stone like a second skin. Outside, the wind prowled the cliffs, low and restless, herding the last stars from the sky. He paused at the threshold of the courtyard, inhaled once, slow and deliberate—then let his voice roll through the halls like a crack of thunder.

"Up. All of you. Now."

Doors creaked open. Boots hit the floor. Groggy faces blinked in the dim light.

Connor emerged first, shirt half-buttoned, hair in wild disarray.

"You've gotta be kidding me…" he muttered, rubbing at his eyes.

Mr. K stumbled into the corridor, still pulling on his boot. Jenna slid off her makeshift bed, already reaching for her tablet even though her eyes were heavy-lidded with sleep.

Nikki came last, hoodie pulled low, dark smudges still beneath her eyes—but awake. And standing straighter than the night before.

They gathered in the courtyard, the cold biting at exposed skin. Alex stood at the center, arms folded, his voice steady and sharp.

"We don't have time for slow mornings. This is it. Starting today…We train."

Connor squinted.

"What…like push-ups and cardio?" he asked.

Alex's stare shut him up before he could add more.

"This will be the hardest thing any of you has ever done," Alex said, his voice low, deliberate. "You'll be pushed to the edge—physically, mentally, emotionally. You will break. Then you'll break again. And again. Until there's nothing left but the version of you strong enough to survive what's coming."

The group exchanged uneasy glances, but stayed silent.

Alex's eyes found Jenna.

"You're staying here," he said. "The monastery is fortified, and you're not trained for what's next. You've done more than enough for us already. But this next battle…you'll be safest here."

Jenna's jaw tightened, but she didn't argue.

Alex swept his gaze over the rest of them.

"If any of you want to back out, do it now," he continued. "No judgment. This isn't a fight you can bluff your way through."

No one moved.

Nikki set her shoulders, hands curling into fists. Connor rolled his neck and gave a short nod. Jacob rested one hand lightly on the hilt of his chain blades, expression unreadable.

Even Mr. K, pale and restless, adjusted his gloves like he was bracing to walk into fire.

Alex's nod was short, final.

"Good," he said. "Because this isn't about being ready anymore—it's about being alive at the end of it."

He let the words hang.

"There is no end to this fight until the Virus is dead…or we are."

The wind surged again, snapping the prayer flags against the walls.

"Lower training grounds," Alex said. "Five minutes."

And then he turned and walked away, disappearing into the cold corridor, leaving the others in the growing light of dawn with nothing but each other—and the long, brutal day ahead.

20

Forged Through Fire

The sun hadn't cleared the ridgeline when Alex's voice cracked through the mountain air like a war drum. "Again!"

Nikki's knees slammed into the dirt. Breath tore ragged from her chest, each inhale scraping her lungs. Sweat rolled in hot rivers, mixing with dust and flecks of blood—hers and not hers. Violet energy snapped and hissed around her like a wire on the verge of burning out.

Across the yard, Jacob's chain coiled and uncoiled with a metallic shriek before striking the ground inches from Connor's boot.

"Focus," Jacob barked. "You're thinking too much. Stop thinking and move."

Connor flinched but kept his fists raised. Bruises swelled across his jaw and ribs, but he squared himself again, smearing blood from the corner of his mouth.

"I'm moving, aren't I?" he shot back, breathless.

"Not fast enough." Jacob lunged, chain flashing in one hand, elbow arcing toward him in the same motion.

On the far side of the grounds, Mr. K sagged on a flat rock, the training baton shaking in his hands. His face had gone paper white, hair plastered to his forehead with sweat.

"I...I think I'm gonna pass out," he rasped.

"You won't," Alex said, arms folded above him. His voice was neither cruel nor kind—just unyielding. "If you pass out on the battlefield, you're dead. So you breathe. You stand up. You do it again."

Mr. K's eyes glazed.

"That's easy for you to say," he said. "You're built like a tank."

Alex crouched to meet his gaze.

"You want to survive this war? Walk away from that final fight alive?"

A shaky nod.

"Then stand up. Pain means you're breathing. Breathing means you're still fighting."

Gritting his teeth, Mr. K forced himself upright.

Behind them, Nikki screamed—part fury, part frustration—and let loose a burst of violet energy. The row of training dummies detonated into splinters and dust.

Jacob's brow lifted.

"That's new," he said.

Alex turned in time to see her stagger, panting but still on her feet.

"That's what I want," he called. "But again. Control it. Uncontrolled energy gets one of us killed—maybe even you."

Nikki wiped her mouth with her sleeve and reset her stance.

Days bled together.

The yard looked like it had weathered a siege—craters from Alex's impact drills, scorch marks clawing the stone walls, splintered weapons scattered like bones.

Jacob pressed Connor harder, forcing sharper dodges and smarter strikes.

"You don't have abilities," Jacob growled, blocking a punch with his shoulder. "So stop trading hits like you do. You've got speed. Use it."

Connor roared, sweeping Jacob's legs—almost working, until Jacob caught himself on one hand, twisted, and slammed him to the dirt.

Mr. K weaved through swinging sandbags rigged with counterweights. Too slow, and they hit like wrecking balls.

"Again," Alex called.

And again, Mr. K staggered back up.

The sun climbed. The air thinned.

By the fourth day, Nikki's fingertips were raw from constant ignition. Jacob's chains bent at the links. Connor's knuckles split open. Mr. K's arms shook so badly he could barely lift them.

Alex didn't slow.

Nearly a week later, Nikki collapsed near the courtyard steps, every muscle trembling.

Alex knelt beside her.

"You want to stop?"

Tears burned in her eyes, but she shook her head.

"No," she said shakily.

"Then get up."

She did.

By dusk, they stood in the center of the yard—bloodied, hollow-eyed, but standing.

Alex paced before them, scanning each face.

"You've come farther than I expected in this time," he said. His tone stayed hard, but pride edged his words. "Tonight, rest your bodies. Your minds are next. The monks will help sharpen them. We can't win on strength alone."

#

While the group spent their days preparing, Capital City was dying.

It breathed, yes—but only in the way a corpse might twitch after death.

The streets were husks of themselves. Skyscrapers, once gleaming with ambition, now jutted like shattered teeth, their glass eyes gouged out by fire and rot. Highways curled in on themselves like burnt scrolls. Storefronts hung open like rib cages picked clean. Every sound—the sigh of wind against warped steel, the distant cries of survivors, the slow, deliberate steps of things that no longer belonged to this world—rang against the silence like stones dropped into a well.

Above it all loomed the Task Force Headquarters.

Once a beacon of defense, it now rose as a citadel of desecration. Where banners once rippled with the symbols of unity, chains of bone and broken steel now swayed like sinister prayer beads. The upper floors glowed with a sickly red light, pulsing in slow, diseased beats. Mist poured from the open portal at its heart, staining the clouds in hues that no natural sky should ever know.

Inside the war room—once a place of strategy and order— the Virus stood at the center. Monitors flickered around him, their cracked screens bleeding static. Cables as thick as arteries pulsed from the walls into the floor, carrying some unseen lifeblood into the tower's core.

On the screens: cities in ruin.

Halvade—its slums still smoking, twisted clawed creatures scaling buildings and tearing concrete apart like wet paper. Others stalked alleyways, dragging the screaming into the dark with hooked limbs.

Veilhaven—fire devoured the coastal district's lower streets. A full block had collapsed into the sea. From the cliffs, the last survivors screamed as the creatures hunted them one by one.

One city after another—claimed.

Surveillance drones swept overhead, hijacking every public screen. The Virus's hollow, glowing face filled them, his voice repeating the same message in an endless cycle:

"The era of man has ended. Your protector has abandoned you. Your obedience will be rewarded. Your resistance will be punished."

Frederick watched from the shattered overlook above the atrium. His face was carved from stone, unreadable, but his hand hovered close to the grip of his rifle. His eyes moved over the chaos with the calculation of a gambler staring down a loaded deck.

He turned toward the Virus, who stood at the edge of the atrium, watching his creatures spiral and shriek into the crimson night.

"So…" Frederick's voice was low, rough. "That's it then? The realm's ours?"

The Virus didn't turn. The red glow from his core throbbed steadily—a light too ancient to have been born in this world.

"No," he said, voice calm, cold, absolute. "Not yet."

Frederick stepped forward, boots crunching over broken tile and glass.

"We control the cities. The people are broken. The Task Force is gone. What else is there?"

Only then did the Virus turn. Shadows clung to him like they belonged there. Smooth metal caught the dim light beneath his black robes.

"There is still the protector."

Frederick exhaled sharply through his nose.

"That bastard's hiding," he said. "If he was coming, he'd be here by now."

"He will return," the Virus said. "The protector will come for what he believes is his. They always do."

Frederick's eyes narrowed.

"So, we wait?"

"Yes." The Virus faced the portal again. "Let him come home. Let him gather his strength. Let him hope."

His gaze fixed on the swirling red light.

"The portal is stable. The next phase begins soon. When it does, he will have no choice but to face me. And when he does…"

He lifted his hand.

Below, in the courtyard, hundreds of creatures stood utterly still. Not alive. Not dead. Weapons, waiting for a breath.

"…we will tear him apart."

A low vibration bled into the air, an invisible signal thrumming through the bones of the city.

And then—screams.

Not human. Not animal. Something older. Something wrong.

The sound shattered windows. Made buildings tremble. Sent every living thing still clinging to the streets diving for cover.

From the tower's peak, the Virus watched.

Smiling.

The war had already begun.

#

Night draped the mountain in silver and shadow.

The courtyard—scarred and blackened from days of brutal training—lay still. Fires had guttered into glowing embers, their warmth barely clinging to the stones. Above, the moon hung low, a pale sentinel drifting between clouds that prowled across the sky like ghostly beasts.

The team sat in a circle near the courtyard's edge. Their bodies were marked in bruises and aches, their muscles taut and trembling beneath worn fabric, but their minds now drew themselves into silence. In the center, a monk had placed a shallow bowl filled with still water and scattered flower petals. A single candle flickered beside it, its wavering light painting restless shadows across their faces.

Nikki sat cross-legged, palms resting open on her knees. Her breathing was slow, deliberate, yet her fingertips sparked now and then with faint bursts of violet light, flashing and fading like whispered thoughts.

Connor sat with his usual quick remarks absent, his face softer, weighed down by burdens that strength alone could not shift. Beside him, Mr. K—once restless and unfocused— now held himself straighter. Not serene, but grounded.

Across from them, Jacob sat like a carved monument, his chains folded neatly at his side. His weathered face betrayed little, yet there was a calm in his stillness, a coiled readiness waiting for the call to move.

At the head of the circle sat Alex, his breathing deep, his mind combing through the past days—Nikki's growing power,

Connor's quiet resolve, Mr. K's stubborn endurance, Jacob's quiet loyalty. And beneath it all, his own silence.

It was then that he heard the footsteps.

Soft. Slow. Familiar.

Alex opened his eyes.

The elder monk stood behind him, his thick robes stitched with centuries of wear. His face bore the weight of years, but his eyes shone with the clarity of someone who had already lived this moment countless times.

"Walk with me," the elder said.

Alex cast a glance at the others—still in their meditations—then rose and followed.

They crossed the courtyard without a word, ascending the winding stone path to a high overlook where the mountain dropped away into an endless expanse of night sky. Stars pierced the mist like watchful eyes. Far below, the world lay still—or bleeding. It was hard to tell from here.

The elder sat on a low bench carved from the rock itself. Alex stood for a long moment, uncertain, before sitting beside him.

"This is your most important trial," the elder said, his voice just above the whisper of the wind.

Alex's jaw tightened. His hands curled into fists.

"I'm afraid," he admitted at last.

The words settled in the air like ash. Bare. Irreversible.

"I'm afraid I won't survive this," he said. "That if something happens to her—if I lose Nikki—I won't come back from it."

His gaze dropped to the stone between his boots.

"I already lost Laura. I didn't get to mourn. Didn't get to fall apart. I've been holding it in so long, it feels like a storm's been trapped inside me...and if it breaks, I don't know who

I'll be."

The elder's eyes never left the horizon.

"Then let it break."

Alex looked at him.

"You must stop running from your emotions, Alex Sinclair," the elder said. "You cannot win by burying fear, grief, or anger. You are not a god. You are a father. A husband. A man. You fight not because you are unshakable, but because you are real."

Alex's throat tightened. His eyes burned.

"You say you fear losing your daughter. Then use that fear. Let it remind you what you fight for. Let it guide you. Let the pain in—but do not let it consume you."

He leaned closer, raising one finger.

"And most importantly…stop pretending you do not feel. That is not strength. That is suffocation."

He touched the center of Alex's forehead.

And the world shifted.

Images bloomed in Alex's mind.

Laura, laughing barefoot in the morning sun.

Nikki, six years old, leaping into his arms with a shout of "Daddy!"

The three of them gathered around a fire too early in the season, marshmallows melting as the night deepened, none of them moving to go inside.

Laura's hand in his, steady and sure.

Her voice, warm in his ear: *Whatever happens…don't forget to live.*

The vision faded.

A single tear traced down his cheek, cooling in the mountain air. He brushed it away with the back of his hand and exhaled, slow and steady.

The elder gave him a single nod.

"You know what must be done."

Alex rose. The weight on him hadn't lifted—but it had shifted. It no longer drowned him. It anchored him.

He turned to the elder.

"Thank you," he said, his voice firm now, certain.

Below, the monastery glowed with scattered torchlight.

"It's time to go home."

And he started down the path—toward his waiting team, toward the war, toward the Virus, toward fate.

21

The Ashes

The monastery lay behind them, wrapped in mountain mist and the pale light of a dying dawn.

From the loading ramp, Jenna stood alone, arms folded tight, her gaze fixed on the ship as though she could keep them here just by looking long enough. She didn't speak. Didn't wave. The silence between her and the team said everything.

Before boarding, Nikki crossed the distance in quick, certain steps and pulled her into a fierce embrace. She didn't let go right away. Her breath trembled against Jenna's shoulder. When she finally drew back, her eyes searched Jenna's with quiet urgency.

"Thank you," Nikki said. "For everything. For being there. For helping me through the toughest part of my life. I may not have said it enough, but...you've been the greatest friend I could have ever hoped for."

Jenna's composure cracked, her eyes brightening with tears she refused to let fall. She nodded, pulling Nikki close once more.

255

"Just survive," she said. "Please."

Nikki smiled and took a step back.

"I will."

Then the dropship's engines roared to life, a low, bone-deep vibration that rattled the stones beneath their feet.

One by one, they boarded—Connor, Jacob, Mr. K, Nikki... and finally Alex. The ramp sealed with a hydraulic hiss, cutting off the last glimpse of the monastery.

Inside, the air was tight with the kind of quiet that knew the shape of death. This wasn't just another mission. This was the reckoning.

The ship cut through clouds, climbing higher, the monastery shrinking until it was swallowed by mist. Mountains unspooled beneath them—white peaks giving way to charred forest, cracked highways, and distant plumes of smoke that smudged the horizon.

Connor leaned against the wall, watching the warped skyline crawl closer.

"So what's the plan?" he asked. "Because walking in and hitting that metal bastard in the face doesn't feel like it's gonna cut it."

Alex stood near the cockpit, one hand braced on the ceiling as the ship tilted in the wind.

"The Virus owns Capital City now," he said. "Every street. Every building. His creatures are everywhere. We're not walking into a battle. We're walking into a warzone."

"And we're outnumbered," Jacob said, arms crossed. "Even with powers, it's suicide."

Mr. K knelt beside one of the reinforced weapon crates, snapping it open. Sleek, hand-forged weapons gleamed under the cabin lights.

"They're not perfect," he said, lifting a launcher tipped with dark red metal, "but they'll pierce most of their armor. And these should slow down the enhanced ones—long enough for us to put them down."

"They'll help," Alex said, inspecting the gear. "But they won't kill the Virus."

The words hung in the cabin.

"Then what will?" Nikki asked, her voice low.

Alex met her gaze.

"We weaken him. Push him. Force him to burn his energy until he's exposed. You three"—he nodded to Nikki, Jacob, and Connor—"draw his fire. Keep him moving. Keep him angry. The longer the fight drags on, the more vulnerable he gets."

"And then?" Mr. K asked.

Alex's answer was steady.

"Then I finish it."

Through the front viewport, Capital City emerged—a jagged silhouette against a churning sky. Fires licked at the edges of broken towers. Helicopters swerved in the distance. Smoke bled across the horizon like the breath of some great, waiting beast.

Nikki tightened her gloves, violet light flickering over her knuckles.

"He took everything from us," she said. "Now we take it back."

Alex nodded once.

"Gear up. We go in fast, and we go in hard. If he's going to kill us, it won't be without a fight."

The ship banked toward the burning skyline.

And ahead, the battle for the realm waited in flame.

#

The dropship broke through the cloud cover with a scream of thrusters, slicing across the smoke-streaked sky of Capital City. Firelight flickered across the skyline—what was left of it. Entire districts lay in ruin, gutted by flame or swallowed by the blackened earth that still steamed from the Virus's uprising.

Alex stood at the edge of the ramp, the wind snapping through his coat. Behind him, the others prepared in silence. Armor strapped tight. Weapons locked in place. Faces grim and eyes hard.

The ship descended into a wide courtyard at the edge of what used to be the Task Force district. It was silent at first, eerily so. But the buildings around them groaned like they were breathing, and ash rained from the sky in soft, gray flakes.

As the ramp lowered, the team stepped out together. Alex, Nikki, Connor, Jacob, and Mr. K.

Across the courtyard, they saw them.

The Virus stood tall at the far end, flanked by Frederick. The metal in his body glinted with unnatural red light, smoke drifting from the seams of his plated skin like steam from a rotting furnace. His eyes burned twin cores of red, unblinking and ancient.

Frederick's face was calm, but pale. Tense. He rested his fingers on his enhanced rifle, though even he seemed to flinch at the distant groans echoing around them.

The Virus stepped forward, hands folded behind his back like a twisted monarch surveying a kingdom he'd yet to fully claim.

"Protector," he said, his voice a low vibration in the marrow of every bone. "You've returned to me. You've even brought practice dummies. How thoughtful."

Alex didn't blink.

"You've taken enough," he said. "We're here to end this."

The Virus tilted his head slightly, almost amused.

"You know you can't stop me," he replied. "You've trained, yes. You've bled, yes. But this…this is not a battle you win with stubbornness alone."

He gestured outward with one hand.

And the city *moved*.

From beneath the fractured concrete and shattered glass, *they* came.

Dozens of creatures, then hundreds, crawling from cracks in the street, from open manholes, through windows and the hollowed shells of buildings. Their bodies slithered, galloped, limped, or sprinted in unnatural spasms. Some were thin and eyeless, others wide and plated in armorlike bone. All radiated the Virus's red light.

They hissed. Growled. Shrieked.

The air soured.

Alex stepped forward, his team at his sides.

"I'm giving you one last chance," the Virus said. "Hand over the realm. Kneel. And I will spare them. Your allies. Your precious daughter. Don't allow them to suffer the same fate as your beloved."

Alex didn't move.

"You know I won't do that," he said.

The Virus smiled.

"Yes," he replied. "I was betting on that."

He lifted a single hand.

The sky *screamed*.

The ground quaked beneath their feet as the army surged forward like a wave of claws and fangs.

"Form a line!" Alex shouted.

The team spread out instantly, Nikki's hands erupting with violet light, Jacob's chains unfurling like living snakes, Connor dropping to one knee to ready his rifle, and Mr. K drawing dual enhanced pistols from his belt with a spin and snap.

The Virus's army *collided* with them.

Nikki blasted through the first wave, her energy rippling across the street like a shockwave. Creatures were thrown into the air, but more replaced them instantly. She teleported midstep, reappearing behind two snarling beasts, blasting them into ash.

Jacob moved like a storm, chains flying in precise arcs, wrapping around limbs and tearing creatures apart. His face was clenched in silent fury, eyes locked on each movement.

Mr. K ducked low under a lunge, firing both pistols into a beast's body before flipping backward and cracking another with a steel-toed boot.

"Connor!" he shouted. "We need cover!"

"I'm working on it!" Connor yelled, aiming and firing into a cluster of enemies.

Mr. K reached into a small pouch and tossed a small explosive into the crowd of creatures. It ignited the street, turning rubble and flesh into molten ruin.

Alex charged straight into the thickest mass of the horde, fists glowing with inner fire. Every strike crushed skulls and shattered bones. He moved like a weapon forged of purpose alone: calm, brutal, unstoppable.

But even as the team fought valiantly, the wave never

slowed.

Creatures climbed over one another in a frenzy, some hurling themselves at the group like living bombs. Blood and smoke filled the air. The city burned around them.

Nikki ducked under a swipe from a hulking, four-armed beast, its jaws snapping inches from her face. She rolled, skidded across shattered stone, and teleported midmotion, reappearing behind it and driving a charged fist into its spine. The creature howled as violet energy burst through its chest, rupturing bone and nerve.

"Jacob, left flank!" she shouted, hurling another blast toward a pack of smaller, spiderlike monsters crawling along the walls.

Jacob responded instantly. His chains shot sideways, wrapping around a section of the wall itself and yanking it down in a controlled collapse. Stone and debris crushed the creatures beneath it, and Jacob used the momentum to swing upward, flipping into a whirlwind of steel and fury. His feet barely touched the ground, his body a blur of trained, brutal motion.

Across the courtyard, Connor sprinted between cover points, rubble, abandoned vehicles, a crumbled Task Force barricade, taking shots when he could, but mostly trying to funnel the creatures into chokepoints.

"K!" he called again. "That prototype! Now would be a good time!"

Mr. K gritted his teeth, ducking under a leaping creature that crashed into the dirt behind him. He reached into his coat and pulled free a small metallic device with three glowing prongs.

"I didn't test this yet!" he yelled.

"Welcome to the testing field!" Connor shouted.

Mr. K slammed the device into the ground.

A pulse of energy burst outward in a tight radius, knocking several of the advancing creatures backward. Their limbs jerked spasmodically as the disruption pulse fried whatever link the Virus had used to animate them.

It gave them seconds, precious seconds.

Alex tore through another line of beasts, fists crashing down like meteors. He spun into a wide arc, sending a shockwave across the pavement that cracked stone and flung enemies into the air.

But then, something larger moved.

The street behind the Virus cracked wide open. Something massive crawled from below. A creature twice as tall as the others, draped in a thick carapace of obsidian armor. Red veins pulsed beneath its surface like lava through black glass. Its head was a mass of eyes, none blinking, and its mouth split open into six serrated mandibles.

The Virus raised a hand casually.

"Meet the Hound," he said.

It charged.

Alex turned just in time to intercept it.

Their impact shook the courtyard. Alex dug his heels into the concrete, but the beast rammed into him with brutal force, pushing him through a rusted barricade and into a nearby wall. The structure collapsed around them.

"Dad!" Nikki screamed.

She bolted forward, only to be cut off by another swarm. She twisted, teleporting between enemies, blasting and dodging with a desperate grace.

Jacob flung a chain out, grabbing Nikki mid teleport and yanking her back just in time to avoid a claw that would have taken her head clean off.

"Keep your head!" he snapped. "We lose focus, we lose this fight."

Connor, pinned behind a crumbling monument, reloaded his rifle with shaky hands. He looked to Mr. K, who was down to one working pistol.

"Any more tricks up your sleeve?" he shouted.

"The weapons bag is by the ship," Mr. K replied. "I need to—"

A thunderous crash interrupted him.

Alex erupted from the rubble, slamming the giant beast into the ground with a roar. Dust exploded around him. His coat was torn, his chest plate dented, but his eyes burned with steady fire. His fists blazed like molten steel as he drove them into the creature's chest over and over, until the light in its eyes flickered and died.

He stood, blood dripping from his knuckles.

"Regroup!" he shouted. "Regroup on me!"

One by one, they converged, limping, bleeding, bruised, but alive.

#

Smoke still curled from the beast's broken body as the group pulled together.

Their breaths came ragged, their limbs heavy, but they were alive.

Frederick stepped forward through the haze, rifle hanging loose at his side. His scowl wasn't the usual calm mask—something restless, almost hungry, flickered beneath it.

"You're running out of monsters," he said, voice level but

edged. "Give me the power, and I'll finish this. I can end them."

The Virus tilted his head.

"You?" he asked.

"I know these people," Frederick replied, taking another step. "I know their weaknesses. They're worn down, bleeding. You give me what you gave my men, and I'll put them in the ground."

"You're not ready," the Virus said, a smirk tugging at his mouth.

Frederick's jaw tightened.

"I don't care," he growled. *"Do it."*

A long silence. Then, slowly, the Virus raised a hand and pressed it to Frederick's forehead.

The air hummed, deep and low. Overhead, the clouds twisted into a crimson spiral, lightning flickering red through the ruined skyline. The ground trembled as if the city itself feared what was coming.

Frederick's body jolted. Veins lit beneath his skin like molten wires. Muscles swelled, tearing through fabric. Metal fused to flesh, sculpting brutal plates across his arms and chest. His eyes burned with scarlet light. And yet, even as his neck thickened and his spine cracked into place, his expression never broke from that calm, calculating focus.

When it was done, he straightened to his full, monstrous height and flexed his fingers into a ready guard.

"This," he said quietly, his voice crackling, "will do."

The Virus stepped back.

"Go."

Frederick exploded forward.

Jacob barely saw the blur before a massive hand caught

his chain midswing, twisting it into a knot and yanking him forward into a knee strike that folded him to the ground. Frederick didn't waste the follow-up—a boot slammed down on the chain, pinning it, forcing Jacob to fight free while the others scrambled.

Mr. K's pistol barked, rounds sparking against Frederick's armor. Frederick sidestepped and shoved an overturned truck toward him like it weighed nothing. Karsten dove aside as the vehicle crashed into a pillar.

Connor's grappling bolt zipped through the air toward Frederick's back—but Frederick caught the cable without looking, yanked, and sent Connor flying.

"You telegraph your moves," Frederick said, pacing toward him. "A soldier's flaw."

Nikki appeared behind him in a violet flash, palm glowing. He pivoted, catching her wrist midstrike and twisting just enough to force her to stumble into Alex's path. Alex caught her, breaking stride, and Frederick was already moving again—every attack calculated to disrupt their rhythm.

"You're protecting her," he said to Alex. "That's your weakness."

Alex stepped forward, fists aglow.

"And yours is thinking you've already won."

They met in a shockwave that cracked the ground. Alex ducked a hook and drove a kinetic palm into Frederick's ribs— enough to make even the brute stagger. But Frederick pivoted with the force, turning it into a backhand that clipped Alex across the jaw, sending him skidding.

Jacob was up again, blood running down his temple, chains whipping through the air. He wrapped Frederick's arm—only for Frederick to flex and snap the links like twine. "You can't bind someone who doesn't fear you," he said, hurling Jacob into a wall.

Karsten lobbed a concussive grenade; Frederick kicked it aside midair, sending it exploding harmlessly behind the group.

"Predictable."

They were all moving now—Connor firing stun rounds to draw his attention, Nikki flashing in and out with bursts of violet energy, Alex pressing in with heavy strikes. Frederick flowed between them like a general on a battlefield—turning Nikki's momentum against her, forcing Alex to break formation to protect someone, knocking Connor off his reload just as Karsten found a line of sight.

But then Nikki landed behind him again, channeling everything into a blast at the base of his neck. It drove him forward a step. His hand shot back, seizing her by the collar, and he slammed her into the pavement twice before she teleported free, gasping.

Alex moved in fast.

"Now!"

Connor and Karsten flanked, forcing Frederick to guard against incoming fire. Alex drove in low, his fist slamming into Frederick's ribs with enough force to crack the armor plating. The enhanced man dropped to a knee.

For a second, it looked like they had him.

Then Frederick slammed both fists into the ground, the shockwave flinging everyone off their feet. He tore a slab of rubble the size of a truck door from the street and hurled it straight at Nikki.

She didn't have time to move.

The impact crushed her to the ground. Alex's roar split the

air as he blurred forward, hurling the slab aside and pulling her into his arms. Blood streaked her temple. She coughed, alive but reeling.

And Frederick froze.

The way she reached up and clutched at her father's arm. The same way…

His mind flashed—

Mrs. Carillo. Buried under stone.

His own hands lifting rubble, scraping his arms raw. The man, crying. She gave a whisper: *You're not like them. You're better.*

The memory pierced him.

He stumbled.

"What…" Frederick whispered. "What is this?"

Frederick looked at his hands—the grotesque plating, the red glow beneath. His breath quickened.

"This…isn't me…"

He turned toward the Virus. And for the first time, the Virus's smirk faded.

"I see," the Virus said. His tone was almost bored, but his eyes were sharp. "You're dangerous."

"No—" Alex shouted.

A thin beam of red light lanced across the field. It punched through Frederick's skull in a flash.

Frederick swayed, then crumpled.

Silence.

The Virus lowered his hand, the crimson mist already bleeding from the cracks in the street.

"What a waste," he murmured.

He slowly raised his arms.

"So, you like to play mind games?"

He spread his arms wide.

The crimson mist filled the air.

It bled from the cracks, from the shadows, from the sky itself. A rotting fog that coiled around their ankles, slithered into their lungs, and thickened until even light couldn't pierce it.

The world around them vanished.

22

Reflections

The silence was unnatural.

Connor stood in the middle of Task Force Headquarters. Or what was left of it.

The once-bright corridors were fractured tombs now—ceilings split, walls slashed open like wounds, shadows leaking into the hallways like thick, black smoke. The lights above sputtered, their faint glow casting more darkness than clarity. Broken screens bled static. Desks lay on their sides like fallen barricades. Blood smeared the floors and glass in shapes that felt deliberate, almost like some mocking hand had painted them there.

He was alone.

The black commander's uniform clung to him, crisp and suffocating, silver Task Force insignia glinting dimly under the flicker. He stood before a cracked window, looking out over a skyline that didn't exist anymore. Capital City burned, its towers bent and broken, and crimson ash drifted from the sky like poisoned snow.

"Commander Avery."

The voice came from behind him.

He turned. A woman stood framed in the doorway, her features blurred like wet paint. Her voice was familiar, weighted with expectation. Behind her, Task Force agents lined the hall, standing rigid, eyes on him.

"What's the plan, sir?" she asked.

He opened his mouth.

Nothing came.

A heat rose in his chest, thick and choking. His jaw worked, but the words were lodged like stones in his throat.

"Sir?" Another voice.

Then another.

They stepped forward—the woman's face shifting into someone else, then someone else again.

"People are dying out there."

"What are we doing?"

"Why haven't we moved yet?"

Connor stumbled backward, palms raised as if the air itself might shield him.

"I...I just need a second—"

They advanced, their crisp uniforms rotting away into bloodstained rags, their skin peeling into ash. The agents dissolved into civilians—mothers clutching children, bloodied soldiers crawling on shattered limbs—all of them staring, hollow-eyed.

"You said you'd protect us."

"You let them die."

"Laura never would have let this happen."

Her name hit him like a blade.

He turned toward the shadows, and there she was.

Laura.

She stood with her arms crossed, expression carved from ice. The air between them was colder than the rest of the room.

"I left this to you," she said, her voice low, deadly. "You weren't ready."

"I'm trying!" Connor's voice cracked, loud in the empty space. "I'm trying my best!"

"But your best isn't enough," she said.

She stepped forward, and the lights above her blew out in a shower of glass.

Connor looked down.

Blood was on his hands. Fresh, warm, soaking into his sleeves. Around his feet lay the fallen—every agent, every friend. Nikki's face among them, pale and still.

At his boots, Laura's Task Force badge lay cracked clean through.

"It never will be." Her voice faded.

The building began to collapse. Steel screamed. The floor lurched. Beyond the shattered window, the city was gone— replaced by a swirling ocean of red mist.

Connor dropped to his knees.

"I'm not enough," he whispered.

The mist thickened, curling around him like claws. A voice emerged from its depths—not Laura's, not his own.

The Virus.

"I didn't need to kill them," the rasp came, low and intimate. "You did it for me."

The world fractured, falling away in shards of glass and shadow.

And Connor fell with it.

\#

The ground was dust.

Ash swirled across a barren expanse of cracked stone and dead ruins—monuments so ancient they felt older than memory itself. A cold wind whispered through jagged monoliths, their faces carved with symbols Jacob almost recognized.

Almost.

They were like fragments from dreams he'd forgotten, from a time before the chains, before the blood, before the cause.

His boots crunched over broken earth, yet the sound seemed to vanish into the emptiness.

No birds.

No wind.

No echo.

The weight of his usual gear pressed down on him more than it should have, every strap digging in, every buckle pulling. The chains trailing behind him weren't metallic here—they were organic, sinewed, pulsing faintly with a sick red glow, as if they'd been infected by this realm itself.

Above him, there was no sky—only a vast, roiling void, a heaven scraped clean.

He came upon a mirror.

It stood upright in the middle of the wasteland, framed in rusted iron, its glass too perfect to belong in a place like this.

Jacob's reflection stared back—but it wasn't the man he was now.

It was him, years younger. No scars. No chains. Eyes stripped hollow.

The reflection spoke, lips moving with quiet precision.

"You pretend you know where you're going," it said, "but you're just a ghost walking."

Another mirror rose from the ground behind him.

Then another.

Dozens. Hundreds.

Each one showed a different Jacob—one drenched in blood, one screaming midbattle, one walking away from a burning home, one kneeling in chains, one smiling that cold, brittle smile he'd worn for years.

They spoke together, voices stacking into a suffocating chorus:

"No home."

"No purpose."

"No name that matters."

Jacob turned his back on them. His jaw was tight, but his chest ached.

The ground split. Chains erupted from the cracks, snapping around his arms, legs, throat.

They weren't his.

These were alien, cold, and hungry.

"You wear chains to control," the chorus hissed. "But you've never been free. You've always belonged to orders. To missions. To wars. To lies."

His pulse thundered in his ears. He fought against the bonds, teeth gritted, but they only constricted tighter.

A whisper came from behind him.

"Who were you before this?"

Jacob turned.

A boy sat alone in the dust. Six, maybe seven years old. Barefoot.

Crying.

Jacob knew that face.

It was his own.

No one came for the boy. Not then. Not ever.

Jacob stared, his breath shallow. That child had waited his whole life for something he didn't believe he deserved. And he was still waiting.

"I don't remember..." Jacob muttered. His voice felt foreign in his mouth. "I don't remember where I started."

The desert bled away.

The mirrors cracked and fell into nothing.

Chains unraveled into shadow.

Only silence remained—a silence that followed him into the dark.

#

Nikki's began with rain.

Soft at first. Cold drops falling from a washed-out sky, the color of old ash. They soaked her through, clinging to her skin, but she didn't shiver.

She was barefoot, standing in the middle of a suburban street where every house was wrong—blank, faceless walls stretching endlessly; no doors, no windows. A neighborhood that had been hollowed out and forgotten.

She looked down.

She was smaller.

Child-size.

Her arms were thin, her sleeves frayed. She wore a purple hoodie she hadn't seen in years, torn jeans, sneakers too big for her feet. Her bangs hung in her eyes. When she raised a trembling hand to push them back, she saw no smoke, no violet light—just powerless fingers.

"Nikki?"

The voice drifted through the rain, soft but heavy.

At the far end of the street stood Laura. Arms crossed. Her face was blurred, like a memory half-remembered.

"I'm sorry," Nikki said. She didn't know why the words came out—only that they had to.

Laura didn't answer. She simply turned and walked into the mist.

Nikki chased her, feet slapping wet pavement.

"Wait! Please! I can fix this!"

The sky darkened.

And then came the screams.

Shadows poured from the cracks in the street, tall and eyeless, their mouths stretching into impossible grins. The ground shook with their approach. They flooded the road, swallowing everything.

Nikki raised her hand, willing the smoke to come.

Nothing.

No light. No power.

Stillness.

She backed away, heart hammering.

"Please…no…"

The creatures halted. Parted.

Through them walked a girl.

Ten years old. Wearing Nikki's face.

The younger Nikki held a cracked mirror in both hands. She lifted it.

In the reflection, Nikki saw her failures.

Jenna—buried in rubble.

Connor—screaming as he fell.

Laura—reaching for her, swallowed by darkness.

Alex—bleeding out, whispering her name.

Her breath caught. She fell to her knees, tears cutting warm paths down her cold cheeks.

"I didn't mean to. I tried…I tried—"

The younger Nikki stepped forward and whispered:

"You're not strong enough. You never were."

The shadows closed in, their voices hissing and overlapping.

Pretender.

Burden.

You don't deserve this.

You're just a scared little girl pretending to be a hero.

Nikki screamed—and the violet smoke erupted from her palms.

But it wasn't power.

It was rot.

It seared her arms, crawling up her shoulders, threading black veins across her skin. The pain coiled into her chest, suffocating.

"I didn't want this!" she cried. "I didn't ask to be the protector! I just…wanted to be normal…"

The street shattered. The rain. The sky. Even her voice broke apart.

She fell into a void of floating glass, each shard reflecting a moment she could never take back.

#

Silence.

Then the hum of stage lights, flickering to life in pale, sterile bursts.

Karsten—Mr. K—stood at center stage under a single spotlight. The rest of the theater was swallowed in pitch black. A lone ghost light burned at the lip of the wooden floor, casting its feeble glow over forgotten props and shattered set pieces.

He looked down.

A faded, sequined suit jacket clung to him—silver glitter dulled, shoulders too tight, sleeves singed at the cuffs. One of his old costumes. From the days when he smiled for strangers.

"Karsten Vale!" a booming voice rang from above.

Karsten looked up. An enormous sign hung crooked over the stage:

THE GREAT MR. K – ILLUSIONS, ESCAPES & LIES!

A slow, mocking applause rolled out from the darkness.

The seats were no longer empty. Row upon row of shadowed figures stared forward—faceless silhouettes in tattered suits and blood-stained uniforms. Task Force agents. Civilians. Monsters. All sitting like silent jurors.

The Virus's voice slid down from the rafters, smooth as oil:

"Let's begin, shall we? A little show…for the man with nothing real to offer."

A mirror dropped from the ceiling and shattered at his feet.

"You're not a soldier. Not a leader. Not a hero. You're a fraud in a lab coat who built toys and hoped they'd fight your battles."

The backdrop behind him flared to life. Explosions. Broken weapons. Nikki on the ground, bleeding beside sparking gadgets. Connor pinned under debris. Jacob standing alone against a tide of enemies.

"They'll all die," the voice hissed. "And it will be your fault."

Karsten folded his arms.

"Sounds about right," he said flatly.

A pause—subtle, almost curious.

"You accept that?"

He shrugged, stepping casually over the broken mirror.

"Sure. I've never been the hero. That's not new. I've spent most of my life making jokes so I wouldn't cry. Tried the spotlight. Didn't work. Tried science. Still working on that."

He looked up, tone steady.

"But I keep going."

The Virus growled. The stage warped, curtains curling into the shadows. The theater became a collapsing lab—walls splintering, sparks spitting, fire crawling up the walls.

From the flames, the Virus emerged—towering, red-eyed, wreathed in smoke.

"You'll die alone," it hissed.

Karsten dropped to the cracked floor, cross-legged, calm as ever.

"Honestly?" he said. "Sounds peaceful. I thrive on loneliness."

"You are nothing."

A tired, genuine smile tugged at his mouth.

"Maybe," he replied. "But I'm still here. You've thrown your worst at me, and I'm still here."

The Virus stepped forward, its gaze narrowing…then halted. Its head tilted, studying him.

"Interesting," it murmured. "There's something inside you."

Karsten didn't blink.

"Probably indigestion."

The growl returned, but this time with an undercurrent of doubt.

The theater collapsed into darkness—burning curtains

falling, seats sinking into a pit of smoke.

And Karsten sat there, alone in the void.

Still smiling.

#

Finally, came Alex's.

The first thing he noticed was the light.

Warm, golden sunlight spilling across a worn kitchen table.

A chipped coffee mug rested between his hands—heavy, familiar. The smell of fresh coffee curled upward, soft and rich.

Laura stood by the stove, humming as she flipped pancakes in a cast-iron skillet. Her hair was longer here, loose over her shoulders. A white tee, flannel pajama pants. Her eyes had the kind of happiness he hadn't seen in years.

From down the hall—footsteps, light and fast.

"Dad! Dad, come see what I drew!"

Nikki. Ten years old.

She burst into the room with a grin too big for her face, notebook in hand, colored pencil smudges on her cheeks.

Alex's chair scraped back without thought. He dropped to one knee, arms wrapping around her before the rest of the world could move.

"Looks amazing, sweetheart," he said, voice cracking in the middle.

"You always say that," Laura called from the stove, a smile in her voice.

"Because it's always true."

They laughed—all three of them—and for a moment, time stilled. The air felt whole.

Then the light flickered.

Birdsong outside warped into static. Heat drained from the room. A hairline crack rippled along the wall like a wound opening in the house itself.

Alex turned. Laura was gone.

The plate she'd been holding hit the floor and shattered, porcelain fragments skipping across the tile.

"Laura?"

Nikki's laugh faltered. He looked down.

She was turning to dust in his arms, fine gray flecks swirling upward like smoke. Her smile stayed, but her eyes...her eyes were terrified.

"No," Alex whispered. "No, please—"

The kitchen folded inward. Sunlight curdled into red mist.

From the haze stepped the Virus.

"Poor protector," it whispered, circling him. "You could have had all of this. You *did* have it. And you left it behind. For what?"

Alex's fists tightened.

"You abandoned them. Your wife. Your child. And now"—its voice deepened into a jagged growl—"your entire world."

It leaned close, the heat of its breath like embers on his skin.

"You trained. You meditated. You pretended to grow. But here's the truth...you're still the same broken man who ran away."

The air thickened. His knees buckled. His chest ached.

Then—

A voice cut through the static. Calm. Gentle.

"Let it in."

The smoke thinned.

The elder monk stood there, robes of sun-faded orange and gold, eyes warm and weathered.

"You cannot banish sorrow by turning your back to it," the elder said. "Fear, grief, rage—they are not your enemies. They are part of you."

Alex's breath shook.

"I failed them."

"No," the elder said, stepping closer. "You loved them. That is not failure."

The Virus hissed from the shadows, but the monk didn't even glance his way.

"You are not meant to escape the pain. You are meant to carry it."

A trembling exhale left Alex's lungs. His head lifted.

"Let it in," the elder repeated, placing a steady hand over Alex's heart.

The kitchen reformed—but now it burned. Ash drifted like snow. The windows glowed red.

Alex stood. Slowly.

The Virus waited across the room.

Something inside Alex flared—gold light bleeding from his chest. It swelled with each breath, filling him, steadying him.

Then—

The light burst outward in a shockwave. The illusion shattered like glass, the red mist ripping apart under the force.

The Virus screamed and dissolved into shadow.

Alex's eyes snapped open. Cold stone under his hands. Air in his lungs.

Around him, Nikki stirred first. Then Connor. Then Jacob and Karsten. Pale. Shaken. But alive.

The mist was gone. The world was back.

Alex rose, the gold glow in his chest fading but not gone. His gaze locked on the figure standing ahead—the Virus, real this time.

And Alex knew.

The final battle had come.

The last stand.

23

The Last Stand

The Virus laughed.

It wasn't a human laugh.

It was a low, metallic rasp that crawled up the spine, vibrating through the broken air like a curse. The sound bounced off the shattered husks of Capital City, carried down the firelit streets, higher and higher until the silence itself seemed to hold its breath.

Rubble still smoked. Somewhere in the distance, a building gave way with a groan of steel. Fires chewed through what remained of the skyline. Overhead, the sky churned in a fever of red clouds, the light casting long, warped shadows across the broken skeleton of Task Force Headquarters.

The team stood in a jagged line, ash-streaked, blood in their mouths, breathes coming ragged.

Connor's jaw locked, his blaster trembling only from exhaustion. Nikki stood beside him, shoulders squared, violet energy fizzing between her fingertips. Jacob was half-crouched, one hand on his knee, chains hanging like the tail of an old war animal too stubborn to lie down. From a smear of smoke at their flank, Mr. K reloaded with hands that shook but never faltered, his cracked goggles glinting in the haze.

And at the center, Alex Sinclair stood tall—golden light pulsing in his chest like a war drum.

They all knew.

This was it.

No retreat. No reinforcements. No more training to hide behind.

The Virus stepped forward, molten armor bending with every motion like liquid steel. His movements were too precise, too quiet—a predator's grace. Glowing wires ran through him like veins, and his face—part human, part machine—tilted in amusement.

"You broke the illusion," he said. "Crawled back to reality like rats from a sinking ship." His head cocked. "But freedom means nothing. You are outmatched. Outnumbered. Outlasted."

A ripple of red shimmered in the air behind him.

"You will die."

Alex's voice cut through the ruin like a blade.

"That might be true." He stepped forward, fire burning in his eyes. "But we'll die fighting."

No signal was needed.

They moved as one.

The first collision was thunder.

Alex reached him first, golden energy exploding from his fist—but the Virus slipped aside, a blur, the counterpunch cracking the ground where Alex's ribs had been a heartbeat before.

Nikki blinked out of existence in a rush of violet smoke and reappeared behind him, a strike already coming. He caught her wrist midswing and hurled her like dead weight toward a mound of rubble—only for her to vanish again, reappearing across the street with a grunt.

Jacob's chains whistled through the air, one catching the Virus's arm. Jacob yanked hard—but the Virus twisted, pulled him forward, and tried to slam him into the ground. Jacob turned the momentum, planting a boot squarely into his torso. The impact forced the Virus back a step, but no more.

From the flank, Connor opened fire, bolts slamming into pavement and armor, forcing the enemy to weave.

"K—now!" he barked.

Mr. K lobbed a flash bomb overhead. It burst in a searing bloom of white. The Virus staggered—for a fraction of a second, but enough.

Alex's fist found his chest, sending a shockwave through the street. Jacob's chains came down in a molten double strike, splitting concrete and tossing the Virus into a roll.

He landed in a crouch, claws carving trenches into the ground. The smile was gone. His eyes were cold.

Nikki dropped from above, heel aimed for his head. He blocked, but her strike still knocked him sideways into Connor's barrage. Stun rounds. Explosives. Focused fire from every angle. For the first time since the portal opened, the Virus moved back.

Then he roared.

The blast tore the battlefield apart, red energy exploding from him in a storm. All five were flung like leaves in hurricane wind. Connor went through a barricade. Mr. K slammed against the shell of a burning car. Nikki skidded across ash until she stopped near Alex's boots.

The Virus straightened. Smoke rose from fresh cracks in

his armor. Not beaten—yet. But hurt.

"You are insects," he spat, voice distorting. "This realm was dying before I came. I am only here to finish the rot you allowed to fester."

He came for Mr. K first. A claw ripped through the car beside him, metal screaming before the vehicle exploded. The shockwave sent Mr. K tumbling, but Jacob's chain snapped out, catching him midair and flinging him to higher ground.

Nikki reappeared low, sweeping his legs. This time she landed the hit, staggering him just enough for Connor to slam a concussive bolt into his ribs.

Alex was already there. Golden fists, relentless—one, two, three in a blur, each strike like lightning tearing through stone.

The Virus adapted, driving an elbow into Alex's jaw so hard the Protector smashed through a streetlamp, folding it like tin.

Connor was at his side instantly.

"Alex—"

"I'm fine," Alex said, blood wetting his teeth.

Jacob landed beside them, armor scorched, eyes locked on their enemy.

"He's responding too fast."

"Then we overload him," Alex said.

"Chaos," Connor replied, grinning. "My specialty."

Smoke grenades rolled. Shadows danced.

Nikki came from behind, violet blades sparking in her fists. One strike connected. Metal shrieked. Sparks sprayed. The Virus spun to retaliate—too late. A beam of charged plasma from Mr. K's perch hit him square in the face.

"Boom," Mr. K muttered.

The Virus howled, lashing out blindly. Jacob's chains coiled, molten and unyielding, locking his limbs.

"Now!" Jacob roared.

Alex launched himself—hands locked, all the light inside him condensed into a single, furious point.

The impact was an earthquake.

The street cratered. The Virus hit the ground, dented, leaking red steam.

For a moment, he lay still.

The team staggered forward, barely standing.

Then, the Virus's body jolted upright—red lightning exploded outward. He floated to his feet, eyes burning hotter than ever.

"You have wasted your last breath," he snarled—then paused, head twitching toward the north.

The portal's glow had changed. The air trembled with a deep, unnatural heartbeat.

"He comes," the Virus whispered, almost to himself.

Alex's voice cut through.

"No—!"

Too late. The Virus blurred away in a streak of red and gold.

"After him!" Alex roared.

They ran. Through fire and ruin, chasing the shadow toward the final gate.

The end had begun.

#

The Task Force Headquarters groaned under its own failing weight.

The once-proud structure leaned toward the burning skyline like a dying giant, windows blown out, its concrete bones jutting through torn steel. Whole floors sagged at impossible angles. Each distant crash was the sound of the building tearing itself apart.

Alex and Nikki burst through the blackened main entrance just as the Virus tore through the stairwell door above them. The steel shrieked in his grip before shattering into jagged halves.

"Move!" Alex barked, already charging forward.

They bounded up the stairwell two steps at a time. The cracked stone groaned under each boot-fall, dust cascading in pale curtains from the fractured ceiling. Electric cables dangled overhead like severed arteries, spitting sparks that painted the walls in staccato flashes of light.

Ahead, the Virus moved like liquid metal—limbs a blur, shoulders rippling under plates of armor that caught the dim light. He ascended with unnatural speed, more like a pursuing shadow than a fleeing enemy.

"Almost there," Nikki panted, her breath tight, eyes glowing violet.

The Virus glanced back once. A flicker of red danced across his face—mockery, maybe recognition—before he wrenched a door from its frame and hurled it down the stairwell.

"Duck!" Alex grabbed Nikki's shoulder, dragging her low. The door shrieked past overhead, hitting the wall so hard the concrete cratered.

No pause. No wasted motion. The Virus reached into a side office and wrenched out a desk, sending it tumbling down the stairs like a battering ram. A vending machine followed— rolling, smashing, scattering glass and metal in its wake.

Alex thrust out a palm. Golden energy bloomed and detonated the vending machine midair. Shards of metal and copper coins exploded outward, clattering against the walls.

Nikki teleported in a snap of violet smoke, blinking three steps ahead to dodge a collapsing chunk of railing. She reappeared midrun, hair whipping behind her.

The stairwell spiraled higher, the air thickening. The walls here pulsed faintly red, as if veins had grown beneath the paint. The hum was louder now—a low, resonant vibration that thrummed in their chests. It felt like a heartbeat that didn't belong to this world.

"He's close," Nikki muttered, her voice hardening.

At the top of the stairs, the Virus punched through the final door. Metal and splinters flew as the doorframe buckled. He stepped into the light beyond.

Alex and Nikki were seconds behind.

They burst into the control room—a wide, circular chamber ringed with shattered glass walls. The city stretched far below, a graveyard of flame and smoke. Wind screamed through the gaps, dragging ash in wild spirals across the floor.

At the center of the room stood the portal.

It was...bigger. No longer a ragged wound in reality, but a living, breathing thing, its swirling surface blistering with dark crimson light. The fractured generators flanking it pulsed like twin hearts, coughing arcs of lightning into the air. Tendrils of shadow stretched from the rift, curling across the cracked floor like searching fingers.

And in front of it stood the Virus.

Silent.

Still.

Head tilted slightly, as if listening to something deep within the maelstrom.

Nikki raised a hand, violet smoke snaking between her

fingers.

"It's over," she said, her voice steady despite the roar of wind and machinery.

The Virus didn't move.

Alex stepped forward, golden light building in his chest. "You've lost."

The Virus exhaled—a sound halfway between a sigh and reverence.

Slowly, he turned. His eyes burned so bright they cast thin red lines down his cheek plates.

"You think you've climbed this far to stop me," he said, voice soft, cold, and sharpened like the edge of a blade. "But you are not the end. You are…an audience. The curtain has already fallen."

The portal behind him surged, lightning crawling up the walls, shuddering through the floor.

Alex and Nikki stood their ground.

"We've fought your soldiers," Alex said. "We've survived everything you threw at us. And we're still standing."

"You're afraid," Nikki added, taking a step closer, the violet glow in her eyes brightening. "Because you know—even now—you can't win."

The Virus tilted his head, almost curious.

"I don't need to win," he said. His claws spread wide as he turned toward the rift. "I just need to open the door."

#

The wind screamed through the broken control room.

He stood before the portal, one clawed hand outstretched, fingers crackling with red lightning, eyes locked on the swirling rift of chaos. The energy churned like a living storm—black veins writhing through molten crimson, pulsing with each heartbeat. He felt it. His master. A presence older than the first breath of the universe. Closer now.

He would welcome him through.

BANG!

The shot ripped through the air and smashed into his wrist. Sparks burst, and the claw jerked backward. A growl, low and animal, vibrated from his chest as he turned.

Connor stood in the doorway, rifle steady, his pale face hardened into defiance.

"Back away from the portal," Connor said.

The Virus bared his teeth.

Alex was already moving. A streak of gold cut across the room, shoulder slamming into the Virus with a collision that split the air. They hit the far wall hard enough to send cracks racing up the steel supports.

"NOW!" Alex roared.

Jacob burst in from the side, chains spinning in brutal arcs. Mr. K stumbled in behind him, nearly tripping on the shattered floor. Nikki blinked into the room in a puff of violet smoke, eyes glowing.

"K! The panel!" she shouted, pointing toward the console wired into the portal.

Mr. K's gaze darted over the alien mess of circuits, glyphs, and tubes hissing like snakes.

"This isn't tech—this is a nightmare with a power supply!"

"Figure it out!" Nikki snapped before vanishing in a flash and reappearing by Alex, driving both fists into the Virus's ribs. The impact cracked his plating and sent a flare of violet light burning through his frame.

The Virus roared, flinging Alex away with a shockwave that flattened a row of consoles. Jacob's chains lashed around the Virus's leg, yanking him down into the floor. Connor opened fire again, bullets sparking off armor, punching dents into exposed metal.

"Don't let him near the portal!" Alex shouted, blood streaking his temple as he pushed to his feet.

Nikki flickered in and out of existence, striking from every angle she could. His claws snapped where she'd been a heartbeat before. Jacob cut him off, chains weaving into a wall between them—only for the Virus to smash through with a single, devastating swipe.

"I'm getting real tired of this guy!" Jacob snarled.

The Virus moved like an earthquake with intent—shattering supports, hurling debris, each step cracking the floor deeper. Still, the team pressed him, attacking in rhythm: Alex from the front, Jacob from the flank, Nikki darting in like a phantom. Connor dropped to one knee, sending controlled bursts into weak points in the armor.

It slowed him—barely.

With a roar that rattled the glass shards in the window frames, the Virus ripped Jacob off his feet by the throat. Red light blazed in his chest cavity.

"Your strength is borrowed," he hissed. "Your defiance—meaningless."

"Yeah?" Jacob coughed. "Borrow this."

He wrenched his last chain free and wrapped it around the Virus's arm, locking him in place. Alex hit from above like a meteor, golden light detonating across their bodies. The Virus slammed into the portal's support beam. Metal screamed.

Smoke and sparks rained down.

For the first time—just for a flicker—his movements slowed. But so had theirs.

Alex dropped to a knee, gasping. Jacob spat blood. Nikki's teleport stuttered, her form flickering midblink. Connor's reload shook in his hands.

Only Mr. K moved with any certainty—scrambling over the console, ripping out wires, throwing switches like a man trying to defuse a god.

Then—sparks erupted. The main screen shattered.

"That's it," Mr. K said, yanking a pouch from his belt.

"What are you doing?" Nikki demanded.

"Being productive!" He slapped the explosives on the panel. "This thing doesn't turn off—it dies."

The Virus's head snapped toward the console.

"No."

BOOM.

Fire and shrapnel tore through the air, the explosion lighting the chamber in violent orange. The wall buckled. The portal stuttered—then screamed.

Reality itself bent inward. Colors twisted into impossible shades. The rift widened, showing flashes of alien seas, skeletal mountains, skies crawling with beasts.

The Virus staggered. Smoke curled from his armor. His claws reached toward the portal like a drowning man for the surface.

"No…not yet…I am not—"

The portal pulled harder.

Air, debris, even the light in the room was dragged toward the spiraling void. The Virus dug in his claws, but the force tore him free.

"NO! HE IS COMING! I AM NOT FINISHED!"

His voice warped into a shriek as the vortex swallowed him whole. The rift buckled inward—then imploded in a deafening thunderclap of light.

Silence.

Ash drifted in the still air. The red mist was gone. The portal—a memory.

Alex staggered upright, chest heaving.

Connor leaned against a beam.

"Tell me that worked."

"It worked," Mr. K muttered, slumped on the floor, singed but grinning. "I think I broke three ribs, but it worked."

Nikki helped Jacob to his feet, both of them staring at the scorched crater where the portal had been.

There was no sign of him.

Alex exhaled, voice low.

"It's over. "

24

The New Dawn

The doors to Task Force Headquarters hung askew, smoke curling from shattered beams and flickering lights.

Alex stepped through first—blood crusted on his brow, cape torn, golden energy now only a faint shimmer beneath his skin. One by one, the others followed: Connor, Jacob, Nikki, and Mr. K. All limping. All bruised. All standing.

The city beyond was quiet.

For the first time in what felt like forever, no sirens wailed. No monsters prowled. No red mist poisoned the sky.

Only ash drifted in the pale dawn.

They stood in the entrance, eyes sweeping the ruined streets of Capital City. Rubble choked the sidewalks. Hollowed cars still smoldered where they had been abandoned. Storefronts gaped open like broken shells.

Yet…people were emerging.

From alleyways, basements, and barricaded shelters, civilians stepped into the light. Some wore bandages; others clutched loved ones as if they might vanish. Parents wept openly. Children held hands in silence. At first, their gazes fixed on the team with wariness.

Then came the sound—a rising wave of voices, swelling into cheers, sobs, and cries of disbelief.

People rushed forward.

Nikki bent to embrace a child who flung themself into her arms, clinging to her jacket. Connor caught an elderly man stumbling on cracked pavement and steadied him. Jacob moved debris from the road with a weary grunt, his chains dragging behind like exhausted sentinels. Mr. K crouched beside a damaged hover-lift, coaxing it sputter by sputter back to life so it could carry a wounded family to safety.

And Alex...Alex only watched. His eyes, shadowed with age and regret, softened as he took in the sight.

A new dawn had come. But its cost still echoed in every heartbeat.

#

Weeks passed.

Rebuilding was slow, but it began.

Brick by brick, block by block, the cities scarred by war and fire began to breathe again. The red mist that once choked the sky had vanished, replaced by the pale gold of sunrises that felt new. The streets were still cracked. Buildings leaned at awkward angles. The air carried the weight of memory. But life was returning.

Former Task Force agents, many of whom had once lost faith, returned to help. Scientists salvaged damaged tech and reprogrammed it for farming, medicine, and construction. Children painted over bullet holes with murals—sunsets and birds, heroes and stars—turning fractured walls into stories. Craters became gardens, filled with fresh soil and tiny green sprouts, defiant against ruin.

The world had been broken.

But it was healing.

In Halvade, Alex and Nikki worked side by side.

The old district had been hit hardest, its foundations shaken by the quake and years of neglect. Now, Alex walked its streets daily, lifting fallen beams from homes, helping elders clear debris. People recognized him not as a ghost from the past, but as a protector returned.

Nikki moved with the quiet presence of someone reborn. She no longer wore a mask. She helped children out of shelters, taught teens how to defend themselves. In the market streets, people greeted her by name.

At night, she and Alex stood atop the ruins of an old watchtower, gazing out at the skyline dotted with lanterns.

"This place feels different," she said softly.

"It is," Alex replied. "Because of you."

In Capital City, Connor and Mr. K emerged as unlikely leaders.

Connor oversaw the reconstruction of Task Force Headquarters, often found carrying supplies on his shoulders, hammering planks into place, and joking with volunteers.

Mr. K, his goggles perpetually lopsided, worked on rewiring the city grid with a team of engineers, salvaging what tech remained, and building new devices from scraps. The underground lab had been converted into a medical and research center—a hub for civilian treatment and technological progress.

One afternoon, Connor stood with Mr. K in the shadow of

the rebuilt plaza.

"Can't believe we pulled it off," Connor muttered.

Mr. K grinned.

"You mean saving the world?" he asked. "Or convincing the city to let me run a lab?"

"Both," Connor joked.

In Veilhaven, Jacob became a local legend.

The quiet city, once home to whispers of smugglers and weapons traders, now looked to him for guidance. He led efforts to rebuild schools, houses, and bridges, using his chains not for battle, but for hauling heavy beams and twisted rebar. The people called him the Forged Man, and children followed him like ducklings.

And through all of this, the group stayed connected.

Messages were exchanged. Supplies were traded. Jokes were shared across radio lines. They weren't just rebuilding cities—they were rebuilding trust between places that had once stood divided. The walls between them, literal and emotional, were falling.

Then came the ceremony.

In the heart of Capital City, beneath a newly rebuilt monument of polished stone and rising wings, thousands gathered. Flags flew at half-mast. Pictures of the fallen adorned the base, Laura's image near the center, eyes forever focused, calm and strong. Around her, the names and faces of those lost in the quake, the war, the darkness.

The crowd stood in silence as Connor stepped onto the podium.

He wore a clean black jacket, bruises still faint on his face. His eyes scanned the crowd—citizens, agents, friends—and paused briefly on Jenna, standing near the front with Alex and Nikki. Jacob crossed his arms at the edge of the gathering. Mr. K stood with his hands in his pockets, eyes red behind cracked goggles.

A Task Force agent stepped forward and handed Connor a small black box.

He opened it.

Inside, a phoenix-shaped badge gleamed—silver with crimson trim. Carved into its surface:

Connor Avery – Task Force Director.

The agent pinned it to his chest.

Applause rippled through the plaza.

#

The monument caught the last of the sun's glow, casting long shadows across the square. Lanterns flickered to life along the street, their golden light warm and steady.

Connor sat on the steps before the monument, loosening the collar of his jacket. The phoenix badge caught the glow, a quiet reminder of all they'd fought for.

"Look at you," Nikki said, stepping up beside him with a faint smile. "Big-shot director now."

Connor smirked.

"Don't act like you're not impressed."

Jacob approached and clapped him on the back, nearly knocking him forward.

"We are," he said, more serious than usual. "You earned it."

"Mister big shot," Mr. K added, strolling over with his hands in his pockets. "I still don't know how we survived half the crap we went through…but I'm glad we did."

Connor let out a low breath.

"Now I just have to figure out how to be half the leader Laura was."

A golden shimmer passed over the stone, and Alex stepped into view.

"You lead with heart," he said, extending a hand.

Connor took it and rose to his feet.

"Thank you. For everything."

The five of them drifted toward the base of the monument, where the night breeze smelled faintly of soot and flowers.

Jenna approached quietly from the crowd, lingering at Nikki's side. Nikki glanced at her and gave a small, knowing smile.

"You did good," Jenna said softly.

"I had help," Nikki replied.

Connor turned, noticing her. Without a word, Jenna stepped forward, and her bag slid from her shoulder, forgotten. She ran.

He barely had time to react before she wrapped her arms around him, holding on with a force that spoke of more than relief—it was gratitude, grief, and the comfort of finding the one person who felt like home.

For a moment, Connor just stood there, stunned. Then his arms came around her, pulling her close, steady and warm.

"I'm proud of you," Jenna said, voice muffled against his jacket.

Connor smiled and embraced the hug. For once, he stayed silent.

When they parted, they joined the others in silence before the monument.

"She would've been proud," Nikki said.

"She'd be yelling at us to check the foundation and get back to work," Connor replied with a faint smile.

Alex nodded.

"And she'd be right," he said. "But even I can admit we've earned a break."

They laughed quietly, the kind of laugh that came after a long silence. Alex knelt and placed a single white flower at Laura's photo.

"She gave everything," he said. "And never asked for thanks."

"No," Connor said. "But she deserves it anyway."

They stood in the quiet a moment longer. No speeches, no ceremony—just a circle of people bound by war, loss, and love, under the shadow of the woman who had given them something worth protecting.

Nikki eventually stepped back and looked to the sky.

"So…what now?"

Connor's gaze swept the city—lantern-lit streets, faint laughter in the distance—then returned to his team. His family.

"We build," he said. "We protect. We make sure this never happens again."

"You just mean more work, don't you?" Mr. K sighed.

"Yup," Nikki said.

They started down the steps together—Alex, Connor, Jacob, Mr. K, Jenna—heading into the city. All but Nikki.

She lingered by her mother's image.

"Don't think I forgot about your promise, Mom," she whispered, fingers brushing the frame. "You still owe me."

"Hey," Jenna called from halfway down. "You coming?"

Nikki looked at her—at the people waiting below—and smiled.

"Yeah. I'm ready."

And with that, she left the monument behind, ready for whatever came next. She knew now she wouldn't face it alone.

Epilogue

The Task Force Headquarters still smelled faintly of scorched metal. Whole sections of the building were draped in scaffolding, the hum of repair drones filling the air.

Deep in the operations wing, Connor sat hunched over a desk littered with datapads and half-drained coffee mugs. The flicker of a dozen holo-screens reflected in his eyes. Mr. K was across from him, soldering a fist-size cluster of circuits with surgical precision, the smell of burnt wiring sharp in the air.

Footsteps echoed down the hall.

Alex stepped through the doorway, hands tucked into his coat pockets.

"You called me over," he said, brow raised. "What's so urgent?"

Connor straightened, clearly trying to put it into words.

"We, uh…we've been working on this thing—think of it like the portal, except not…portal-y. It's more like a—"

"A controlled dimensional resonance link with a hard-coded isolation layer," Mr. K cut in without looking up.

Alex blinked.

"Right. Which is?"

"A way to communicate with other realms without actually opening them," Mr. K said, setting down the tool and swiveling toward him. "No unstable gateways, no cross-contamination. Just signal, nothing more."

Alex crossed his arms.

"Is it dangerous?"

"Not unless you consider long-distance calling dangerous," Mr. K said with a shrug. "The line goes one way. Nothing can come back through."

Connor leaned back in his chair, relieved.

"It's safe," he said. "We made sure. Well, he made sure. I just kind of…sat there."

"That's not why we called you, though," Mr. K said quietly. "Come here."

Alex walked over, staring blankly at the screen.

Mr. K hesitated, then tapped a sequence on the nearest console. One of the holo-screens lit up, projecting a distorted image—jagged red static rippling like an open wound across a black void.

Alex stepped closer, his eyes narrowing at the shifting pattern.

"What am I looking at?"

"A trace," Mr. K said. "Residual signature buried deep in the signal from one of the realms we scanned."

The static pulsed, forming the faintest outline of something that might have been a face.

Alex's jaw tightened.

"The Virus."

"Yes," Mr. K said. "The good thing is, he isn't near us."

The room went still. Only the quiet hum of machines filled the air.

"Then where?" Alex asked.

Mr. K's eyes flicked to the screen, then back to Alex.

"He's far," Mr. K replied. "But likely still alive."

"Then we can't risk letting him live," Alex said. "We need to get to him and kill him."

"That would be amazing," Mr. K said," but we'd have to create a new portal. A more…sustainable one."

"Can you do it?" Alex asked.

"Yes…but I'll need some time."

"Okay," Alex replied. "Let's get this done."

Alex stood there a moment longer, hands curling into fists.

The next battle was coming.